The Road to Delphi

The Road to Delphi

A Gentle Mystery

Nigelle de Visme

BY THE SAME AUTHOR

Patrick and the Cat Who Saw Beyond Time
Memoir: Book One – The Tiger and the Taxi Driver
Memoir: Book Two – The Tiger and the Taxi Driver

Moleskine (*Italian: mol-a-skeen'-a*)

"MOLESKINE is the legendary notebook that has held the inspirations and ideas of everyone from Van Gogh, Picasso and Hemingway to Bruce Chatwin and Alexa Buddicom. Artists, authors and geniuses of all variety have long appreciated the simplicity and superior functionality of these notebooks.

Originally produced by small French bookbinders who supplied the Parisian stationery shops frequented by the international avant-garde, in 1986 the last manufacturer of Moleskine, a family operation in Tours, closed and Moleskines were gone – but not forgotten. As a result of their previous popularity their reincarnation was demanded. In 1998, a small Milanese publisher brought these books back for writers, artists, travellers and all free-thinkers around the globe."

DEDICATION

To D.C. for telling me his story, a story that belongs to a different era, a story so terrible he, and those like him, can be forgiven almost anything. There were no methods then to deal with trauma, nor were ways to remould a human heart and soul known.

Thanks in abundance to special friends Gillian Bouras for mega-support and Helen Zannetakis for coffee, cakes and the camion. And to Liz Williams, sci-fi author extraordinaire, for enthusiasm and encouragement that, having survived, I publish!

CONTENTS

PROLOGUE
June 2004

The history of the Island of Roses is as compact and shapely as the sea nymph Rhode after whom the island was named. She was daughter to Poseidon and Amphitrite and wife to Helios the sun god who drives his ·chariot and horses across the skies in a blaze of light and warmth, while his sister Selene waits each night to light the world with her moon shadows. Athena Polias and Apollo left their temples on Rhodes, and men their legacies: Apollonius, Librarian of Alexandria; Hipparchus the Mathematician; goldsmiths from Rhodes lent Byzantium its majesty; sculptors immortalized the island's beautiful women, the Bathing Aphrodite surely the loveliest. The legendary Colossus of Rhodes, larger than the Statue of Liberty, spanned the ancient harbour; the Knights Hospitallers built and maintained the largest and finest hospital in the world for two hundred years. Byzantium rose and fell there, the Turks brought their coffee and baklava, their elegant minarets and their domed hamams; the Italians came and went and left the island green and watered; the Germans and Swedes are still there pushing up the property prices and pulling down their knickers. Young Brits fornicate all over Faliraki. But ... it is a beautiful island and large enough to escape the depredations of contemporary tourist hedonism.

Alexa Buddicom leaned her head on her window of the plane as it banked in preparation for landing, unfolding a view of blue such as she had never seen anywhere else during a lifetime of travelling; a blue as quintessential as the quintessential green of the ancient Isle of Avalon, her beloved Glastonbury.

Everyone falls in love with Greece sooner or later, and for Alexa it was very late indeed. She was a writer, called to a Conference in the memory of Lawrence Durrell whose little villa amongst the eucalypts and the cats in a Turkish graveyard was being dedicated to his two years of residence there. The villa was named Cleobolus after one of the Seven Sages of Ancient Greece; grand antecedents for such a diminutive building as Durrell described always sent a *frisson* through her, leaving an unaccountable sense of connecting with a fate beyond her own. As the plane touched down gracefully its slight tremor relayed itself to Alexa and she knew in her bones that her far from ordinary life was about to change – again.

CHAPTER ONE
October 2007

Detective Inspector Pericles Kostakides led a quiet life, for all that his education had equipped him otherwise, but there were unsuspected depths in his soul that an interesting case to study might reveal. This day began as any other, except that repeat phone calls had alerted his office to the discovery of an abandoned Grand Vitara whose sentinel appearance had concerned a growing number of local fisher folk who used the same lonely littoral during the days they chose to fish there. It was time to tow it in.

"He was a war hero you know," said Ilias, "we grew up on tales of his courage and we celebrated his return when he came back to the island. That was a long time ago; the Cypriot crisis, the Royal Hellenic Navy, *po! po!* no one even thinks of these things today. Mind you, Kyrios Aristo lived a long time in France and when he came home he could barely speak Greek. Imagine! Why he should leave his car by this empty beach makes no sense at all."

His companion, senior in station, pulled out the registration details of the Grand Vitara and confirmed its ownership by one Aristo Theohalis; details of his address and person clearly paralleled the Identity Card records accompanying every police report. "Call Savvas, tow the vehicle to the holding yard," the Inspector instructed, "we'll check it over this afternoon, see if we can come up with any sort of clue as to where the owner could have gone. Maybe we should search the shore line, heart attack maybe, who knows..."

Inspection of the vehicle later that day revealed a curious anomaly: its sunroof had been left open wide enough for a small frame to enter. Ilias slipped inside and unlocked both the doors. Their search told nothing of the owner's whereabouts, and nothing that suggested foul play. A folder containing a number of loose A4 sheets was lying on the passenger seat. Ilias handed the folder to his superior without paying it too much attention. Registering the manuscript, perhaps a potential book, a work in progress, the senior officer put it to one side.

Pericles Kostakides climbed into the Vitara and sat at the driver's wheel. He took in the vehicle's comfortable, pristine, appearance, its mock leather trim fed and polished, no sign of fading from the harsh summer sun of Rhodes. Knowing the owner's address at one of the enclaves built for Italian officers during their thirty five year occupation of the island Pericles knew the vehicle was ungaraged, its maintenance was therefore impressive and gave a clue to the owner's character, fastidious. The open sunroof didn't gel with his assessment.

The rear passenger seats had been folded down flat to create space for fishing gear, snorkels, two oxygen tanks, a spear gun, towels, flippers, bottles of water – this man was a responsible swimmer and the equipment suggested its owner would not venture into the sea without precaution. His disappearance made little sense.

Pericles climbed out, stepped back and opened the passenger door to run his hand under the folded down seats as far as his reach permitted. His searching fingers made contact with a small object. With his fingers flattened against the carpeted floor of the car he nudged the object towards the narrow space between the front seat and the rear until he could just identify it as a small black notebook, its binding and pages held together by a self attached black elastic loop stitched into the back cover. Once he had wriggled it into a position where his hand could clasp it he recognised it as one of those rather classy notebooks students sometimes carried around the Museum as an *aide memoire* for their theses. He handed it to Ilias.

Leaving the vehicle in the compound the two men pondered what to do next. Nobody had reported Aristo missing, though he was known to live alone so who would immediately know? The thought continued to nag both men.

Later that same day as Pericles drove along Democratius Street he swung left on an impulse into the *cul de sac* adjacent to the University, pulled in to the square and parked. Walking up the incline he came to an old man sunning himself under a large blue umbrella on a small balcony.

"*Kalispera sas,*" the two men greeted each other as Pericles introduced himself, adding the courtesies of Greek greetings before stating his reason for being there: "there is nothing to worry, but can I ask if you have seen your neighbour in these past days? His car was reported down by Istrios Point, empty, men were curious. A good vehicle, no sign of an accident, but it's a lonely coast and it was an invitation to, well, a closer inspection."

The old man raised both eyebrows, his expression spoke surprise: "Kyrios Aristo? He would never abandon his car unless he was towing his boat and going off for fishing."

"No, no trailer, no boat, no indication of any intention except swimming, but all the fishing and swimming gear was still in the back. Not even covered. We wait more days and then we tow it to the compound. You have no ideas ...?"

Pericles was slightly embarrassed at interrupting the old man and promised to attend to patience, the quality of which was eluding him of late.

"Kyrios Inspector, my neighbour is a very particular man; he doesn't even go out shopping without locking his shutters. If he goes down to his olive grove and intends to stay overnight he turns off the water stopcock on the balcony here. Have a look, see if it is on or off, then at least you know if his intention was to return sooner ... or later. Maybe he is working on his new house down in Phanes. I have not seen him for some time now. He comes, but then he goes, and we only hear his door."

The two men exchanged more pleasantries, Pericles learned of the olive grove in Lardos (that hadn't come up on the ID check) and of the restoration project in Phanes, (that hadn't revealed itself on the ID check either). But Phanes was a long way from Istrios Point.

It was siesta time, those sacrosanct hours between two and five when the Island slept, but rather than rest Pericles felt the urge to continue on past Ialyssos where, since his beloved wife had died, far too young, he had returned to live in the family home, nestled within a large walled compound along the road to Philerimos.

He drove on to the small village of Phanes. Walking into a *kafenion* he ordered a *briki* of coffee, never referring to its native origin, which struck a nerve whenever he heard the English still call it when he had lived as a student in London. Not for him *Turkish* coffee. Chatting amiably to the woman who brought it to him on a small tray with a glass of iced water he learnt that a man from Rhodes Town had in the past year bought two shops, rather tumbled down and empty for years, and had converted them into a single house, adding a whole storey to the single floors.

"He invited all the neighbours in just before he moved in, to look over and admire his work – especially we women," she blushed slightly, "who had walked past every day for months trying to peer in to see what he was doing. We did admire it too; it set the cats among the pigeons because our husbands were held up as lazy by his standards. We all wanted *his* terrace, *his* modern plumbing, *his* new tiling in our own homes. He lives alone, and since he has come here he has hidden himself away, but he is a good man, and a good neighbour. He lives up there," she flicked her head to indicate a side street running away from the beach side. "You'll know it – it is the cleanest and newest of all the old houses."

Pericles paid for the coffee and strolled up the lane, the new paintwork on the front door was easy to spot, he knocked tentatively, mindful of siesta. The knock sounded hollow, not a perceptible sound, more an intuition, an instinct, that assured him the house was empty. There was no access to the rear of the property and he could not detect the hum of an air conditioner within. He returned to the *kafenion*.

Greeting the woman again he asked if she had seen the owner of the house of late. "No, *Kyrios*," she replied, "he comes and he goes and his car is not in the field at the end of the lane at this time. We know a woman came here, a foreigner, she stumbled over even asking for a loaf of bread but she smiled so we forgave her for not speaking Greek. She was here some days and then they both left. We haven't seen him since four or five weeks, nor the lady. She looked a little Greek, perhaps from Saloniki, but she couldn't speak Greek. She used to walk past here on her way to the sea. My cousin has the café down there, he noticed her. She was not young, younger than Kyrios Aristo though, and her smile was pretty."

Thoughtfully, Pericles Kostakides returned to his car. He sat awhile, in no hurry to drive away, allowing thoughts to percolate like the coffee, rushing to the surface, bubbling with grains of unspoken perceptions.

A new road had recently opened just a kilometre or so ahead of Phanes; it swept across the island from Kalavarda to Salakos, on to Laerma and directly to Lardos. Rather than make the trip down the opposite side of the island another day he could cut straight across and return along the south west coast road, cutting west through Kalithies to Pastida and Philerimos. He didn't expect answers from an uninhabited olive grove but the case of the abandoned vehicle now had a curious edge, the notebook under the passenger seat had been a diary, and it was written in a foreign language – English.

Lardos revealed nothing. It was devilishly difficult to find any olive grove. Pericles drove back into the village and parked in the square. Almost everything was closed but for a restaurant in which a large, jovial man was singing as he wiped down tables and tidied chairs for the evening diners. Pericles excused himself and found he was looking into a pair of twinkling sea green eyes and listening to a Greek with a distinctly recognisable drawl. "American?" inquired Pericles having invited himself in and introduced himself.

The sea green eyes twinkled, "Canadian. And what can I do for you?" Pericles was not wearing a uniform but a small badge on his lapel gave a clue to his authority. He asked about olive groves, a Greek, a Grand Vitara and now, a foreign woman.

"It's the end of the season and we don't get so many foreigners so the odd one or two are more noticeable. Olive grove I don't know, but I do remember an attractive couple coming here for dinner a few weeks back. She didn't speak Greek so I talk to her, she said she had lived in Australia, she heard my accent and felt a colonial rapport, you could say, although she spoke a most beautiful English. The man, he is Greek, but funny thing, his accent was more even than mine – his Greek was *French*. So I remember these kind of people, they have manners, not like so many of the foreigners who come here, even the older ones, *Theo mou*, which side of the bed do they come from in their own country!" He flicked his cloth, raising both eyebrows theatrically as he emphasised his opinion of graceless middle-aged foreign *barbaros*.

He paused, then held out this hand and introduced himself as Manolis, offering a potted bio of his family's desire to return to their roots even though their kids, two girls and a boy, were Canadian born and bred. "But they love it here, how could they not! The beach is so close, the weather so good, sure they miss friends and skiing and decent TV reception – but I tell them in a coupla years they can have the best of both worlds to live. So we all work this restaurant together while they finish their school and then we see what the good God brings."

Pericles pushed aside the tiniest mote of nostalgia at the man's fortune – his children. There was no time to save his from the collision which emptied his life of meaning that Sunday when Dimitra was driving Adriana and Ion home from the Church. *Theo mou*, but the *Panaghia* must have wanted them in heaven for Herself so much, he thought, and sighed quietly.

Manolis offered a few more thoughts: "the man, I don't remember if he told me his name or not, he seemed proud of her, the woman, but in an odd way, as if she was doing him a favour which he ought to acknowledge. As for her, it was obvious he was her sun and moon, but there was great sadness in her. They had that familiarity of intimacy, but not affection. I don't think she lived here, but he did. He drove a silver Vitara and had the muscles of Heracles. He was not an easy man to speak with and he didn't encourage her to talk to me but I could tell that for her to speak English made her happy. He spoke English, good English, he just didn't like speaking. No," he said, anticipating the obvious question and pre-empting the answer, "I don't know where his olive grove is but if it is in Lardos they will know at the *Dymaheion*, we are a very small population. Cross the road, turn right, the office will probably be closed now but the secretary lives next to the office building."

Pericles thanked him, wandered about the village, glad his siesta pattern had been propped awake by the coffee. As luck would have it a young woman was just leaving the municipal offices as he approached. She took in at a glance the good-looking man purposefully approaching and waited until he reached her. Explaining his quest, having proved his *bona fide*, Pericles wondered if she could help him.

"Of course, *Kyrios*," she smiled pertly, "I am late closing this afternoon so you are lucky you find me, why don't we just go back upstairs and I will check the title deeds – we are not so many people here and almost all the names will be familiar to me, it won't take me long."

On the second map she withdrew from a row of large flat drawers in the old cabinet there was registered a name not from the village. Aristo Theohalis. She photocopied that particular section for the Inspector so he could follow the goat paths and stone walls that ran along the boundaries: "it is dry now so your Alfa will easily manage to get through," smiled the pert young woman who had noticed the one car in the village square that she did not recognise as belonging to any of its permanent residents. Pericles thanked her, walked back to his car and drove out in the direction of the eastern coastline. Over the bridge which spanned a dried and stony riverbed he turned left down a coarse and corrugated track, a track which disagreed with the suspension of his old Spider Lusso in spite of the young woman's assurances. No wonder Aristo had a 4WD. Following the track, which narrowed even as he drove, he came to the building indicated on his map and inwardly groaned as he saw deeply entrenched tyre tracks leading to the showiest piece of wrought iron. This would have to be the right place – only someone with a French Connection could create a Versailles of gold and silver scrolls and mock heraldry set into a vast pair of black wrought iron gates to protect a tiny small holding of a dozen olive trees – and this would have to be a walk. He parked the Spider amongst the thistles edging the fields, walking up the grassy centre between the trenches that passed as tyre tracks. As he reached the vast gates he was able to make out a large, very large, tin shed with a roof whose span actually steeped over an old caravan in the further corner of the fenced in olive grove. The gates were chained and bolted on the outside, and padlocked through. They were completely impregnable, Kyrios Theohalis was not at home.

Setting his car homeward Pericles was no closer to solving any riddles, but perhaps, ran his thoughts, he had eliminated in one afternoon the need to follow more false trails. Coming down the steep descent from Philerimos he remembered his mechanic, the best mechanic on the island, who worked at the back of the main road through Ialyssos – would he, could he, possibly know Aristo Theohalis and his 4WD? A man as discerning as Aristo Theohalis would choose the best mechanic for his own vehicle. A buzz of anticipation thrilled the hair along his arms as he checked his watch to find it was close on five, a time when life began again on the island. He pulled up just as the mechanic's roller doors began to crank their way open.

"Kalispera sas!" the men greeted each other warmly, shaking hands. Pericles outlined his story and felt a winner's glow when Kosta fairly bounced up and down, volubly launching into all he knew of one of his most admired clients.

"Of course I know Kyrios Aristo, I service his cars for years, he's a regular, does about 100 kilometres a week, his olive grove is down in Lardos, he visits there weekly, like clockwork he is. There, see," he rummaged through a few oil-smeared papers still unfiled on his desk and flourished the latest service sheet for the Suzuki in question, "around two, two and a half, thousand kilometres a year. Good car, he and I take care of it. What's the problem? He's a good man, my father remembers him, calls him the Captain, he blew those fucking Turks clean out of Cyprus you know. He was here a month or so back, asked for this special service, said he was going to take a trip, with a friend, a lady, said she helped him write his story. I reckon it must have been burning him up, his story. You know the Navy never honoured his top secret mission, well how could they? It was secret. Whoever this lady was she must have helped pull it out of him. He was, well, you never really knew what he was, didn't talk much, always paid me cash, enjoyed his drink and his own company."

Pericles smiled for the first time that day. He asked Kosta if he happened to have a copy of the last mileage count for the abandoned vehicle, and was given a copy of the service details. He pulled out his notepad and checked the figures he had written down earlier – there was a difference of two thousand kilometres. In the past four or five weeks the car has clocked up over two thousand kilometres. *Two thousand* kilometres! The normal quota for its annual service on a dewdrop island that was barely eighty kilometres long. Where had it been?

There was only one answer to that question – off the island. Pericles thanked Kosta and drove home. He made a call to the booking office of Blue Star. His hunch was right, the records showed the registration of the vehicle as having left Rhodes for Piraeus on August 31st, and returning to Rhodes on September 7th. The owner of the registered vehicle booked a luxury double cabin out – and no cabin back...

Pericles, more thoughtful than usual, came to the dinner table in silence. His mother, an elegant woman whose own tragedies sat lightly on her neat shoulders, watched him. They each thanked the cook, whose meals were unfailingly excellent, and set to. "Mama," he eventually spoke, "you must excuse me tonight, I have a puzzle to consider, and some papers to read, but do you remember ever hearing of Aristo Theohalis?"

"*Vevaios!* Everyone has heard of the man, your father even met him, do you remember the Melina Mercouri fiasco? Well, Aristo was to be the diver to the wreck near here that your father knew had good salvage, artefacts, antiques – but all the fuss, and then she forgot. Too busy. Never mind, we have the Theatre. The diving needed special equipment, and a very special diver. Aristo was that. Why do you ask?"

Pericles outlined the past days, the discovery of the manuscript, the notebook which began to assume its name, *Moleskine*, when he referred to it, the missing man, the mystery woman, the abandoned car.

"*Paidi mou*, at last," smiled Danaë Kostakides warmly, "a case on this quiet island worthy of your education!"

Pericles grinned, a rare flash of sunlight across his serious face, kissed his mother goodnight and went to his rooms where he settled down on the large comfortable sofa, lit his evening pipe, a habit he had developed in London, and began to flick through the hundred or so loose pages of the folder from the car. Some hidden awareness alerted him to return and begin at page one – he was about to enter a world hidden in the recesses of a man's memory, a world unknown to his own generation and one which brought to the surface a history that belonged to the immediate past. The pages he was about to read, written with the intimacy of the narrator's memories, brought it very close to home.

CHAPTER TWO

Aristo Theohalis: In the Beginning 1943 – The Red Balloon

I am born in a village on Kos in the time of the Second World War. I am the third child of the third wife of my father. My father has three children with his first wife and she died during the birth of their fourth child. He has seven children with his second wife, who also died. Then he married my mother, and they have seven more children. I am somewhere in the last seven, after the one before me dies and before the brother after me dies. In 1948 my parents sell all they have in Kefalos. It isn't much, the Germans destroyed everything: my father's pottery, our livelihood, all is ruined. My father decides to take us to the bigger island of neighbouring Rhodes. It is a terrible crossing in very rough sea, I am perhaps five years old and I know fear, we are all afraid, for our lives. We are tossed like capers in a can in this small fishing boat, maybe 14 metres long. I remember her name, Sofianoula. Somehow this little boat brought us to Mandraki harbour on a very dark night. There is no food, and the crossing took many, many hours.

All together we walk through the night in the dark from Mandraki to my grandmother's house in the Old Town of Rhodes. It is just one big room and there we all have to live together. There are no toilets, no water, no bath. The public toilets and amenities are primitive and filthy at that time and they are a little way further down the mediaeval alleyways. My father used to leave Rhodes to the north of Greece to look for work; he left my mother and us children alone for many many months at a time.

I am now five years old and in this time still the war is everywhere, you can still see the weapons of war in the street, in the seaside, in the mountains: grenades, machine guns, helmets and old boots from the soldiers and all the soldiers' personal items, strewn everywhere. At that time nothing exists for us in the way of clothes, or shoes, or toys. We play with the weapons and with the grenades, many times the grenades explode, killing my friends. For food, we have more than nothing. We eat anything we find around us, like snails, spinach, wild grasses, and at the night we go fishing with torches made from old tyres to burn and give us light. We try to catch small fish, crabs, octopus in the rocks nearby the dry dock. We have no shoes and our clothes are old and very tattered and these we never take off even to sleep, for we have no others. In the morning we wake up and we go to the school. We have no breakfast, and I cannot clean my teeth for I do not even know of such things. By luck the school gives us a little breakfast of powdered milk and some bread, sent to us by the allies. This is my main meal for the day. In the school I cannot say I am the best pupil in my class, I am not.

In my grandmother's house of one stone walled room we sleep one on top of the other, like kittens. My mother sends us out to collect wood and kindling in the mornings before school so she can cook. She bought me a pair of shoes, very cheap, made of canvas. These shoes and a white t-shirt and a pair of white pants are only given to me to wear on Sundays so I can go to the Church. I have a good voice and the priest likes me. I stay with him during the holidays and on Sundays to help him with the Mass. He gives me a little money sometimes to go to the cinema, especially when he stays a long time in the houses of the widows. He always comes out smiling. When I come home my mother takes my white shoes and my white clothes and hides them until Sunday when I go again to the priest.

In the class of the schoolroom I am so terribly tired, it is impossible to stay awake with nothing in my stomach. With impatience I wait for the bell so I can free myself of the tyranny of this school. Every year at the end of the school season I have my diploma, I just scrape through, or perhaps the teachers understand the reason why I am such a poor student and give me a pass. Many of us cannot do it better. I am one of the best in history and in gymnastics because I am a strong child. I have a very good memory, and do not need to re-read what I am told.

One thing I can say is that the teachers at my school were the nicest people I ever met in my life. Many times they invite me and some other children to their own homes to give us lunch and then we want them to be proud of us in their classes, so we behave well for them.

One day I remember I was passing a shop, it had a glass window, like a mirror, and I look in the window and I see something so terrible I cannot believe it. I am looking at myself, but I do not recognize myself as a human being. I have seen other children, sometimes when I pass the other houses I see children sitting with their parents at a table, eating food, from plates. These things do not exist in my life. We never have a table, and my mother, because of her own problems, had very little food for us to eat, we never sit down. Anyway, I look at this terrible picture in the window and I see it must be me. I am dirty, I have rags instead of clothes, no shoes, so dirty I am. Then, I remember it is Christmas, but I do not know what Christmas is apart from the church. I do not know about presents. As I look in the window at my image I see there comes a little girl, she is playing with a balloon. She is dressed nicely, her parents are with her and they are to go into the shop. The little girl stands next to me, this filthy urchin of the streets and the harbours. She looks me up and down and smiles at me. I feel like a clochard. I look at her and I know we are from different worlds. Then, slowly, she puts her hand out towards me, she is holding the balloon. She gives it to me. It is red. Then she smiles again and she leaves me standing there holding this red balloon. I cannot say thank you to the little girl because she has gone, but in my heart are many words and many things that I want to say to her. She lives in my heart with the red balloon.

When I am twelve years old I finally complete my primary school, but I cannot go any further because I must work for my family.

One distantly related cousin of my mother has a little grocery shop which sells everything; he takes me to help him. I am working there from morning until night for 100 drachmas per week. This is very little, but I give all this money to my mother for food and clothes for the family.

My father comes home every few months. I love my father, he is a good man, but some things happened in that room which are so terrible for a young child to see and hear that I run away and sleep the night in my rags without a blanket at the bottom of a small boat. When a father comes home after three months away you understand what kind of ambiance can happen in that room when he sees his wife again. But in that one small room the children do not understand. I do understand, and I am feeling so ashamed, for there was no curtain, no separation at all. I have to run away these nights.

Later my father is ill although we are too small to know what kind of illness my father developed. Perhaps it is to do with his liver, because for the very very poor people ouzo is a way to forget the suffering. Anyway the hospital or the government pays for him to go to Athens. But who of us has money to go to see him? Two weeks later somebody comes to tell my mother my father has died. A cousin calls to me in the shop and said: Aristo, I have some bad news for you, your father is dead. My boss said to me: "Okay Aristo, you can go home now to be with your mother." I found the family and our neighbours crying. Now it is even more difficult for my mother, for now there is no money at all.

I stay with this job with my uncle until I am fifteen years old, but because my passion since a child is the sea I spend a lot of my free time on the beach, not for swimming but for trying to catch octopus or fish. I make myself a mask with the rubber inner tube of old tyres. I save up to pay a man to make me a round glass for the mask. I make a spear gun from a small tube made from either a plastic or brass water pipe, about 2 cm diameter and about 20 cm long. Then I find a rod, and file a little runnel in one end and attach 2 pieces of elastic which were connected to the pipe, the bottom is joined by a piece of wire. The rod I put down the pipe, and seat it in the wire and I stretch the elastic back like a catapult. The Tahitians still use this method today; I am very successful in catching the prey.

At that time most of the young boys who have no work leave the country to work as sailors or deckhands on the old cargo ships or to go for sponge diving and collecting coral. This is the most dangerous job because at that time there is no decompression chamber anywhere in Greece. The captains who employed the divers are only interested in the catch, not our safety or our lives. Then no one even knew about decompression tables anyway, this is why so many so many men died or remain paralyzed all their lives. I decide to take one of these boats and try to make some money with sponge ship around the islands, and also in Crete. My first job is to turn the hand compressor that gives air to the divers. At that time the divers used the skafhandro, a very heavy helmet. Inside the skafhandro is an incoming valve through which the air from the hand air compressor is pumped. The diver then presses the valve with his head to control the airflow and his weight. For example if I am under the sea and I come to a rock over which I have to swim I keep the air inside both the helmet and the suit to create the buoyancy necessary to raise my body. Once over the obstacle I then press my head on the valve to release air and empty the skafhandro and my suit, so I can descend lower again.

After a week pumping the air for the other divers I want to learn to dive so that I can earn more money, and I asked Captain Manolis if I can dive. He refuses me because he does not want to spend the time for me to learn. After pleading with him for some time he agrees that I can do the first dive the next morning. I am so excited I cannot close my eyes all night. My expectations for the first deep-water dive keep me awake all night. In the morning everybody helps me put on my first diver's suit, my boots, my skafhandro. The captain gives me important advice, how you go down, how you move about holding your net on your left side and how you catch the sponges with your hook on the right side. So I come down the ladder of the boat half afraid, and a little panicky, and I let myself go down slowly, pushing my air valve to release the air.

In those days there is only one diver's suit for all the divers. I am very small, the suit has to be folded around my waist but the men do not tie the folds very well. As I am going down my suit it comes loose and begins to float up around me.

When you go down you have to hold your nose so the pressure is released in your ears. Of course I cannot hold my nose with the helmet on, so I press my nose against the inside of the helmet. But to my horror the skafhandro is beginning to float above my head because the loosened suit is lifting it from my shoulders. I panic and try to pull it down, but my suit keeps pushing it up. With my hands I pull the skafhandro down and begin to press my nose against the inside and also to press the valve on the outside. Now I am about 25 metres under water. If you cannot release the air you blow up like a balloon, not just the suit but the diver's body as well. When the air is released I continue to descend to the seabed, which is around 45 metres. When I reach the seabed I was conscious but very unfocused. It is like I am half drunk and half panic, my hands are shaking and I cannot think. This is my first dive and I do not realize, nor do they warn me, that the pressure inside the suit presses my body so much it is like suffocating. I am struggling with this sensation and at the same time trying to concentrate on what I am to do. In my state I cannot understand the signals that the surface crew are trying to give me down the line. My response does not conform to the code of signals. After a few minutes (and one minute at the bottom of the sea is a very long minute in this kind of situation) I feel that the surface crew are trying to bring me up again. I begin to feel much better about halfway up when I can see the light again. Down below is very very dark. But I am very aware that I have to think up some excuse for the captain.

Once on the surface the face of the captain is as dark as the depths I have just come from. He is losing time and money. The second diver is waiting for my equipment. I have to explain myself to the captain. I tell him everything and ask him to please let me try another time. The captain said he was not expecting much from my first dive, and I promise him that the next time I will be successful. He is not a happy man. As I stand there I feel an enormous release in my body, as if the tension of my pre-dive panic has been taken away. I feel I can do anything, and I know my next dives will be successful. I feel free, and elated.

The following day I pump for the divers and the day after that I do my second dive. Everything then is almost perfect, I am well prepared in my mind and I take precautions with the tying of the suit myself. Because I am feeling so exhilarated I know the second dive will be a success. When I reach the seabed I am so much clearer, I can choose the sponges and see which are good or bad, and I can say that at the end of the dive, about 30 to 40 minutes, I do not want to come to the surface. When I do I can see that the captain is happy, I am happy, everyone is happy. I stay with this boat for 5 or 6 months.

My elder brother is working for an American Coast Guard vessel of The Voice of America as a maintenance hand and one day the vessel has a problem with a rope caught around the propeller. The ship's staff cannot find a diver to do anything about untangling the rope and so my brother calls me to ask if I could help. I am able to clear the vessel with the metal saw that I was given to do the job. With my poor English I talk with the officer of the ship and he asks me if I would like a job on board with them. The work is mainly in the laundry, washing and ironing the uniforms of the crew. The salary they offered me is so much more than I had earned before, around $2 a day and lunch is included. During the times we left port I am given a bed and fed three meals a day. Sometimes when there is not so much maintenance work or laundry I am to make the beds and change the sheets of the crew. I make a lot of friends on the ship and am given clothes and shoes. After washing the clothes I put them, clean and ironed, on the bed of each man. I can read the names on the lockers which correspond to the labels on the clothes. I am able to buy cigarettes cheaply on board and sell them on shore for more money. I keep a little money for me, but all the rest I give to my mother, for now we were seven children.

My mother was becoming ill; she stays in the bed the whole day. Doctors come to make examination sometimes, but we have no way to take her to hospital and she dies with us. My elder sister looks after the children and cooks for them during the day and in the evening she will go to work, for very little money, in a restaurant in Mandraki.

The year passes slowly, but I am very happy with my job. When I am eighteen years old I am called for military service and I leave to Athens in January 1964, it is cold in the wintertime, much colder than our island of Rodos, but the military life is better than I expect, we have much exercise with the uniform of the Royal Greek Navy, the food is not so bad, and I make a lot of friends.

One day two of the officers of the underwater commando training come to our training school and they ask for volunteers to come to their special training school. They explain that the conditions of this training are terrible. If you succeed after the six months you will be able to travel around Europe, they tell us. Even more enticing, the salary was a little more than we are used to. About 850 men applied. We sign papers to absolve the Royal Navy from responsibility if we die or are killed in the training and the training is so difficult soon we are only 50 men left. I am in group thirteen.

The training really is difficult, they did not joke about that. We cannot sleep day or night, we have to swim for many hours in the cold water, we have to learn how to diffuse mines and explosives. During the night around 2 a.m. the trainers come to our cabins and put smoking poison torches in our rooms. They close our doors and windows with a key so no one can escape. This is to train us for a bad life, a life of war, to toughen us up. The name of the command, OYK, is for underwater demolition. Americans call this UDT. Once the smoking fuses are lit we are supposed to apply wet cloths to our faces, but the first time this happens we do not know what to do. They do not tell us. And we have no wet cloths anyway. After a few moments they open the door and we fall out coughing and choking. Out of our mouths even our saliva is red, like blood. You stay on the floor coughing for some time and then they order us to go into the room again and get dressed into combat gear.

The second time we have this experience I am prepared with my mask and my wet towel always hidden under my mattress. Immediately the exercise was repeated I put my mask on so I can see, and then with the wet towel pressed against my mouth I can breathe almost normally because the water breaks up the concentration of the smoke. As soon as the door opens we run from the room like rats.

So after the first experience we are assembled in full combat gear for a meeting, freezing cold, snow outside. We are asked if we are cold, no, we must answer, no! Fifty metres away is the swimming pool, it is frozen over.

"Are you sure you are not cold," asks the officer.

"No! No! No!" we all shout back.

He said:

"Company! Right Turn! March, one two, one two."

We face the open swimming pool and one by one, fully dressed, we have to dive in to the pool through the ice. Steam rises from the pool. One of the officers brought his car so that the lights show up the freezing vapour of the ice. The officers are dressed in full winter gear, heavy coats, gloves and scarves, that is how cold it is.

Again the trainers come and ask if we are cold. With trembling voices, trembling from the bitter cold, we call back: no-o-o-o.

"Are you sure you are not cold?" the trainer calls again.

"No-o-o-o!"

"Okay," said our trainer, "then we will see which is the coldest, in the water or outside the water. Company, out of the pool! Stand around the pool one by one."

It is so hard to climb out of the pool.

When you are this cold the blood slows down, the brain does not work properly, you can't react. Standing in that water your balls are drawn right up into the body and it hurts enough to make you crazy. Years later, while I am drilling and standing still in 100 metre depths of sea, I experienced this many times. Only when I am warm at the surface after my dives can I push them back down.

The wind coming from the winter sea is like knives cutting through the body. I have heard from men up in the mountains who had told me about cold, but I never imagined how it is to have bones aching as if they were broken, to have no feelings in my feet and my fingers, and to have my teeth clattering without any movement from my will at all. My lungs are going hard every time we breathe in the frozen air.

"Now," said the master, (for we were his slaves), "stand here until you are dry." We have to stand motionless, at full attention. Not a word is spoken, the night is not finished and we are expecting more.

"How are you? Are you cold?" calls the trainer. "Ah," comes his reply to our trembling response, "good, then we will see if the sea water is warmer or colder than the swimming pool."

We march four abreast to the seashore, our boots squelching, in formation. The officer calls to us:

"Company! March!" And we march into the sea, continuing until the water is up to our necks.

"Are you cold?" calls the trainer. "Which is more cold? The sea or the swimming pool?"

We do not dare to answer. Again he calls, and still we cannot answer. A third time he calls and a third time we all remain silent.

"So," he says to us, "then we must check again the swimming pool to compare the temperatures." And back we all go, to be marched into the pool. Of course the pool is even colder than the sea. And again we stand in the wind to dry out a little, and again we are marched down to the sea. This we continue to do for 4 hours. Now it is daylight. Finally, we are given half an hour break to change clothes, shave and then the day's training begins again after breakfast.

During the day we are taught in classrooms about how to make and detonate bombs and explosives, and how to switch off a live mine, how to put mines under the ships, how to position mines under the hulls with magnets, how to transport the mines underwater and so on.

Some of the other forms of physical training included being greeted in the morning by an officer who would make us do 50 push-ups, and then 50 more before he is satisfied that we have greeted him properly. Crawling through fields of mud and clay in full combat gear all day is another form of training, then through fields of thistles. It takes hours for us to remove the thorns from each other's bodies.

Twice a week a professor of karate and ju jitsu comes to teach us these martial arts. Another kind of exercise is obstacle training, and for this I always have the best time, and with swimming races and free diving, fishing with the spear gun, all these I am able to excel at. How to parachute from helicopters with full diving gear, how to collect and save people from shipwrecks, all these things one must know. First aid is essential training. All kinds of rifle practice, how to kill enemy guards in the dark with a knife. How to determine the quantity of explosives you need for blowing up different types of bridges. All communication is via semaphore and Morse code.

After four months this kind of life becomes easier for me. I am light and strong. I begin to enjoy the life of exercise in this school of a thousand lessons. They are lessons for life itself. Not only how to kill, or how to sink a ship, or how to blow up houses and factories, but also because you learn how to survive in every physical and moral condition. Another of the training practices is learning how to cope with the insults and verbal abuses deliberately aimed to break our morale. Many men leave in this time.

There were two most important exercises before the Passing Out. One is to swim 14 miles. We are dropped into the ocean naked except for a mask and flippers, nothing else. We are 30 to begin, and only 13 made the beach. Perhaps the others were picked up; I never see them again anyway. We swim all day. The second exercise is to be taken by boat to an island about 6 hours from the base and abandoned there for seven days with only a knife. There is no water and no food. We call this the week of the devil. We eat sea urchins, crabs, a few crustaceans. We cannot fish for we have no masks, we turn the rocks to find small things, sometimes an octopus, which we leave in the sun to dry. We rinse our mouth with sea water, but there is nothing to drink. Seven days later the Navy vessel comes to pick us up. All of us who landed, survived. On board is a wonderful lunch to welcome us. Everyone eats well. Six hours later we all develop the most shocking diarrhoea. It is not part of the training, but the béchamel sauce on the lasagne was made the previous day and the cream had gone off. We have three days to recover from this unfortunate episode before we go to Athens where we return to the base for the Passing Out Ceremony and to receive our Diplomas. Thirteen people succeeded – twelve men from the first intake, and myself, the only one from my intake of 850 men. I make up the number thirteen and, since the School began, it was the thirteenth course.

When I return to Athens I am called in to see my officer. I have been chosen to go on a very special and secret mission to Cyprus. Six other commandos are to go with me, we are seven very special people. But we are not given any idea of what we have been chosen for or what the military want us to do. We are given false passports and papers and names. I am a medical student from Athens returning home. The vessel we are travelling on is full of military, but even they do not know that we are commandos, they think we are civilian

Cypriot students. On deck the military also wear civilian clothes, and some are dressed as women with parasols parading the decks to confuse the Turkish planes which fly over us into believing we are all harmless civilians.

We moor offshore and in the night ferryboats take us commandos to a small bay. Our work is to swim around Cyprus and measure the ocean depths from various distances from the shore. We have a line and a weight each, and record the measurements on a small blackboard. We are so tired; we have to swim up to 14 hours a day, and where we land at the end of each day we find a jeep waiting to take us to the nearest hotel. The military requisitions rooms for us to sleep in, but we never had time to wash or change clothes for we are out in the morning at first light. One of the other commandos is so concerned about making the sheets dirty in his diving gear that he put a towel down on the bed before he lays on it.

One day, about when we have completed this reconnaissance, we return to the base and are told to load thirty bombs with magnets for a mission the following day. The following day we are taken to a spot about three to four miles off shore. We tie the bombs to buoys, which we had deflate just enough so that they are a few inches under the water and can trail behind us as we pull our particular loaded buoy. It is a very dark night. We swim silently for those miles to reach the quay of M. harbour. The sea is quite rough outside the quay but within the harbour all is still. Moored adjacent to each other in the harbour are eleven Turkish ships. Each one of us has our orders and our duties, first to quietly quietly position the bombs under the hulls of the vessels, being aware that soldiers with guns and dogs are just a few metres away patrolling the quay alongside the ships. The darkness and our silence cover us. We attach all the bombs and swim back to our grouping within the harbour, but still quite some distance from the ships. Then we have to swim back a second time to link up the connection that will trip the bombs in unison and explode them.

Because I am the fastest swimmer I propose that the other men swim to safety out of the harbour while I make the connection and set the timing device of the explosives to give myself five minutes space to swim clear of the harbour before the bombs go off. It has taken some of the slower swimmers about ten minutes to enter the harbour and join our group, but know I can reach safety faster than that.

I set the device and swim with all my speed. But I cannot see the entrance to the harbour at all. The darkness is complete. I reach the rocky wall and follow its curve when suddenly the entire fleet explodes. The explosion of the ocean itself flings me against the rock wall, completely crushing three ribs. I pause to gain my breath, and when I realize I can still swim I strike out again for the entrance. I reach it and crawl around to the open sea, but there is no way I can swim the three or four miles to our vessel in the much rougher open sea. By now I am in pain, a lot of pain, though I am still fully conscious. I manage to find a small cave in the outer wall and creep in there to rest. I know that my vessel will have to leave without me. I barely sleep and I fight the pain all night.

The next morning I watch as wave after wave of Turkish planes fly over the harbour to bomb the Greek villages. Forty four of them I read later in the newspapers. Who can blame them? It is a war we are fighting. On the third day all is silent. I creep out of my hole, hungry and exhausted. I look around. Nothing to be seen anywhere to indicate I am being hunted. I creep back into my hole. Then some hours later I creep out again, for the day remained silent. I see an old Greek priest on a donkey combing the beach. He is whistling a certain code. Softly I whistle back to him. He has been sent from a nearby monastery to see if he can find me, or my body. Back in Rhodes everyone has been told I have died on Cyprus. The old priest beckons me to remain where I am. Shortly afterwards he comes back with a second priest on a donkey and a hessian potato sack. I manage to get to the shore and the two men bundle me into the sack, heaving me up over the donkeys' backs. They take me to their monastery to rest for three days while they look after me until a special military plane comes to take me back to hospital in Athens. When I hear there is a shortage of beds I say I will leave, they can give my bed to someone else.

CHAPTER THREE

Pericles read on and on before blurred eyes made him set down the manuscript. It was 2 a.m.; he reached a natural break in the narrative and sat staring into the moonlit garden below and beyond the windows, aware of the shifting levels of his thoughts. The man whose life he had entered had the gift of story-telling, a gift the gods have bestowed on all Greeks. The tale Pericles had been reading had pulled him in as surely as listening to a master raconteur over an afternoon of ouzo and mezes. He stood up, stiffly, walked into the quiet kitchen, unsure of whether to boost his faculties with a strong coffee, or to make a tisane from his mother's herbs and bring his mind to ease and his body to rest. She was right; in this manuscript there was a "case" that needed attention. Too much remained unanswered. This man, this war hero, was too formidable a human to frankly, just disappear. His adult years, head-hunted as a barge-master, a diver, an explosives expert, a man who showed uncommon courage, surviving horrific accidents to save a worker, to rescue someone ... any one of these tales would make a hero.

Pericles reflected on the coincidence that, as chance would have it, he was shortly due a week off. It was a longstanding arrangement reaching back to student days, an annual pilgrimage, he liked to call it, to fly to London to visit a remarkable Englishwoman with whom he had boarded as a student while reading for his Bachelor of Law at LSE. He loved London and looked forward to this trip every October. Staying with Alice in recent years had left Pericles with a sense that hospitality was becoming less easy for her, so he took rooms close by, in a large house owned by the local Greek Orthodox Church. Alice and he would make their way to the Church of the Dormition of the Mother of God on the Sunday of his visits and afterwards they would share the hospitality of Vrisaki's table. It had become a deeply satisfying arrangement without incurring great demands other than pure pleasure on either of them.

Alice was now in her eighties, her life's work had been for the underdog, the poor, the foreign students adrift in London, the mentally deficient, the dispossessed – and some of the latter from the blacker of the emergent African nations had dispossessed her of wealth and wherewithal, posing as they did as members of the insular Swiss Church of which her parents had been strong figures of the foundation in the 'twenties and 'thirties. A generous woman without guile, Alice was always deeply hurt at these betrayals which were happening more in recent years; years long since Pericles had proved one of her dearest students, sharing a deep spiritual bond based on their agreed ultimate goodness of the human spirit. He had boarded with her for some years, feeling as at home in Bounds Green, which abounded with Greeks and Turks living amicably together, as he was on Rhodes itself. He would bring her the Moleskine diary, its tiny pencil hand too small for him to comfortably read, or to understand its allusions and nuances in a language no longer so familiar.

Waking too early in spite of the lateness of sleep, Pericles looked into the morning, its light beginning to stain the world's beginning at the far horizon of the sea. The night's reading dominated his thoughts, whoever had written it had been sensitive to the man's own form of English, was able to convey the passion and the power and the terror of the man's personal experiences in an authentic way. Pericles felt he knew the man himself through the skilful truth of the narration.

Shaving, dressing and leaving the house long before usual he patted the pocket book safe in his jacket. Reaching his office Pericles parked his car and headed for the beach where coffee and a sweet pastry in the Finnish café would help him clear his thoughts. Finishing both, and placing a generous note in the small table glass with the bill, he whirled out of the café, returned to his car and drove purposefully back to Ialyssos.

Pulling up in front of the open roller door, a spit of gravel crunching under the tyres of the Spider, he surprised a wrench wielding Kosta intent on persuasion tactics. "Kyrios Pericles! what brings you here so early!" It was a statement, not a question.

"*Kalimera* Kosta, let me come straight to the point, this missing Aristo, I read his story, or part of it, last night. Couldn't sleep. A man like him doesn't just disappear. We still have his car. His neighbours have seen nothing. I learned yesterday from you and from others there is a foreign woman involved and his book, his story, wouldn't have taken five minutes to write, she must have been around for *months* to get his story down on the papers we found left in his car. Yet his neighbours didn't say they saw her, maybe they didn't think it important. Maybe he has a lot of ladies, what's one more? Tell me what you know from your father about this man. And what happened when he came back to Rhodes after his life in the ocean? Where is his wife, she is registered on the property in town but she isn't there and his neighbours make no mention of her? If she was around they would have told me to ask her. Where can I find her?"

"Hmmm Kyrios Pericles – I know a little, but I know the man has no enemies, he is a good man, he will tell you himself. And courage, *po! po!* courage of ten lions, and strength. His wife? She is French, doesn't live here, doesn't live with him, they have been separate for years though she comes and goes because of the son. The son, you must have met him, he had that restaurant in the Old Town and his mother would come twice a year for holidays. Kyrios Aristo has properties in Paris, he lived in France working for that French diving company drilling oil wells in the Gulf. His wife keeps the properties and she didn't want to leave Paris. He was not happy in France, that we all know. He came back to Rodos with just enough money from his French years to buy that old Turkish palace at the top of the Old Town and spent a year doing up those twenty-two rooms to make a successful hotel. This man, Aristo, he works like ten, but his son doesn't like to help, and the wife isn't here – and then some years back I hear that an American tourist comes to stay and she has a story with Kyrios Aristo, you know how it is, these blondes on holiday. She tells him she will buy his hotel. As an American she is not permitted to buy the hotel but she arranges with an English company to buy it on her behalf. Money re-arranges legal loopholes. She offers Aristo a small advance, tells him she will pay the rest over five years. No interest, and no increments for property inflation. Aristo said he had no choice, he was running himself into the ground. Imagine! A Greek falling for that! His empty pockets hurt a lot! But enemies, no I don't think so. Hurt pride and empty pockets don't make *him* enemies though he might think angry thoughts about the arrangement that left him poor after such a life. When we took on the Euro a coupla years back he lost so much, we all did, the drachma vanished and the next day the price of a cucumber rose to cost more than what we paid for Metaxa the day before. Our idiots fell in line with those German opportunists." A deep frown drew one dark line across his forehead as Kosta remembered his anger: "Huh! They beggared us in war and now they beggar us in peace, *and* now they buy our land to build for tourists so we can't afford to live in our own villages! And did those *malakas* ever give back what they stole from our banks?"

Placing his hand on Kosta's broad shoulder Pericles nodded in sympathy. He knew so many whose lives had been almost crushed by the precipitate political pressure to make Greece part of the EU. A few had profited shamelessly, countless number had suffered silently. Kosta's outburst over, Pericles said his thanks and prepared to drive away. Kosta called after him: "Kyrios Pericles I will phone my cousins and set a trail, women love these things, we'll find him don't you worries." Pericles caught a glimpse in the Spider's rear view mirror of Kosta as he downed his wrench, wiped his hands on a cleaner piece of dirty rag and picked up the phone.

Pericles returned to the impounded vehicle, checked the tyres, observed the sand in the treads, the overall cleanliness of the interior, the way all inside was strapped tidily to the wheel hubs, folded neatly, stacked firmly. This was a very ordered mind, not the mind of a man who would do something messy, or leave a mark.

He opened the door of the abandoned vehicle from the driver's side this time. A glint of yellow caught his eye. To his astonishment he clearly saw something he had missed on the earlier search. There, at the side of the passenger seat, caught on the seat belt spring, was a gold earring. A large and exquisite piece of jewellery fit for a Byzantine empress and costly beyond his assessment. How could he or Ilias have missed this? Pericles ran over the earlier scene in his mind, satisfying himself that he and Ilias had looked over the car from the opposite side; it was curiosity rather than sinister prompts that had guided their perhaps too casual search. However, whoever the passenger was she had class and if he found the owner of the earring maybe she would know where Aristo Theohalis was.

Hesitantly Pericles removed the earring, holding it in his hand and turning it this way and that. It was 22 carat gold, a circle perhaps 3cm diameter, made up of rows of gold droplets holding a filigree of spirals which supported a central triple layered rose of breathtaking delicacy. From the outer circle a rose, the Rose of Rhodes, hung suspended, and pendant to the rose a pearl, a cylinder of lapis lazuli and another pearl. Gracing the pendant hung a loop of finest gold chain attached by two tiny circlets. The sleeper was hinged, the whole a master craftsman's copy of a work of great antiquity. The clue of its provenance lay in the Rose of Rhodes. Rhodians of old were famed for their gold work; whoever executed this piece had carried this acknowledged gift in his veins to this day. Pericles held it gently in his palm as he walked into his office and finding a small thick brown envelope placed the earring inside and put the insignificant looking package at the back of his office safe, rolling the barrel of numbers to confuse the code from anyone but himself and Ilias.

Collecting his case from the carousal at Heathrow a few days later Pericles smiled at the grubby familiarity of the world's most important airport as he made his way to the blessedly convenient Piccadilly Line that carried him from the airport terminal directly to Bounds Green, directly, in fact to Brownlow Road, at the lower end of which Alice lived.

"My dear!" Alice advanced like a billowing sale to enfold him, pulled him inside and led him down the small and narrow and so familiar hall to the small dining room overlooking a garden of happy disarray. Pericles pulled out bottles of purest olive oil, packets of various specialty biscuits and pastries, olives and *dolmathes* made by his mother's cook, rich and full and dripping with flavour. It felt good to sit together and drink the familiar English tea in the warmth of this woman's generous company.

On the flight Pericles had time to look again into the Moleskine. The owner had written her coordinates: *Alexa Buddicom, Magdalene Court, Glastonbury*, with a phone number alongside a request for the return of the diary if found. Pericles had telephoned the number on two occasions since finding the journal, leaving a non-committal message with his own phone number to return the call. No return call had come, but it was on his mind to drive down to Glastonbury; he had not been there since his student days. He had been drawn there then by the Arthurian mysteries, and the sense of sacred landscape so dear to his Greek soul. It was Alice who had suggested he go, she had known some of the old Avalonians; Wellesley Pole, Firth, and briefly, Buckton, an inspiration, whose name she shared, though Alice had retained her own particular blend of Eastern and Christian affinities which strangely suited her interpretation of the young Greek's own Orthodox. Shriven of dogma, Alice's visionary spirituality had inspired Pericles to take a deeper look at the legends and inheritances of Glastonbury, the coming of Joseph of Arimathea bringing the original Christianity, and the palpable sanctity of the Abbey ruins themselves.

It crossed his mind that Alexa might be a particularly interesting personage and he was impatient to involve Alice in the mystery of the Moleskine as soon as tea was over.

"It's good to be here, you look as magnificent as ever! How are your feet these days?" Alice's stature weighed heavily on feet too delicate for their task over the years and now their age was beginning to deliver a number of problems. Having been assured that her special slippers gave her comfort Pericles returned to the issue troubling him.

"I have a dilemma on my hands Alice and I think you will be able to help. A man has gone missing on Rhodes, quite well known in his way, his car was abandoned and in it was a manuscript and a diary. I have read some of the manuscript, it's quite dramatic, but the diary is written in pencil, in English, and in a small hand too fine for me to read effectively, I just don't have the facility in English any more. It's an unorthodox procedure I know, but as there are no suspicious circumstances I have brought it for you to read for me. I intend hiring a car and driving down to Glastonbury on Thursday to pay a visit to the lady in question. She may be away, I can't get her on the phone, but some instinct tells me to go. Would you like to accompany me?"

Alice responded by saying she would read the diary first, their conversation continued, warm and familiar, catching up, reminiscing. The autumn evening darkened early and once the tea tray was cleared Alice went to rest as Pericles left to head for his rooms in Nightingale Road. The pair would meet in the morning to plan their few days together.

In spite of the darkness it was still early and Pericles allowed himself a short detour before reaching his rooms to visit the old Turkish Cypriot cobbler, one of the last craftsmen of a trade going back to the time of the Seljuk Turks with their caravanserais a thousand years ago.

"Effendi, *merhaba,*" greeted Pericles pushing the door and making the camel bells ring, "how are you?" The cobbler looked up with a welcoming and wry smile, embracing both meanings: "*hos geldinis* my friend", he wasn't as good as last year, arthritis in his fingers makes stitching difficult, but "welcome, welcome, *effendi*, how good you are here again."

Their reunion called for tiny tulip glasses of heavily sugared apple tea, steaming on a red tin tray brought in by the cobbler's wife. The usual greetings and family inquiries dispensed with Pericles asked Kemal if he remembered anything of the '64 civil war in Cyprus. "Not much my friend, though I was at school when one of your lot blew up our ships in the harbour. My grandmother suffered earache from our airborne retaliation for the next days. Why on earth do you ask? It's good we are all brothers in this country and can talk calmly about these things; they're still shredding themselves over there."

"Actually that's what has been on my mind these last days," responded Pericles. "You see, a man on Rhodes has gone missing, we found his car, and inside was a manuscript and a couple of other things that seem to belong to a foreign woman. We can't be sure yet, it doesn't look suspicious, just curious. I read the manuscript, or some of it, and I read the whole of the Cyprus plot. The missing man was the diver who attached the limpet bombs to the hulls of your ships."

Kemal let out a slow whistle. "Too much water under the bridge my friend, but even twenty five years ago his name had a death warrant attached to it, probably still has, it is better to let the past lie under sand. What was the man's name again? There was a time when we all thought we knew it!"

"Aristo Theohalis," replied Pericles. "Yes we should let the past be, and I don't want to bring up memories, but it seems so strange – his car had too many kilometres on the clock to account for being on Rodos these recent weeks, he had obviously taken it off the island but no one has seen him, or seen the woman again, and her diary was in the car, it had fallen under the seat, but his manuscript, the story of his life, was there on the passenger seat asking to be read. It's a drama alright, his life I mean, real Greek style. I hope it isn't a Greek tragedy too."

"Aristo Theohalis! That's the one!" laughed Kemal, still juggling with the name Pericles had given, "we thought we'd make a million if we found him and handed him over but if the Turkish forces really wanted to find him they would have. You don't think they finally got him?"

"I hadn't thought of that, but that wouldn't account for the mileage, or for the shadowy presence of the foreigner. If you Turks had got him there would be a body for us."

"You're right, we'd leave a calling card," Kemal laughed affectionately at his old friend. Dimitra, Pericles wife, had been a local girl, local to Wood Green, her family had come to England from Kriti, driven by poverty after World War Two. Kemal's young wife had been at school with her. Alice, of course, had been at their local wedding in the splendid Trinity Road Orthodox Church; another full family affair with multiples of cousins was celebrated on Rhodes during that summer when the world glowed with the happiness of two beautiful people on whom the sun shone. The two men didn't speak of the tragedy the Fates held in store, each honouring the silence on a subject too painful for the light of day.

"So my friend, how is your Alice? I don't see her out much these days, I suppose she lives in those slippers, they'll go on forever." Pericles grinned, it was Kemal who created the soft kid and wool lined slippers for Alice from his own design and craftsmanship – a craftsmanship little called for in these days of mass footwear flooding the poor feet of *fashionistas* too silly to know that by the time they were the age of Alice their own feet would need far more than the ancient skills of a Kemal to keep them comfortable.

The two men spoke of old days, promising to meet over a meal after Pericles trip to Glastonbury but first there would be the usual gathering for supper that evening. Returning to the main road Pericles located the car rental office in the nick of time to pick up the pre-booked Peugeot 307 for his couple of days. Getting used to closing time in England, opening time in Rhodes, was always a challenge on his first day or two. He deposited his case in his rooms, hung its contents, set out his toiletries before walking over to the Church of the Dormition for quiet reflection; a habit from his earliest years when the proximity of the Church had inspired his choice of board and lodging with Alice, a decision he had never ceased to be thankful for.

Alice had taken the Moleskine to bed with her. In recent years she indulged in a late afternoon nap, occasionally reflecting on why the English (she was Swiss after all, even if many of her younger siblings had been born in Hornsey, in that great barn of a family house that was now part of the College of Art) resisted simple pleasures like siestas and winter heating twenty-four-seven and double glazing and snow tyres and full down duvets and cooking mushrooms with white wine and butter and garlic. Life here was so *puritanical* at times. Perhaps that was the inheritance they carried: since Henry VIII and that murderous *puritan* dynasty of Cromwells had successfully destroyed Merrie England in the 1530's food was a demeaning experience, and as for dancing and sensuality and wine and song! Well! It was almost as drear as Switzerland where a similarly humourless man had single handedly raised himself to power. It occurred to Alice more frequently now that what she loved about Catholic France and Orthodox Greece was their open devotion to the Mother of God, a devotion which was so apparent in the feminine expression of daily life: love of fine food, a good kitchen, flowers, children, warmth, dance, music, *abundance.* A sensual cornucopia of life and beauty in fact. The Calvinist church of her parents fitted well in Puritan England, although her father, as clergyman, had visions of a religious unity and tolerance far beyond his pulpit. It was this she had inherited herself, always reaching out to other faiths, other races. Her small and fine boned Hindu lover of forty years had called her the Great White Goddess; she tucked him under her arm like a packed lunch when they travelled to India together. Alice was a large and generous woman in every sense; she referred to her statuesque proportions as a Stately English Galleon in Full Sail. Only now she was beginning to feel her age; her lover had died some years before, and Alice's little naps began then, taking one of a succession of rescued cats always named Jenny to bed in the afternoons when sleep or prayer would proffer up, *de profundis,* her reveries on life's frailties.

The last Jenny had also died, and was buried with the others in the tangled garden beyond the bedroom window, always under the apple tree. Alice climbed under her quilt, still clothed, and opened the Moleskine. *"Alexa Buddicom",* she read, and approved the name's *vibration.* She began to read, and read, and read.

The hours darkened the sky, the wind rose, her heating kicked in – and the phone rang.

"Alice? Pericles, I want to invite you to lunch tomorrow, I am taking you to the restaurant at the British Museum, it's time we paid our respects to Demeter of Knidos and her Lion. I love that place, I can forgive Elgin, for here the whole world can see our marvellous Marbles, and for free, whereas only half the world visits Athena! I'll come for you by eleven, is that alright with you?"

"I would love to," responded Alice, "you know I don't get out on my own so much now, and lunch with you and Demeter will be a joy. She's the only other Goddess I know who resembles a Stately Galleon. But my dear, we will have serious conversations about your mysterious foreigner. She is not mysterious at all, just an intelligent woman who loves a man who, no matter how she excuses his behaviour, treats her disgracefully. I'd say he was barking mad, and you know I don't say that lightly of anyone. I usually say such people are hard to reach, but this one, this one has had his emotions lobotomised out of existence. Are you certain your war hero is the same man?"

Alice's unequivocal assessment of the subject whose biography had arrested him floored Pericles for a moment. He didn't question Alice, but his own reading and interpretation based on the known myth. Of course! The lack of emotional response-ability in the fleeting references to the few women in Aristo's life; the brutal training as a Commando and his solo survival of it; abandoning the barge and crew he captained, for nothing more than thwarted personal authority – these were revelations of an inner character to a large extent overshadowed by the dramatics of his physical courage and resourcefulness. Pericles had been carried away by the man's myth of himself.

The two friends chatted on for some minutes, tacitly agreeing to leave further talk of the Moleskine revelations until the following day, to be discussed over tea and gossip when they returned from lunch. Alice would only say that it was imperative that Pericles visit Glastonbury, but no, she wouldn't accompany him, he needed to have all his instincts on red alert and not concern himself over the comforts of an old woman. "I suggest," she said, "you stay overnight down there, I have a feeling one thing will lead to another and you don't need time constraints."

The hair on the back of his neck prickled. Alice was the sanest women he knew, and one of the most intuitive. Some echo of his own disquiet sent ripples up from his own depths. But first, the pure enjoyment of supper with Kemal and friends tonight, and lunch with a couple of Goddesses tomorrow.

Walking from Russell Square gave Alice much pleasure, how many years of accumulative lunch hours had she spent in this most wonderful Museum of the world communing with the great Siva Nataraj before his rightful return home; with Sekhmet, with Demeter; gazing at the glorious horse of the Moon Goddess Selene; the Lion of Knidos; the Gayer-Anderson Cat; the funerary paintings of Fayum, those haunting portraits with their look of a personal farewell, eye to eye, their hieratic gaze looking through ones' very soul to other worlds far away. The grandeur of human expression from all these ancient statues resonated through the very cells of Alice's being. She recalled an occasion when the Museum had moved the great Demeter to her current cramped position at the top of a small flight of stairs whose proximity prevented proper reverence. Having stood for a considerable time at the only angle that afforded a full view of her, Alice made ready to continue down the stairs, but first she placed her hands, palms down, on the lap of the Goddess in respect and gratitude for the tranquillity that emanated from her as a blessing to those who paused by her for long enough. One of the attendants behind her coughed and warned loudly: *uh! oh!* against the forbidden physical contact. Turning to him Alice beamed her widest smile and said: "don't worry, *She* doesn't mind, She remembers me from our past life together!" Her response rendered the man silent as she swept past him down to the next gallery.

When Alice recalled her moment with Demeter to Pericles his delight in her active reverence for the gods and goddesses of his own ancestral consciousness vivified his own appreciation. It set another seal on their affection for each other.

Lunch was a rather splendid affair in the new upstairs brasserie: *cassoulet* and *coq au vin* being the choices of the day, followed by *mille-feuilles* and a *tarte tatin* every bit as excellent as Alice's; a good red and an equally good coffee. The attentions of the French waiters, delighted to speak with Alice in their mutual language, her family was from French-speaking Geneva, and mindful of her being beyond *a certain age*, placed their day's outing into the shared amalgam of mutual memories.

They travelled home contentedly, Alice broaching the subject of the Moleskine almost as soon as they had hung their coats.

"It seems to me," she began, as they settled themselves in her tiny dining room with its window on to the garden, "that Alexa, I will call her by her name as she has revealed her deepest thoughts to me, knew she was playing with fire when she returned to Rhodes for her 60th birthday; *shelf life of ten days before he blows*, she wrote. The diary stops on the 10th day – they are leaving for Metsova and Meteora that morning. You know as I do that those early deep sea divers suffer terrible mental problems, the gas mixes were hit and miss, it was a short life for most of them; those who survived made their fortune and got out. All this glamour of coral reefs and aquatic encounters is not Telly Tubby; it's terrifying. The reality of deep sea diving, saturation existence, laying pipelines, undersea explosives, going into sewerage blocks, is filthy and dangerous. Your man was a guinea pig for those early gas mixes; his behaviour patterns show great instability and cruelty. You say he was known as a loner? Hardly surprising, he wouldn't want to blow his cover, spoil his myth. Anyone coming too close would be privy to the cracks in his highly developed persona."

Alice paused. She could see Pericles was struggling to reverse the thought patterns he had formed, based on the common knowledge of popular opinion. She knew a shift in mental gearing was necessary before she offered her assessment of the woman whose diaries she was privy to.

"Go on, Alice" said Pericles after some moments, "I sense you have touched a possibility of interpretation I would not have considered. I have a feeling … no, tell me more first … go on with what you are thinking …"

Alice took a breath, let it whisper out with a quiet sigh, "She loved him, Pericles; Alexa loved him and was intelligent about their chances, but she had given him three years and it had already left her bereft of most of what she had, as well as being homeless. Why did she go back?"

Alice paused again, resting her fingers lightly on the Moleskine she had placed on the dining room table before the pair had left for lunch. Picking up her thread she took another breath and said:

"Perhaps we'll never know for sure, but he held her heart and for women, saying goodbye to a great love, and he *was* a great love, can be a long journey. A *very* long journey."

Pericles sat transfixed by the story Alice was unfolding. He made no comment, could not break the thickening atmosphere Alice's telling was drawing in to the room, as if the very presence of truth had been invited in. After a moment or two Alice continued:

"There was also the question of the book she had written for him. She is a writer, not well-known, but published, and she felt a professional responsibility to birth the manuscript both for the man and his myth, and also because she felt it was a personal memoir that stood up historically. He lived through pivotal points of his own history as well as the discovery and advances of the diving bell and the possibilities they opened up with the invention of gas mixes after wearing the old *skafandro*. He was a brave man, and a guinea pig, and she was able to distance her own feelings and despair to view their liaison as more than personal, to say professional would not do justice to its complexities, but nevertheless that was a consideration. That he was incapable of seeing this through the blinkered lens of his own narcissism discredits his, not her, integrity. I think, my dear, that if *she* has gone missing you have a serious investigation on your hands. Going to Glastonbury may prove a watershed."

CHAPTER FOUR

Glastonbury was an easy drive from Bounds Green, almost door to door if Pericles thought of it that way. Once he had turned on to the North Circular the traffic ran swiftly along to Gunnersbury Road and linked effortlessly to the M4. Congestion was confined to incoming lanes and Pericles sped the few miles along the motorway, swung onto the M25, joined the M3 and then settled into the charming drive along the A303 sweeping past the great standing stones of Stonehenge breasting Salisbury Plain. He hadn't been here for years, yet those great stones silent in their golden fields with only the clouds to frame them made his heart lurch. The landscape through Parnassus driving from the north had the same effect on him, the grandeur of the stone sentinels of the Tholos of Delphi still held secret the mysteries of the human heart. He slowed, noticed a lay-by to one of the many gates accessing the wheat fields and promised to himself he would stop for ten minutes on the way back to pay his silent respects to the great megaliths of this ancient landscape. But for now the nagging urgency of too late, too late, pushed him on.

By ten-thirty the town was still fairly empty. Parking the Peugeot in the Abbey car park he stepped into the fresh air and was suddenly enveloped in that most quintessentially English smell of freshly mown grass. It took him a split-second to identify it from his memory bank, it was not a smell associated with the dry boned ridges of his homeland. Behind him the ruins of the once most majestic Abbey towered above the car park wall, behind which lay acres and acres of Abbey grassland. The sweet smell of the *holiest erthe*.... Memories of Dimitra swept over him momentarily, he had promised to bring her here on one of their trips back to London but family reunions never left enough time, and time had passed them by.

Coffee had improved since he had been here before; true, it was a simulacrum of Italian, not Greek, but at least it didn't taste of flavoured dish-dregs that he had once received when he innocently asked for coffee in his youth. Even English tea was preferable to that. The toasted teacake dripping butter was welcome too, and the Abbey Tearooms were so charmingly *English* where so much else in the small High Street had become a pseudo pastiche of Calcutta or Sedona, selling crystals and fairy dust, promising enlightenment and exploiting the gullible, the lonely, the unwary, the lost. These alien attractions added to the harlequin appearance of Glastonbury High Street but for Pericles it was the smell of mown grass and the taste of West Country butter that was authentic.

He booked into the George and Pilgrim, the 14th century pilgrims' inn built to accommodate the wealthier pilgrims who made their way to the greatest Benedictine Abbey of Christendom. It was a pilgrimage of sorts that had brought him here.

Idly he inquired of the receptionist if she had known Alexa Buddicom. She hadn't, "not one of the regulars," she said.

Bookshops – where else would a writer go? There were any number along the one L shaped street of the town's singular shopping street. *Red alert*, cautioned Alice, *have your antennae on red alert, you might not have much time, you still haven't found the English woman. Is she victim – or suspect*?

Walking slowly, Pericles paused at the windows of each of the first four bookshops, five if he counted the stationers, six if he thought The Psychic Piglet displayed enough books to warrant inclusion. Passing the bakery, Burns the Bread, Pericles was reminded of how he loved this language, and how he enjoyed speaking it when the opportunities arose. Its underlying humour, its linguistic puns, were so *Greek!*

As he reached the last of the bookshops his attention was caught – Minotaur, what an ideal name for a bookshop, here he was following his own Ariadne's thread through a labyrinth of mysteriously missing people; a Minotaur was a coincidence he could begin with.

Pericles stepped inside, intending to first see if he could find the book Alexa had mentioned publishing. There on the central table amongst other neat stacks of books on various subjects the cover of a white cat stood out. Alexa's book. Picking it up he was charmed by the paintings that accompanied the text, a true story said the words on the cover, of a small boy and a magical cat. The writer painted icons and lived in Glastonbury.

Momentarily taken aback at the mention of icons he mentally questioned the book's biography – did they really mean *icons*? That was a specialised form of devotional art and required a certain grace of mind and spirit as well as hand – he decided to buy a copy of the mysterious Alexa's book for Alice.

As Pericles looked up he became aware of the woman behind the counter. She looked curious. They exchanged courtesies, as one does. On hearing him speak the woman asked where he was from. "Rhodes" had barely left his lips as her astonished reaction ricocheted around the book lined space.

"Rhodes! Oh, excuse me," she corrected herself, flustered, "I am so sorry to have burst out like that but the fact that you are from Rhodes, and that you are buying Alexa's book gives me goosebumps. I'm Eve, Alexa's a friend of mine, she went to Rhodes for her 60th birthday to be with her lover and she hasn't come back – and none of us know how to contact her. She was cell-phone phobic, didn't own one."

Pericles' head spun. This woman in front of him, she *knew* Alexa. He had phoned the number written in the Moleskine before leaving London, and again on arriving in Glastonbury. More ominous was a message from the service provider advising the account holder that twenty held messages was the limit and that the message box was now full. Wherever Alexa was she certainly wasn't home.

Pericles cleared his throat, uncertain of where to begin. "I am here because of Alexa," he said slowly, "I was hoping to talk to her about a man who has gone missing on Rodos. Now it seems you are telling me she is also missing. I am, as you might say, lost. What can you tell me?"

"This is the last postcard she sent me," Eve reached for one of a number of postcards blue-tacked to the wall, "here, read it, she hasn't been seen for over a month, this came from Ioannina."

"Zeus' personal Thunderbolt still as morose but we survived! Country is magical, Suli and Zalongo very moving (my choreography of sightseeing even impressed the Thunderbolt!). Meteora next, and then my beloved Delphi for my 60th birthday when I shall turn into an Oracle and predict the whimpering end of this affair! So sad, so much loss; see you soonest for tea and goss – A xxx"

"Alexa always referred to him as one of Zeus's thunderbolts," explained Eve, "he had a ferocious temper. None of us here saw it but many of us here felt uneasy about him after the saga of the past three years. We knew him as charming, but really he was very unstable."

Customers began to trickle into the shop. Pericles was torn between conflicting interests. Did Eve have a lunch hour? Could he take her to lunch? This could be a matter of someone's life, though he didn't know as he said it whether it would be Alexa's or Aristo's.

"Yes," said Eve firmly, "I'll arrange for a friend to come in and give me a break so we can talk as long as necessary. Come by at one o'clock and we'll go round to the Who'd a Thought It – a significant title for the occasion." She allowed herself a *frisson* of fantasy as she took in the man's profile – nothing like that along *our* High Street – she thought, thick silvery grey hair, cut long enough to confuse identifying his profession, and *so* finger friendly ...

"So who else has gone missing?" said Eve as they removed their coats and settled by the lounge fire in the old low beamed pub with the singularly appropriate name.

"Aristo," said Pericles, "his car was found abandoned in the south of the island a week or so back. Nothing seemed suspicious, except the missing man. A manuscript was on one of the seats, and we found what turned out to be Alexa's diary under the passenger seat, slipped there unnoticed I imagine. I have traced all possible leads and come up with very little."

"So why come to Glastonbury?" asked Eve.

"I come to London every year anyway, and I couldn't alert the owner of the diary on the phone, nothing has come through to us about missing persons, people on Rhodes recalled having met her with him when I tracked down his most recent movements – but nothing made sense. I am a detective but I am here unofficially. I hoped that Alexa might shed some light on his disappearance."

"D'you think he murdered her and then disappeared to avoid suspicion?" Eve's bluntness took the wind from his sails. The thought had not occurred to him.

"We-ell, it isn't a thought that carries much weight because of the man's reputation on the island as a war hero, but has anyone *here* reported *her* as missing?"

"No, I don't suppose they have, she travels a lot, on a shoestring, she could hang her hat on a sunbeam and life would support her, but if it would help then I'll put in a report when I get back to the shop. She – we all – get on with the local police and PCSO's who know her well because where she lives can be a bit of a rat run for druggies from the adjacent park. She's been trying to get security for her courtyard but you know the old saw about the Law of Neighbours: I'm alright Tom, Dick, Harry. They resent incomers to that little quarter and Alexa's arrival, washed up from Rhodes or further afield, drew forth a censorious xenophobia still buried in the older residents who remember The War! She was still battling for keypads to the gates to stop the druggies last I heard, their proximity bypassed the other bungalows, the residents were unaffected. I suggested her neighbours felt threatened by our weapons of mass perception y'know." Pericles smiled at the touch of humour. Eve continued, "anyway that's hardly relevant, but yes, I'll file an official report. By the way, whose manuscript was found, his or hers?"

"Are you suggesting there are two?"

"Yes, the one he press-ganged her into writing of his life while she was trapped out there, and the one about the terror and love of her whole experience with him which she wrote back here after her escape. Ever read *The Collector*, John Fowles? He wrote a lot about characters on Greece, lived in Lyme Regis. Alexa took Aristo there and he fell in love with the place. Well, her time on Rhodes became like that, he collected her, trapped her, maybe she's still there, trapped. Sorry, I'm sidetracking again. You have questions? Fire away."

"Begin at the beginning as you know it" said Pericles, as the waiter appeared with their meals; grilled wild Atlantic salmon, broccoli spears for Eve, and a rare sirloin, organically sourced from the Somerset fields around them, for Pericles. English food had come a long way since his student days. A silent moment of grace, and they tucked in.

Eve began to speak, slowly, garnering her thoughts.

"I know Alexa kept diaries, I had told her to write her own book. I knew she had written Aristo's bio and he had nearly killed her for it." She paused, as if remembering their conversation in a quiet corner of their favourite café just months before.

"In the beginning ... oh those gifts. Alexa had gone to a writer's conference on Rhodes and met Aristo in a jeweller's shop. He was a friend of the jeweller, the reason she had even gone in to look was another story, too long to tell here. When she told him her reason for being on the island the jeweller introduced her to his friend, Aristo, who happened to be sitting in the shop. Ari, he always referred to himself in the diminutive, needed a writer to write the book of his extraordinary life and voila! there she was in flesh and blood. Attractive flesh and blood in those days and the attraction was immediate and mutual. He was a handsome man you know."

Pericles didn't know, he had never met him, but he let it pass.

"She came back from that fortnight looking so radiant, so beautiful, she was a woman in love, and she was wearing an exquisite pendant of a shell she had found on some beach during their intoxicating romance. Ari had given it to his friend who had set it with a sapphire in a gold circle. We all wanted one. We all wanted one that came with a Greek lover. He was gorgeous then and adored her. We were all enchanted by his adoration, his showering of gifts, seven phone calls a day! Alexa didn't even know what a mobile phone was until she met Ari, then she was never without one, she found a pink plastic fluffy mobile phone pouch with a string of hearts as the handle and "wore" it over her arm, calling it her mobile heart. So out of character, and she never told anyone its number, not even me! She was known for stylish dressing, touches of French, *chapeaux* from a little *Chapellerie* in Nice, she had an *eye* for homing in on the one lovely thing in a charity shop full of trash. Her grandmother's name suggested Gallic blood in the bloodline.

Their passion was too intense for separation. He came here, she flew there. Then when he took her back to Rhodes it all went pear shaped. She took everything with her of course, gave up the protected tenancy on her studio apartment. He refused to let her have anything of hers in his house, put everything she owned in an old damp village cottage, wouldn't even allow her a book. A writer without a book? Like, stop her breathing!"

Eve, owner of a bookshop, paused to let the enormity of a writer being denied books sink in.

"She didn't speak Greek and the loneliness must have been agony for her. Two friends from here went to Rhodes on holiday and wanted to spend time with her in the early days. She wasn't permitted to see them for more than one hour in their whole two weeks. That was early on in the Rhodian domicile and she, and they, thought it was a cultural thing which would even itself out as time went by. It didn't. He staged one of his Grand Banquets for them, a sort of show – it was his public persona you know, Feeding the Five Thousand. He did it here, her friends with large homes would lend him their kitchen, she invited the guests, and he cooked the banquets. We were all impressed, obviously. Anyway the friends who went to Rhodes both put their doubts aside and entered the spirit of his offer to dinner; it was the night before they returned to England. One of the women, canny she was, left all the euros she had in her purse for Alexa who, having left Glastonbury had also lost her small income. It was a grim time – months went by and when we phoned she was not allowed to answer, her mobile pay-as you-go-heart had run out, she was completely isolated. A few of her friends got together and emailed her to say they would have a whip round to bring her home, but she would have lost everything she owned to his village house and she couldn't do it. Somehow she met an English woman on Rhodes who helped her escape, rather dramatically, back to Australia – followed by Aristo, whose charm faded abruptly when her old Oz friends hardly recognised her. Apparently one of them said Alexa looked like she'd been exhumed from the grave when she picked her up from the airport! At least one other pronounced her to be in a domestic violence situation and more sinister than all that were the comments of her GP here in Glastonbury. He had read her book," Eve flicked her finger indicating Alexa's book in Pericles' bag, "and promptly left for Oz. Anyway she and Ari stayed with he and Pixie before coming back here. It was a macabre unmerry-go-round and Jeremy took her aside and admonished her about her own safety. He thought Ari had brutality written all over him. How do I know all this? She left me a copy of *her* manuscript."

Pericles had stopped eating. He shook his head in disbelief. He knew in his marrow that Eve was telling it as it was.

"Why would Alexa go back to Rhodes again, after all that?" he managed to ask, more as a statement than a question.

"Ah, well, Inspector," Eve's eyes twinkled as she turned her head faintly, flirtatiously, shaping her next sentence carefully, "Alexa wasn't what you'd call worldly when it came to men. Most of us," she laughed, "had the experience of the Grand Passion and the Impossible Love in our twenties or thirties: violence, wouldn't commit, misjudgement, still married and so on and so on. Alexa was a sort of nun during *her* thirties, looking for the Divine Love you know, and when Aristo met her she was well into her fifties, he was that divine lover. And, frankly, anyone who gives you a pair of earrings fit for a Byzantine Empress is pressing a suit that can hardly be refused unless the suitor was a monster. And he wasn't ..." The words hung in the air until their eyes met, something passed between them, and both almost whispered ... "*or perhaps he was...*"

Pericles' thoughts spun like a dust-devil – earrings? A shock wave through his solar plexus.

"Earrings? Did you say earrings? Did you see them? Can you describe them? Have you a photo?"

"Did I see them! Half of Glastonbury saw them! And when she returned after her escape, via Australia I might add, we welcomed her back and most of us added *sotto vocé: 'hope you hung on to the earrings!'* As a matter of fact I *do* have a photo and it was taken recently – she had aged, a lot, the experience had taken its toll, but the earrings are magnificent. I'll bring it in to the shop tomorrow."

They consulted the dessert menu; nothing inspired them, not even the ubiquitous *crème brûlée* which both knew would not match up to its cultural origins. "Two cappuccinos," said Pericles, thankful the Italians had pioneered the west and were now firmly established. He recalled the Italian POW's held in Somerset who refused to go home when they were released after the War was over. They stayed and married local lasses, introduced grapevines into Glastonbury gardens, garlic into stews, wine to the table and coffee anytime, real coffee.

Pericles repeated the one obvious question again as they each spooned their froth: why did Alexa return?

"It was her 60th birthday in September," sighed Eve, "she had come back from Australia and had a harrowing nine homeless months until she was offered the grace and favour bungalow where she now lives; she has an elegant way of expressing her penury – to the rest of us it's a council house or social housing, for Alexa it's a grace and favour residence. She has style, breeding, call it what you will. Anyway she had tried to sever all contact, but she did love him, or at least the man whose myth she's recorded. The whole affair was so bizarre, and when she was given the malevolent little hovel by the council it nearly finished her off. Councils were no longer obliged to repair or decorate or clean places vacated by noisome or destructive tenants and in despair she told Ari of its ruinous state during one of his phone calls."

Eve shook her head at the anomaly as she recalled: "and he got on the next plane with his tools and paint brushes and heaven knows what and came here to spend a month decorating and repairing it and settling her in. He was formidable. But she knew he had a shelf life of ten days or so and sure enough he erupted. At least she was on home territory, spoke her own language and was surrounded by friends. She collapsed one day from the strain of it all and he finally flew home. The bungalow is tiny but home, she has taste and an eye and a sense of placement. What's so strange is that Ari would do all this, spend a fortune on The Grand Statement – those earrings for example. Yet when she was on Rhodes he took her to his dentist for a pre-existing perio problem that was causing her pain, and the dentist told Ari that she had to see a specialist periodontal surgeon. He point blank refused her. She hadn't the money to go independently and she had forfeited her regular treatments here because he'd promised her the world there. A world that didn't include dentists apparently. She was to suffer greatly."

Pericles' skin prickled slightly. Puzzled over the narrative so at odds with a hero or an empress's earrings made him feel uneasy at the contradictions of priorities, teeth, surely were important, but to ignore the pain of someone you loved? That was something alien to Pericles' thought processes.

Eve had paused momentarily, concentrating on spooning the froth from the cappuccino before continuing: "then last July she disappeared for ten days, telling no one until she returned that she had gone back to Ari. She laughed when she said: *ten days, that's his shelf life, if we can manage ten days together every two or three months we'll survive.* She was turning sixty in September – and you know the rest. He promised her the trip around Greece, which, with her considerable knowledge of ancient, classical and contemporary Greek history, she knew far more about than he did. She would have loved it, and loved sharing it with him – he spent much of his life in France, and he isn't an educated man you know, she wanted him to know his own magnificent heritage the way educated foreigners know it. It grieved her that he was so Greek, and felt so *un*-Greek. Even his accent was French Greek, and oh, you should have heard his English – French enough to make any woman's toes curl."

The reference to her considerable knowledge, reflected Pericles, explained the remark on the postcard, *Suli* – who would know of the women of Suli but another woman who felt passionately about Greece?

As they got up to leave Eve turned to the Inspector: "and saying goodbye, Pericles, for a woman who loves, can be a very long journey."

The echo of Alice's words dropped like a plumb bob into the darkest depths of his thought, exposing him to the softness in Eve's voice as she said his name. In muzzy confusion her words shimmered around his heart like the haze of a spring moon. Her voice caught his attention: "Glastonbury is full of colourful characters you know, for better or worse. When you walked up the High Street did you happen to see a couple who look like twins? I noticed they passed the door just before you came in. Mousy coloured hair to the waist, slim, small? She wears the walking stick and he wears the lipstick and both wear long dresses, he was wearing a puce floor length satin number today."

He? Pericles' look said *startled*, an uncommon expression for him. Eve laughed softly, "yes, I know, you thought they were sisters! Actually they're he and she and there's no accounting for taste in this place. Keep your eyes open, one of the tallest of the old hippies who washed up here, and who still peddles his drugs and his sex Olympic proposals, wears a dashing carmine toenail polish and a flowing nicotine stained beard. It's all normal for Glastonbury. Have fun while you're here, you won't see the like on Rhodes!"

Pericles spent the rest of the afternoon observing the locals, with more than a dash of affectionate appraisal at their appearances, before his more tourist pursuits of climbing the Tor, exploring the churches, lighting candles for Alexa, for Dimitra, Adriana, Ion, for Alice – and for Aristo, in the light-filled Catholic church dedicated, he noted, to Holy Mary, Our Lady of Glastonbury. How dim and grim were the other churches without the warmth of candles and the protecting veil of the Mother of God, he mused. Though he wasn't a regular church goer himself his love for the Mother of God came gene-programmed. Later, as he returned from walking Wick Hollow, he paused at the lower end of the High Street held by the sound of a harpist playing in a café, the Café Persephone. With such a Greek name he chose to eat a light supper there. The owner opened a conversation, it was quiet at that time of evening and he was a stranger, where was he from? Rhodes?

"Well!" exclaimed the woman who introduced herself as Philippa, and her ready warmth invited Pericles' response: "Was Alexa known here?"

"Most certainly she was, and so was Ari, a humourless character much of the time, don't know what she saw in him," said Philippa, "I had uncomfortable feelings about them all the time she was on Rhodes. When I heard she'd escaped to Australia I couldn't believe it – she'd left there years ago to come home here. When she eventually got back again whatever journey she had been on had etched a calligraphy of lines to her face."

As he ate his cannelloni and downed a good organic red Pericles began to wonder at the contradictions; what he was hearing was an altogether different view to that of the war hero of Rhodes.

He turned in early, thankful for the heating and extra blankets in the old pilgrim inn. The bed was comfortable and his sleep was sound and deep.

The following morning the Minotaur bookshop did not open until ten o'clock, leaving him time to shower and shave with leisurely pleasure. He reflected on the conversations he would later share with Alice, the results of his trip confirmed her instincts tenfold. Fortifying himself with a full English breakfast, *no wonder they kept their Empire so long*, Pericles chuckled to himself, pondered on how he would be able to buy in to the war hero myth of the good man when he returned to Rhodes. And yet, maybe he could, when in Rome.... To those for whom Aristo Theohalis was a hero he would always remain thus, and rightly so; to those for whom he was anything other he would also remain thus, and rightly so. There still, however, remained the mystery of his disappearance, and now, definitively, Alexa's.

Eve's smile greeted him like a dewdrop in the desert, her smile dawning in his direction as he entered the shop.

"I've given the report" she said, "PC Marple came by late yesterday, when I told him he agreed he hadn't noticed Alexa recently. Apparently the report of a missing national abroad goes directly to Interpol. Maybe you could put Ari down as going to France and now missing, it might speed things up a bit. I confess that my instincts when I tune in to Alexa are not comfortable."

Pericles was momentarily nonplussed; she had something there, perhaps they were all missing that *something* back on Rhodes. The fact so many people knew Aristo and thought his a good character meant it was distinctly possible they had overlooked more subtle possibilities.

"Eve," he said, liking the sound of her name, "you are right, I'll call my office and put the facts on file, we have too much information now to continue this naïvety. Alexa missing, Aristo missing ..."

Eve handed him a photo, and a CD. "Thought you might like this, it's not a man's story and you might well find it boring but some of us women who read it were moved to the marrow. We've *all* been through some of it, and we can all identify with her. It's a copy of Alexa's manuscript. I have to tell you that I used her title yesterday, *Goodbye is a Long Journey,* when I sanctioned her actions in response to your question".

Pericles' heart *plipped* somewhere around the ventricle guarding the memory of love as the CD passed from Eve's hand to his and their eyes met over whatever mystery was held in the small round silver disc.

"Let me know, Inspector Pericles, when you find what has happened to Alexa, she was," the past tense slipped through unbidden, "she knew the Art of Living."

Eve held out her hand, Pericles reached for it with both his hands, for a split second he thought of kissing her on both cheeks, but it wasn't an English custom, how silly, for how would anyone ever feel the *frisson* of real contact that speaks feelings more than words. He let the moment pass, let pass, too, the revelation that the magnificent earrings adorning the attractive but well lined face in the photograph matched his solitary find perfectly. Where was the other? He had not mentioned his discovery to Eve, not yet, not until he was sure – one way or the other.

He stepped from the bookstore with a lighter tread than yesterday, feeling the clear blue of Eve's eyes penetrate the caul around his heart, peeling away one of the layers that grief had placed there.

As Pericles sped back along the A303 he realised ruefully that he would be unable to stop by Stonehenge, the lay-bys' were on the opposite side of the road, there was nowhere on the left for him to pull up, the traffic too fast to attempt to cross lanes, he would have to leave it for another time. Why would he think that? At the thought came a flash of clear blue eyes from recent memory and his smile reached the accelerator as he sped onwards.

Leaving Glastonbury before lunch Pericles found the motorways relatively clear, and he swung on to the North Circular after only the slightest delay around Hammersmith. Home again, he parked in Brownlow Road to share an early and welcome afternoon tea and gossip with Alice.

His legal mind recalled every detail, every nuance, spoken and unspoken and his retelling of his Glastonbury experience held Alice spellbound as the autumn sky darkened and she drew heavy faded velvet curtains across the window. She held the photo of Alexa under the lamp to focus more clearly on *those* earrings.

"These are astonishing earrings," she observed, "her face wears them well; it has a spirit of attractiveness about it, not pretty, and not particularly English. Mama was French and this woman wouldn't be out of place across the Channel. You know, my brother's daughter, my niece, is in Australia, in Townsville. Alexa's diary mentions the same place, I finished reading it while you were in Glastonbury, and my niece has an interesting network of friends. I wonder, it is such a long shot, I just wonder if they ever met. I don't suppose Townsville is very large – curious name, town in English and town in French. Anyway, until Nanette went there I was unaware of it. My niece is a creative woman; it is just possible her artistic inclinations crossed over with Alexa's at some point. Would you like me to give you her *coordinates*?"

The *frisson* of a smile in his mind's eye as Alice slipped into her mother tongue sent affectionate warmth through Pericles even as his mind raced ahead. "Please," he said, and after what seemed to him an interminable delay he found his voice again to speak the unspeakable:

"Alice," he paused, his mouth dry, "*one of those earrings was in Aristo's car.*"

CHAPTER FIVE

Pericles swallowed. Alice stared into the middle distance. She was the first to break the silence threatening to embalm them. "Have you dealt with many crimes on Rhodes," she inquired.

"No," sighed Pericles slowly, "we don't even bother with parking matters Alice, everyone knows everyone else and to a large extent we are our brothers' keeper. Family feuds, who knows? but really crime such as you know it here hardly happens there. Wives are beaten, but it isn't yet a criminal offence so they go home once the hospital patches them up. Things are changing, the young will not take these ways now, university education will improve everything, some things will become a crime and people will bring such things out of the family fold."

"Well my dear, you now have a mystery on your hands. A missing foreign woman, a missing war hero – *phhhh*," the sound puffed from Alice's lips, "you must not let this reach the media before you have made your own conclusions. They'll twist it beyond recognition and cast their slur over everyone. Ours will add the Greek demon to their litany of TV sob stories of holiday romances gone wrong and yours will blazon Alexa as a foreign trollop. You need to go home before the Interpol report makes news."

Pericles looked at Alice. Then he looked at his watch, 18.08. His mind raced ahead: "Alice there's a 22.10 flight to Athens which connects to the 05.30 to Rodos, I could be home before breakfast if there's a stand-by seat free, I need to get that earring out of the safe, something is bothering me. I'll scan the photo of Alexa back to the Missing Persons Bureau here in London; if Eve has already done that it'll already be on the circuit. I need to download Alexa's manuscript too, see what I can make of it, I'll send you a hardcopy, Eve would be happy you've taken such an interest in her friend. I hope you'll both meet next time I'm over, I *am* sorry to cut our time short. *Theo mou*, I haven't even had the time to see Dimitra's mother! Please phone her, tell her everything. Kemal will fill her in on the war hero stuff." He glanced at Alice's wall clock: "I must run, the rental office will still be open and thanks be to the gods for the Piccadilly Line. There are usually give-away price seats on that flight, I'll just turn up. Oh, and here's Alexa's book, I thought you'd love the Silver-Moon Cat. Alice," he paused, folding up the slip of paper with Nanette's phone number and placing it inside Alexa's Moleskine which Alice was holding out for him, "thank you, thank you for more than you will ever know, this is a case that mustn't be bungled, these people, they are different, they deserve the best that their truth bequeaths to them. I'll phone you the minute I know anything more. *Kalinikta*, dear friend, wish the angels to sit on my shoulder!"

The two walked to the shabby front door, Alice smiling fondly at the uncharacteristic rush of words tumbling from Pericles as he found himself galvanized by imperatives. A warm embrace, a wave, the car door slamming, an unaccustomed haste in acceleration and he was gone. Alice closed the door and walked back into the warm parlour, still webbed with the invisible weavings of fate and coincidence. Tomorrow she would phone Nanette.

The angels remained on Pericles' shoulders from Brownlow Road to Diagoras airport. His unexpected arrival home so early in the morning surprised his mother as she drank her morning coffee. Her questions brought a rush of clipped sentences tumbling from his mouth. The journeys of the recent days had dislocated his thoughts; yesterday he had been leisurely shaving in a mediaeval Glastonbury coaching inn and here he was breakfasting on a beautiful Greek island most people only dream about. He told his mother the bare bones, said he must go straight to the office, would explain when he returned, explain about the Glastonbury connection, and that the little Somerset town had captivated him all over again.

Reaching his office before Ilias and the secretarial staff meant he could collect the earring before anyone noticed. He doubted anyone would have gone in to the safe since he had left on Tuesday, and even if they had it was unlikely a very small brown envelope placed at the very back behind piles of files would have attracted anyone's attention. He was right. It was still exactly as he had placed it. Putting it into his jacket pocket he rolled to close the lock's combinations and walked across the room to his computer, switched it on, waited too long for it to power up, and then slipped the CD of Alexa's manuscript from its sleeve ready to load.

The computer hummed into action as Pericles thumbed through his in-tray. A cold douche of horror arrested his heart – the Interpol report from the Missing Persons Bureau had been faxed to his office just as he was leaving London. The scanned photo of Alexa, pixel blurred but recognizable, was the same image that Eve had given him, the earrings easily discernible. A missing foreign woman would have little significance to anyone south of Metsova, and hopefully was of no relevance to his staff here, they were too concerned about a missing war hero, but so much had unfolded in the past four days he couldn't remember how much Ilias was privy to. He knew about the Moleskine, but did he know about the foreign woman, that she had lived here too? He did not know about the earring, that's for sure. As Pericles glanced through the report he groaned audibly: Eve had included Ari's details. Of course. Why wouldn't she. War hero or not the man was a Jekyll and Hyde as far as Alexa's friends were concerned; they had the shared history of the relationship to prove it.

He had to find the woman on Rhodes who had helped Alexa escape, Alice's reading had only revealed her first name, Penelope. Where would he start? The computer was ready at last. Pericles inserted the CD and was opening the file with the title of the book, ready to print, just as Ilias came through the door.

"Kyrios Pericles!" he said in surprise, "you are not supposed to be back until Tuesday, it is Saturday! What happened? And have I got news for you! An English lady called in, worried about a friend, a friend who was supposed to have a birthday dinner with her in Phanes. A friend who is a *friend of Aristo Theohalis*. She has been phoning the English telephone of the friend and cannot get a response, she doesn't know Kyrios Aristo's number but she called to his house and the neighbour told her he was gone and that Inspector Pericles had found his abandoned car. She came here then. I said you were in London so she left her contact details here for you."

Pericles sat back heavily in his chair. Ariadne was leading him by too many threads too swiftly to untangle; a *frisson* of conflicting emotions forced him to sit blankly watching page after printed page throw itself into the printer tray. In there somewhere was the thread he was really looking for. He prayed he could find it before any speculation blew the story out of hand and set itself uncompromisingly in newsprint.

The phone shrilled too loudly through the fog of his sleepless Friday night. Pericles reached for it to hear a fellow police inspector introduce himself from Athens:

"Angelos Apostolakis here, is that you Pericles? Good. You've read the Interpol report of course, have you had time to talk to this Aristo Theohalis the report connects the woman with? Pardon? *Pardon?* You would not jest with me Inspector would you ..."

"No," said Pericles wearily, "I wish I could, but no, I've just flown back from London. I went to see if I could talk with the foreign lady people have seen with Kyrios Aristo – but she is not there. It was her friend who filed that report. She said Alexa Buddicom has not been home since late August. I read her last postcard, it was sent from Ioannina in September – it seems they were on their way to Meteora and Delphi. Whether she got there or not we don't know but Theohalis returned on the Blue Star without booking a cabin. On the way out he had a luxury upper deck berth – but he hasn't been seen since more than a week. We found his car, abandoned. Not being a foreigner we didn't involve Interpol, and with nothing suspicious to go on we didn't call you. He left a manuscript, which she, this woman Alexa, wrote for him. It's his life story, Angelos, it was he who headed the Pegasus plot in '64."

Angelos whistled down the phone, penetrating Pericles' sleep deprived brain as he continued: "It's looking messy Sir, her diary was found in the car and her friend gave me a copy of another manuscript on a CD. The English woman wrote *her* story of her relationship with Theohalis and we're dealing with a capriciousness that may be dangerous. I've read her diary and I'm about to go find another English woman here on Rodos who knew her and helped her to escape this man. Well, it was we Greeks who invented drama and tragedy and this story is becoming something like that."

Some instinct made Pericles play for time, he needed to read through both manuscripts before the case, whichever way it fell, was taken out of his hands. Ignoring the obvious – which was to email all he had to Apostolakis immediately – Pericles disingenuously offered: "I'm copying her manuscript now, would you like me to send you copies first post on Monday? There's a lot to read through," he knew from past association his superior preferred hours of fishing to hours poring over the printed word, "is it any use to you if I'm on the case here? You know, without a body, a suspect *or* a victim there's not much we can do. If our man came back on the ferry alone maybe we should alert Ioannina office as being the last known whereabouts of the missing woman. Check hotels, follow any clue."

"That's in place as we speak; the report came through yesterday morning. It was circulated within the hour. Nothing's come to light yet," said Angelos, far away in Athens.

"Check Dodona too, she had a passion for our old history, they may have stayed there. She mentioned Suli and Zalongo on the postcard, obviously doing a tour guide for wandering war heroes. Sorry Sir, flippancy's out of order – but what to do?"

"Suli and Zalongo? *Panaghia*! The woman knows more than we do! Yes, send on the manuscripts, I need some light reading."

Pericles didn't warn him that he might be better off reading Myrivilis than Theohalis. As for Alexa's manuscript he didn't anticipate it being a bundle of laughs either.

The men hung up. Pericles gathered the completed printout of Alexa's manuscript and set Ilias the task of photocopying Aristo's manuscript ready to post to Angelos in Athens on Monday. He'd send Alexa's after he had read it, a task he was going home to attend to right now. But first he would call Penelope Samarakis, who lived, he noted on the paper given him by Ilias, not five minutes from his mother's house.

Penelope answered the telephone in Greek, her accent good, her vocabulary generous, only the inflections she liberally sprinkled along the sentences gave her away as a non Greek. She had a laugh in her voice that warmed the cockles of Pericles' heart. Yes, she was home, and yes she would be delighted to meet him, how about in fifteen minutes down at the Esmeralda, a well known *kafenion* along the beach front.

Penelope arrived first, found a table by the bay window and watched as the exclusive car drove in and reversed into the walled parking bay. *Très chic*, she grinned to herself, *Alfa*. A handsome man above average height, steel grey hair glinting in the sunlight, climbed out and walked towards the café entrance. Momentarily pausing for his eyes to adjust to the darkened interior Pericles scanned the tables and smiled immediately at Penelope as she lounged in a huge mock leather bucket chair.

Pericles took in at a glance a fair and plump and smiling woman, half camouflaged by the huge potted palms, and looking so ... *English!* She was dressed down, dressed, in fact, in comfy baggy trousers and a white shirt, her capacious bag filling another chair. Their rapport was immediate and his affection for the English enveloped her by osmosis.

"Can I get you a drink?" he smiled, echoing her request as he ordered two frappès.

"Penelope," she said, firmly, offering her hand as he responded in kind. This meeting was going to be a pleasure.

"Where do we start?" and both laughed as their words came simultaneously.

"Well," said Pericles, "you are as up to date as I am but I know nothing of the beginning so, ladies first."

"Right," said Penelope, "I'll begin at the end because that's why we're here. We had arranged, my husband and I, Alexa and Aristo, for a belated birthday meal for Alexa in a taverna in Soroni the night before Alexa was due to fly back to England, the 13th September; the plan for her actual birthday was for the pair to spend it in Delphi itself. I knew they had both gone round Greece for a couple of weeks so we hadn't had any interim contact, and that was fine, she wasn't one for letting arrangements down so Panos and I showed up as arranged. But they didn't. We ate anyway, went home at ten, I knew Alexa wouldn't arrive after eight, she went to bed with the birds. I half expected her to call the next day, but she didn't. I knew Ari was pretty volatile and hated her to have friends call her so I waited until she'd reached Glastonbury and I phoned her there. Four times over as many days, I left a message each time but she didn't return the call. I suppose a week or two went by and I tried again. This time I got an answer-machine-full message when I called – and that was really odd. So eventually I went to Ari's home up behind the University, met the neighbour under his beach brolly and heard that you had also been looking for him."

She paused, reflecting on her memories, turning her head slightly to sever present time to past memory, shifting her position in the oversized chairs before re-engaging eye contact with her quiet and attractive audience of one:

"Well," Penelope continued, "I must tell you that from about the end of the first week in September I had the oddest feelings about Alexa. As if something was very wrong, but what could I do? I didn't have Ari's mobile number, and if I had I doubt I would have called *him*. What do you know so far?"

"Little more than you I'm sorry to say. D'you mind telling me how you met? Do please speak in English, I've just returned and I love to speak the language when I have the opportunity."

"Right then. Oh I remember it well; it was just before Christmas, a few years back. I was at a carol practice with the English group in Rhodes, you know there are French groups and Finnish groups and all that and sometimes we even overlap! I wasn't singing at the time, just watching, and in walked Alexa, pixie like, *different*. She looked lost so I called her over and her face lit up and we just went on from there. Over the next weeks I learned she was in a pretty pickle. Penniless, oh that was rich that one – he gave her €25 every three weeks – *three weeks* – and she had to *ask* for that so she could buy stamps or whatever, so I took her for coffee and cakes as often as I could but he didn't want her to leave the house or make friends. I would go round to pick her up and jolly him along by joking with him, but it was hard work. Eventually she told me some of the cruelties she had to endure, it was monstrous. All this time everything she owned was rotting away in that grubby little village house in Kremasti and she had nothing to wear! God, if I had seen that one skirt or that one cherry-red sweater once more I'd have screamed. In the end they became a joke – her uniform of Silent Protest."

Penelope paused, sipped her frappè, turned to look out of the window before continuing. "I had to help. So we began by smuggling her most precious things over to my veranda which is huge and glassed in – and then the swine banished *her* to the village house, like a parcel, and we had to smuggle everything back there! But by this time I was helping her escape. She had no choice. That was a drama if ever but the angels were on her shoulder. You should read her story; it's a horror but funny as well. When we were packing for the shippers – secretly of course, Ari hadn't a clue what was going on but if she had stayed any longer she would have died, either by his design or her despair – she found a pair of pixie ears, a leftover from Glastonbury and its fairy shops, and put them on. One of the young male neighbours knocked on the door in a shitty mood because he thought we were taking up his parking space, outside Ari's house mind you, and I was volubly putting him in his place, in Greek of course, and out she came, in her pixie ears, having forgotten she was wearing them. Poor boy couldn't take his eyes off her. His jaw dropped, along with his argument, and he took off back down the street."

Penelope laughed as she remembered the scene in the quiet village street and paused momentarily to pick up her narrative: "so we got the shippers to take her stuff away, oh and was *that* a saga. Then she had to face Ari. I tell you I wouldn't have wanted to. I made her leave her passport with me. He erupted of course, but because I was involved he couldn't harm her or I'd *know*. He desperately needed to keep up appearances. Easter Monday was the most frightening for her, too long to tell you here, but the pair of them went down to a friend in Salakos, to the jeweller who introduced them actually. The one who made *those* earrings! Do you know about them? It's a story for another day. She never drank you know, but that day at Salokos she knocked back a tumbler of Spiro's homemade Muscat which loosened her tongue and emboldened her to speak to Spiro about what was really going on after which she turned to Ari and let fly enough verbal caustic to strip varnish. Ari turned puce apparently, grabbed her arm and forced her into his car to leave. He drove back murderously and while he was turning his car to park and was just out of sight she ran all the way down to her own car. You know she had to abandon it here ...?"

Seeing Pericles' right eyebrow rise infinitesimally Penelope side tracked to say Ari had driven Alexa's own car from England when he brought her permanently to Rhodes with wooing promises and wondrous presents. Veering back to the principle narrative she then continued the high drama: "so she ran down to her own car, jumped in and drove to me. She was in fine fettle, had left him high and dry. They met again of course, and he turned the whole thing around to *his* taking *her* on holiday to Australia. It was almost hysterical. Anyway *he* bought the tickets, *they* got on the plane, and he was savage to her throughout the flight. When they landed her own friends didn't recognise her. They were gracious, she had somewhere to stay, he made use of their hospitality, the perfect guest, except behind the closed doors of their bedroom. He stayed a few weeks and when he left she tried to pick up a life. But her life was in England. Why did she escape to Australia? Well at some point the bastard had conned her into thinking he could work in some capacity for AIMS which was in Townsville where she had friends. He had a fantasy of getting back into professional diving at sixty-four. She so wanted to believe it. Townsville is on the Great Barrier Reef and AIMS is some kind of scientific marine study base attached to the University there."

Pericles listened as the story flowed over him, indicated a repeat order to the hovering waiter, and to bring water, *parakalo*, this was thirsty work. Penelope paused, and sighed. "She loved him so much, you know, and she really had trouble believing he was treating her abominably. Yet it wasn't one of those repeat family pattern scenarios, her life had been difficult but had not included the slightest comprehension of violence before they met. He would disarm her with gifts of his choosing yet keep her so impoverished. I think if she hadn't met me she could have died. I suspected undercurrents when she told me she had been to his dentist over some problem she had. The dentist told Ari to take her to a periodontist urgently and he refused. It wasn't for lack of money, it just wouldn't be *visible.* He needed the approbation of a visible grand gesture. The Empress Earrings were that."

Penelope took a few sips of her frappè before continuing.

"When Ari returned to Rhodes after the fiasco in Australia he couldn't live without her. Something in him probably sensed she loved him and she was, as Spiro, his *only* friend, said, his last chance at real happiness. He phoned her daily and wore her down with promises of coming back to fetch her – she would never come back to live in Rhodes – and he would take her to England. *Which, incredibly, he did.* Though I believe the showdown at the luggage carousel at Heathrow was grim. He raged and threw one of his terrifying tantrums right there and then and Alexa calmly said: *sweetheart, I am home, I am going down those stairs and I am going to catch a bus to Glastonbury and I am going to stay with friends. I do not know what you want to do now, but I am going home to Glastonbury.* She told me this once she had a phone to call from and we could catch up on the dramas. Of course she had no home at that moment, she had nothing, but he went down with her to the West Country on the bus from Heathrow. She stayed with friends, but she wouldn't let him take advantage of them again so found him a B & B. After a couple of nightmarish days he returned to Rhodes."

Pericles waited. Penelope sipped her frappè slowly, the ice had melted, the coffee froth now thick and sweet. A small sigh escaped her as she took up the narrative to its conclusion. "She then had the most awful nine homeless months. We had little contact as she had no stability or way of keeping in touch, it was later that she told me all this. She was at her lowest ebb when she was given some tiny and dilapidated accommodation by the local council. We made contact again then and the next I heard Ari had flown there to make the place habitable. So he bloody should have, she had given up everything because he wanted her with him. Then in July she came back for 10 days, he behaved well, she had stipulated ten days because that was his shelf life as she put it. She and I had a great day together; she was a different person now she had a home and security and she filled me in as only a wordsmith can, with all the nuances of emotion. The Grand Tour for her 60th *should* have been wonderful. The only trouble is that it was for fourteen days and he couldn't maintain normality in such close proximity for so long – the cracks would open."

Penelope stopped. Her tale had reached the great question mark. Where was Alexa?

Pericles was disinclined to break the silence. Penelope had brought the tale up to date and he was now lost in thoughts and reflections too kaleidoscopic to untangle for clear narrative. It was apparent to Pericles that Penelope had read Alexa's manuscript, and learned that Alexa had emailed it to her before returning for her birthday trip. Had Penelope read Ari's?

"No, but that was a huge bone of contention, he wanted production line completion, and after weeks and *weeks* of just typing up the bare bones while he dictated she needed to distance herself, as any writer will tell you, before attempting to put it into a workable book – biography, novel, or whatever. She told me some of his life, it was pretty dramatic, but actually when I thought about it, and how he was treating her, I couldn't help thinking she was just another tool for his own purpose. He told her she was like a toy he could use anyway he liked, and when she puzzled over that during one of our permitted coffees together I felt chills along my spine. He *knew* he was using her. She asked me to tell her if he really was the most beautiful man in the world or was she trapped behind rose coloured spectacles? I laughed and told her he wasn't, but I did recognise that he had a lovely smile. And he did, and he was a very well presented man. She sighed, I remember, as if struggling with a something that held her in thrall."

Pericles smiled, a sensitive woman who chose Glastonbury as her home could well be held in thrall, the veils between realities were thin there and the *charisma* of the place palpable. He spoke the word in its original Greek: "*χάρισμα*," he said, half to himself, "it means more than the attractiveness of a person, it embraces a divinely conferred power of place too. Have you ever been to Glastonbury?" he said, directing the question to Penelope.

Penelope's eyebrows rose into her wispy blonde fringe, "no, I'm from the south-east, why do you ask?"

"No reason really, I found the landscape there rather magical, sacred you might say. It might take a special person to live there; apparently Alexa was not worldly wise in the usual way."

"You're right, she was blown away by the impact of Ari, he was *very* sexual, she hadn't experienced that before. For most of us at our age it's a memory. And we look at our kids and think – did we ever feel like that? Possessed and obsessed and adored and consumed by passion! I once asked how were her legs – she looked at me blankly for a whole moment and then roared with laughter when she finally got my drift – *oh!* she groaned! The whole experience for her was, well, she was such an *innocent* is the best way of describing her."

Pericles laughed. This woman's company was hugely enjoyable, how fortunate Alexa had been to meet her, but then, we all have our angels. He silently prayed that they still be on Alexa's shoulder wherever she might be now.

"I have read some of Ari's story," Pericles told Penelope, "she recorded it well, it would make a good film. But the women in his life, they were nothing; they fulfilled no part of his world view, or his image of himself. I now have Alexa's story, I'm on my way home to read it. Interpol are on *her* trail, but there is no trace of Ari."

Penelope shivered, "I know, that's what is so perplexing. Go home and read her story, you'll have some laughs when you get to the escape scene, it wasn't all a *film noir*, she had an impish sense of humour."

They finished their drinks; he left money in the tiny glass provided with the bill as they rose and walked to their cars. Penelope admired the Spider, Pericles grinned and patted the deep blue soft top, the yellow gold metallic body of his beloved Alfa, "It's called Zoé yellow, looks so good with Greek blue leather; ten years old but such style, no other Alfa comes close! It's been good to talk to you, we'll keep in touch. I'm going home to sleep off the night flight and then read Alexa. *Kalinikta* Penelope," he said, as they shook hands, "it's been a real pleasure meeting you."

"Paidi mou," greeted his mother as Pericles removed his jacket, "you must eat and sleep. You are tired and have much on your mind, but first tell me of your meeting with the Englishwoman. Is that the other manuscript you are holding? Good that you enjoy reading, and good that Alice primed you on the contents of the diary, getting through this one in typewritten English will be a lot easier. How was your meeting with..., here, let me take that while you get a drink... Alexa's friend?"

Mother and son moved to the salon, listening to the sound of Maria preparing the table for food as Pericles ran through the events, meetings, synchronicities, doubts and discoveries of the past days and his delight in meeting Penelope who had, unknown to either party, lived in the street behind them for many years with her now retired husband. Seeing Danaë's surprise Pericles added: "but he worked in London until his retirement, so our paths wouldn't have crossed because they only came here for holidays until he retired."

"You know the big house being built some years ago? The top half is theirs, that's how close a neighbour we are." He stepped to the window and craned his neck, nodding as he turned back.

"... and Alice sends her love and kisses to you," he ended, just as Maria invited them to the table.

"I wonder if time is on our side my child, and I wonder if it's on Alexa's either, or even for Kyrios Aristo. For him to disappear is too strange. You have until Monday, effectively, to read this second manuscript, link it to the information in the diary, follow up any calls that Alice may initiate for you, and to pray, *paidi mou*, for both of them before Interpol takes over. If you would like me to read any of the Alexa's book I shall be happy to, you know I always enjoy meeting interesting women, in person or in print."

"Thanks Mama, maybe it would help if you could," reflected Pericles, "to do him justice I have to finish Ari's manuscript, I only managed to get through half before I left. It would help if you would scan through Alexa's. Eve, the lady from the bookshop in Glastonbury, said it was a woman's story, it resonated with the Grand Passion and the Impossible Love, as she put it."

His mother raised an elegant eyebrow as a smile played around her lips. "It has been so many years since such words came to my ears but, you know my dear, that was how your father and I were all the years of our marriage. We were so blessed ... so blessed with the passion and the romance and all that will endure of human love. And," she looked at him with meaning, "so were you. I know, I know, it isn't something we speak of, but you and Dimitra had that same blessed love. If you want me to read Alexa's story I will, happily. It is not an official document after all. Just think of all the unofficial leads Poirot followed to come to *his* conclusions! Tell you what, if you want to catch up on some rest I'll make a start on it, summarize what I think and you can take it on from there if it will help."

The telephone rang, halting conversation. Pericles turned briskly to retrieve it: "Alice, how lovely! Yes, you did ... she *did*, oh Alice ... HQ phoned me as I reached the office this morning. Eve's report of a Missing Person is all over Greece now, and probably the rest of Europe. Ari hasn't shown up, just hold on while I get a pen, right, fire away, yes give me your niece's number again: Nanette de Visme 0061 7 4772 4781, Karen McDonell 0061 7 4721 9434. Mama is going to look through Alexa's manuscript while I sleep, I haven't slept since Thursday y'know," he chuckled. "Yes, yes, I realize the time difference, I'll call Australia in the morning. Nanette didn't know Alexa, but you say Karen knew them both, hmmm, interesting. She may have had other mutual friends.

"Alice, thank you from the depths, I will call you as soon as I have spoken to them. Mama sends her love to you too, *kalinikta* Alice, goodnight, and thanks again."

"Well," Pericles allowed a small tired sigh to slip from him unawares, "Mama, Alice phoned her niece in Townsville, she has a mutual friend who is a close friend of Alexa's and I'm to call in the morning our time, afternoon their time."

"Townsville," echoed his mother, "isn't that strange, that's where the Vogiatzis family lived, his name is on their War Memorial you know, and now they have the tourist shop back here on Rodos. It is irrelevant of course, a complete *non sequitur*, but fancy of all the unheard of places in the world I can identify *Townsville*. No, these people would not have known Alexa, they came back to Rhodes years ago, it's just a curiosity of mine to make connections, you know that! There are a few thousand Greeks in Townsville and the name is well known. They'll happily tell you so if you meet them. Now my dear, let me have that manuscript while you get some sleep."

They bid each other goodnight affectionately. Danaë picked up Alexa's manuscript and retired to her own rooms asking Maria to bring coffee to her at ten o'clock; she anticipated a long night.

CHAPTER SIX

Danaë took the sheaf of A4's to the small private sitting room that led from her bedroom along the northern side of the charming home her husband's family had built decades before, moving with feline grace to curl up into the old French *méridienne* inherited from her grandmother that filled the window alcove.

For the first few sentences Danaë found adjusting to Alexa's use of tense and second pronoun curious. As she moved into Alexa's voice the story brought up a chiaroscuro of images; echoes never allowed full expression from the many girls whose lives Danaë had followed after their short schooling into marriage and motherhood. For some of those young women the injustices and the imbalances of a life subservient to their husbands had been a litany of violent echoes, more sensed than known by Danaë personally, but observed as the young familiar faces grew old too soon under strains and secrets behind closed doors. The echoes drew potency from Alexa's ability to articulate those secrets, the abuses, the entrapments and the boundaries of pronoun blurred as Danaë became the "you" Alexa was inviting her to experience. Increasingly as she read Danaë knew Alexa's story was giving words to countless thousands of women who had been allowed no voice of their own. She knew also that Alexa's unusual choice of pronoun was a protection, a way of out-distancing the pain of a love story written between the acts. The whole must have poured out piecemeal between the time Alexa returned to Rhodes in July and before she returned at the end of August. Perhaps she had a premonition, had left Eve with the raw manuscript on a CD before coming back yet again, just in case.

CHAPTER SEVEN

ALEXA'S STORY - Appointment with Aphrodite

It is your first evening. You have come to Rhodes to attend a writer's conference; a five day event entitled On Miracle Ground. You had been to one on Corfu four years before, and Greece, you are late in life discovering, is definitely miracle ground.

Walking down the cobbled lanes of Omirous and of Sofocleous to Pan Hotel, which has garden terraces, rooms with views, and ceiling fans, will prove a good choice. The windows of your room open on to the whole of the old mediaeval walled town of Rhodes. The Palace of the Grand Masters rises tawny stoned on the horizon; minarets grace the foreground and middle distance; two kittens skitter along the ancient stone wall below you where a dusty orchard leads into a crumbling courtyard. Your gaze spans most of the mediaeval city, arches and castles, cats and cobblestones. A sizzling anticipation greets the heat of the sun on your skin as you lean from the high window, before turning back into the room to unzip the small carryon case containing all that you have brought for a fortnight.

Laying out a silky number on the bed you then shower away the four hour flight and tedious delays of the day, towel yourself dry, dress, step into fresh sandals and trip down the staircase for your first exploration. Mike, the hotel owner, greets you, and gives you a key to the walled gate should you be late.

The late afternoon sun is warm, you haven't felt this buoyant for some time and you sense that it heralds change, and in your life even small change is welcome. You find a taverna and sit baffled by the alphabet. The menu is written in English as well as Greek but momentarily thrown off balance and ravenously hungry you opt for something recognisable – Greek salad. You grin broadly under the shadow of your hand that you can be so *lacking* in imagination, but tomorrow, you promise, you will have something completely different, something like *charcoal grilled octopus* or *courgette flowers in batter* or *stuffed squid* or *vine leaves with grilled lamb* or *saganaki*.

The salad comes topped with a large slab of feta cheese and a basket of village bread, deep textured and tasting like the bread mother never baked fifty years ago. The standard of the olive oil has been reserved for the undiscerning tourist, but tomorrow is another day and you will wise up pretty quickly. You ask for a coffee, withdrawing the word *Turkish* just before it escapes your lips, Greek coffee you smile, not even knowing how to say ευχαριστώ, *thank you*, to the waiter who set it down before you. *Eucharist,* the same familiar word, *thank you*. You chose the café for its burgeoning purple bougainvillea cascading over the

Shirley Valentine tables-for-two on the sidewalk and idly wish you were not one-sitting-alone. Still, there are worse things to be, so you sit and enjoy the sun's warmth and the human bustle around you.

You pay, and begin to explore the walkways and plakas. Eventually you find your way back through the little alleyways to Sofocleous Square, the ruins of a mosque with a tall and elegant minaret adding a silent foursquare presence to shabby shutters and doorways of the neighbouring façades. The gold displays in the huge glass paned windows of the shops of the main boulevard had lost their power to attract after viewing a dozen or so and you are drawn to smaller displays of icons and antiquities.

Pausing opposite the darkened mosque you are compelled towards a half shuttered jeweller's window. Two objects vie for your attention: one is the grandest and most stunning pair of gold earrings that quite take your breath away, and the other a tiny bronze coin in the lower left corner of the window. An insignificant little object but one that lured your gaze from the dramatic earrings and you know in your bones it has meaning for you. The earrings have a nonchalant swing tag attached showing four figures without a dot, too bad for you and your small change, but you admire the beauty of the workmanship enough to pluck up courage, open the door and go in.

The interior reveals itself as an atelier. A man looks up from the workbench, removes the magnifier from his eyes and greets you. You have brought a small collection of jewellery must-fix items including an ancient Sufi ring and a working jeweller is exactly whom you were hoping to meet. The man is older than you, tall, with a thatch of white hair topping a broad smiling face. You tentatively ask if he could make you some gold hooks with filigree flowers for a pair of nineteenth century carved coral drops you have been unable to wear for at least twenty years. And could he reset the ancient carved carnelian you had bought in Le Marais from a Persian who had bought it from the widow of a Sufi sheikh killed in Afghanistan? And other similarly odd requests. Of course he can. You return then to the real reason you entered his shop. The uh, um, er, little piece in the window? He knew exactly the piece you meant and in one swift movement places it in your hand.

"Do you know what this is?" he asks. It is a coin, but that can't be what he is asking so you admit you don't know. "It is at least two and a half thousand years old, we used to find them everywhere in the seas around our island. I have had this one for many many years. The ancients put them under the tongue of the dead to pay Charon, the Ferryman, to carry their soul safely across the River Acheron to the Underworld. I think you may call the river the Styx, but there are others in our mythology too, you know."

On one side of the coin face is the Rhodian Apollo, Apollo Pronaia, and on the other, the Winged Goddess of Victory, Niké herself. It is melting into your palm and the jeweller is sensitive to its effect on you.

"I will clean it and set it for you, very simple ring, smallest finger," offers the jeweller, "tomorrow evening it will be ready, bring your jewellery for me to see how to prepare as you wish."

The gorgeous earrings catch your eye again. Is it possible to try them on? You hesitate, confess you are unable to buy them. "Of course!" comes the enthusiastic reply, "these are my special piece. I made them when I was younger and had the eyes for such fine work. Now I cannot do this. They are a copy of very ancient Greek work, very ancient, before the Byzantine."

He reaches in and brings forth the display stand, removing the earrings and holding them in his large hand with tenderness. He tells you he has spent forty years learning everything he knows about gold and silver and precious stones and carving and cutting and setting but only in the last five years has he called himself a jeweller.

"Really," he confides, "I am retired, but I will continue until I can no longer see."

You let him place the earrings in your hand, feel their weight, marvel at the hinged keeper, admire the exquisite filigree flowers, the looped chain in which is suspended a cylinder of lapis lazuli between two tiny seed pearls. They are the earrings of all earrings. The hooks are thick, to carry their weight, but they slip into your ears easily and look ... *divine*. You just *know* these earrings, or ones very like them. Your passion for Byzantine history makes sense now that you have been reunited with the earrings of no less a personage than Empress Alexa. Another life, you smile to yourself.

Some moments later the jeweller looks up beyond your shoulder and greets a man who has come in quietly behind you. You turn and your body becomes an amalgam of goosebumps. Your mind, soaring somewhere out of known reach shutter-snaps an indelible image that flawlessly fits the hollow in your heart that has accompanied you all your life. Love-at-first-sight comes to all women sooner or later and for you it is very late indeed.

The jeweller introduces you, and tells his friend you are a writer. Come to dinner with us, he says, you will be our guest, we will have special Greek food for you.

Later you confess that your heart went pitter-patter so hard against your chest you wonder if you could remain standing. *Something* in your heart stands to attention. You are lost. Aristo is small, powerfully built, golden brown, quietly spoken, beautifully dressed, a black knit top and grey pants (and you notice your naturally matching colour themes, an uncanny synergy that will go on for as long as you are together) with silver grey curls hugging a well-shaped head.

"I am Aristo," he says to you with a smile so wide you fall right in. You offer your hand, which he shakes warmly. And then you do the most extraordinary thing.

You turn around to the safety of the glass counter and just carry right on talking to the jeweller about jewels. And about any other thing you can conjure up without having to turn around and see the beautiful man again. You hope he will slip away as quietly as he had come in because you know that the feeling that passed between you both can only veil something quite other than a casual meeting, a polite greeting. Here a reality covering a palette of meanings you have never explored before. Your back is all you have as a shield against a world of unknowns not yet sensed. If you remain with your back to him perhaps when you turn again the initial effect will prove a figment of your imagination.

But he hasn't left. He is there, exactly behind you, having sat down in the armchair near the door, watching you, watching your back. "And I watch your back for a long, long time," he tells you later. "I thought you were not interesting in me, so I watch you, a long time. I think you are French, and Spiro tells me you are a writer and he says maybe she will write your book, Aristo."

The three of you walk to the taverna adjacent to Spiros' atelier. Mezes pile up on the table; two cats walk underneath and sit. When the large platter of fish arrives Aristo naturally and effortlessly reaches over to lift two fish from the plate and give one to each cat. His gesture goes straight into your heart and lodges there. These are the threads of Fate that bind you and you do not know if you have the courage that will be required to be drawn to a golden and silver man who has, so you learn, a wife in Paris. The evening passes on to promises of tomorrow. Sightseeing, offers Aristo, before your Conference begins.

Tomorrow. Aristo is waiting beyond the mediaeval gate to the Old Town. He drives you to at least four beaches, each one prettier than the one before, but you head for the hills to have lunch.

The table groans under plates of delicacies Aristo orders for you to try, but just when you reach satiation the many little empty dishes are whisked away and a vast platter of charcoal grilled lamb is ceremoniously placed in their place. You are meant to eat this? you ask Aristo mutely. He orders retsina and soda for you, Greek champagne, he says smiling. The chill gold liquid is delectable, and perfect to wash down all those whitebait, that grilled aubergine, the salad, cheese puffs, humus, dolmathes, char-grilled octopus, tzatsiki, green beans and artichokes that have settled fulsomely inside you, pinioning you to the chair. Eventually you brave the charcoal grilled chops, the food is so delicious what else can one do, and reflect that temperance in the ordering department will be a wise procedure in future. To finish Aristo orders Greek coffee, *metrio*, medium sweet; coffee so strong you can hear your heartbeat through it.

Your sightseeing meanders south across the island to a long, wild beach, windswept and empty and Aristo drives with skilful negotiation down the sandy dunes from the high escarpment by a track to a beach only accessible by four-wheeled drive. The littoral is thick with seaweed and the wind blows in strongly from the sea. Fishermen don't come this way, Aristo tells you, the fish do not like disturbance, but he will often take his boat out to the horizon where it is deep and calm and dive with his speargun for bigger prey. He spreads out two towels, side by side, removes his cotton waistcoat and shorts to lay down in the briefest swimsuit on one of the towels. You sit on the other towel, suddenly self-conscious of your isolation on the wild lonely strand. Aristo offers to put suntan lotion on your back; you lay down and roll over on to your too full stomach. He takes a long time, a very long time, your back is quite small after all, his hands move slowly over your body and down to the back of your thighs, all the way down to your heels his hands travel, the lotion feels silky, smooth, warm, and you are awake in every cell of your being. He stops, you sense a slight movement, you pretend to be asleep and then moments later you hear a sound, a *cat snore* you think in surprise, and turn to look at him. He is *asleep* for goodness sake! Innocent of gene-programmed after-lunch siestas you are embarrassed to think your company so boring. You get up, walk to the white sea foam, attempt to wrangle with the seaweed tangle on the shoreline to reach open water, admit defeat, and go for a long, long walk instead.

Aristo wakes as you sit back down; you show him a pretty amber colour shell you have found. He takes it gently in his hand, turning it over. "This shell has been in her ocean for thousands of years, look how the movement of the waves has made the ripples on the back, and the colour, the colour is unique. It is special, for you."

The intimacy of his words stirs your attention as you lie down beside him, head supported by your hand, elbow propped on the sand. He reaches over to touch you, moves closer and runs his hand along your waist and hip. Intimacy is strange, and confusing, and, when he reaches over to kiss you draw back, unaccountably shy in the face of the forest of feelings within you.

The air between you crackles with the tension of unrequited desire and Aristo remains silent as you return to the car. You sigh softly, knowing your heart is a reliable organ and you will trust it with your best interests, for you know there is no future for you with a man whose wife is in Paris. Along the silvery coastline Sfakianakis sings his silvery songs and you listen with attention, ask for a translation:

"Our songs always speak of life," says Aristo, "and love and death. I will never be able to hear them again without remembering you, Alexa *mou*."

His words stir something that has been asleep within you, forever. He responds, slowly, all his movements are slow and deliberate and gentle, you have observed during your short acquaintance, by reaching over to pick up one of your hands to bring it to his lips. He kisses your fingertips, one by one, gently places your hand back in your lap.

The intensity of the turquoise sea almost hurts as you keep taking sideways glances at the so handsome man beside you, resistance seems infinitely remote, you have been alone for so long; you look at his face, a face you have known, forever.

"With you," he says softly, too softly to invite dialogue, "I am seeing the colours of my Greece as if for the first time. The blue is more than blue, the sun is more than golden, the scent of the pines and the herbs is sweeter than I knew, and the songs I am listening for the first time. I listen them in a new way. Being with you makes this possible." He reaches for your hand, touching it briefly before he has to change gear to round a sharp bend to bring you back to the entrance of the Old Town.

And thus it all began. Kisses honeyed by oblivion. Hours pass through aeons, day and night are flung into another universe ... and your first afternoon siesta together passes into the briefest night.

"Where have you been all my life?" he asks touchingly.

"I believe you have been underwater for most of it," you smile, adding, "and I suppose you've a lot to make up for." He chuckles, smothering you with kisses. "You are right," he twinkles, "I have a lot to make up for. And so do you."

Earlier when Aristo had said that he knew he loved you, and that you are the one he has waited his whole life for, it was because you had refused anything more than the most chaste of kisses on that desolate stretch of beach. "I would have been horrified," he confessed, "if you had proposed me anything more, for I did not know what else to do, you were so close, so beautiful, really I could feel the energy flow between us like fire."

He has been unable to eat, sleep, think, drink ever since, he adds. And it's true, you are the one who has done justice to most of the gargantuan meals you have been faced with since you met; it was he who starved – for you. You hear the power of words spoken in love in another language, husky with passion: *s'agapo*, Alexa *mou*, *mon amour*, and his French causes him to laugh with happiness: Alexa *mou*, I have not said those words for twenty years, twenty *years!* I love you Alexa *mou*, I love you! And he laughs between kisses that armistice you until dawn.

"Theo mou," Dimitri laughs "Athens will burn tonight!" Greece had won the European Cup, just as you had predicted to every Greek you met after having your conversation with the great statue of Niké the Winged Goddess of Victory down on the harbour. The sea wind had shrieked through her stone feathers, and you took it as her response. Later Aristo offers the briefest bio of his relationship with his wife and son. After years in the ocean as a highly successful deep sea diver working out of France he returned to Rhodes to restore a Grand Viziers' Palace and turn it into an attractive hotel. Many years later he was exhausted running it alone; a rich American woman came, with promises like piecrusts, but by then his health was in question and the American woman wheeled a deal that benefitted her enormously. *I have to sell*, he tells you, *I have no other choice.*

Aristo spoke to his son, Petros, about the situation before he sold. Petros erupted violently. Aristo did not consider his son's presence at the hotel profitable, and his behaviour wasn't contributing to the common weal. To sell was imperative. "If you sell, I will kill you," hissed Petros to his father, in the melodramatic manner of Mediterranean men. Aristo responded in his quiet way: "If I do not sell, I will die anyway. If you kill me you will spend the rest of your life in prison. Do what you wish."

With the first year's payment from the American Aristo fitted Petros out with the restaurant in the old cobbled Square, paying for the lease, the attractive renovations, the handsome new kitchen, the atmospheric decorative pieces, tables, chairs, authentic imported Moroccan crockery and tableware. Air conditioning was essential, so was modernising the toilet, and the interior décor. Aristo had done more than he could ever do again to heal the unbridgeable chasm between them.

Aristo concludes his sorry tale with the confession that Petros was full of anger towards him, he does not know why but he has always been like this. He thinks sadly it is because he is favoured by his mother, while he, Aristo, was off-shore making considerable money. He had been wealthy, *I work all my life*, he said, sadly enough to break your heart, *and for what? for what? She has everything, all my apartments in Paris, everything.*

You have a horrible sense, a kind of fugitive shadow on the threshold of consciousness, that you are on the brink of a world unknown to you, a world where jealousy, intrigue, betrayal, anxiety live hand in glove with sensual love and passion and human frailty. You sense it might even be worse than a wife in Paris but are happy to delay any thought on the topic as you drive off together for another lunch at another mountain taverna. A white statue of Aphrodite stands behind Aristo's chair, you photograph him, with her; he has never looked more beautiful and you will send a copy of this photo to friends in Australia.

The fortnight passes quickly, the Conference has high points and medium points and you choose the sessions you will attend carefully, making sure there is time to be with the man you are not so slowly being carried away by. You can't eat, can't sleep, and your golden man confessed the same one afternoon as you sat together on a beach bench and he stared at the ocean in forbidding silence. "Is there something wrong?" you ask and he answers with your own words: *can't eat, can't sleep.* You burst out laughing and say you can't either – and his reply stops you right there: "I love you, Alexa, and I can no longer be alone. We must talk before you leave me to go back to England." He paused, so did your heart, before continuing. You had only just met – but, if you took into account your familiarity with each other, the knowing would extend to lifetimes.

It is your last lunch; your time together can now be counted in hours. You have spoken little of any future, nothing specific. Aristo is not a man of words, decades under water doesn't enhance conversation. He takes your hand and tells you again how he loves you.

"Do you think we could live together?" Aristo asks you, with a smile on his face and his fork in the octopus. It is your last meal before you board the plane to Bristol. Before you can answer he looks at you and laughs: "we would be dead in a month! Imagine, no sleep have we had, not for ten days!"

You squeeze lemon over the salad; ask him if he would like some over his souvlaki. Again he takes your hand: "I love to be looked after," he tells you, "all my life I cook for my wife, I do the shopping, always always I am looking after everyone. I do my own sewing even, she does less than nothing for me. Now my life must change, I

can no longer live this way. I love you Alexa *mou*."
And he tells you a story of two innumerate village
women from Kephalos, his birthplace on Kos:

In the days before indoor bathrooms
women and men went to the fields to perform their
toilet. On this particular night the sky was filled
with millions of stars. Maria and Roula had gone to
the field together. Maria's granddaughter was
learning to count at school, and prided herself on
telling her *yahya* of the big numbers she was
learning. Roula's grandson was learning the same
wonderful things, but he wasn't quite so
responsible at repeating the sequences of increasing
numbers to his *yahya*.

Look at all those stars! commented Maria,
looking up at the night sky: *there must be at least
thirty!* For thirty was a number unimaginable to her
in its abstract form. Not to be outdone, Roula said
briskly: *Don't be foolish Maria, there's more than
twenty!*

"And I love you," sighs Aristo, "*more than
twenty.*"

Suddenly he becomes sombre, silent, stares
into the darkening sky, his face darkening with it as
memory unravels a story so shocking you remain
silent through the telling of it. He has recalled a
nightmare tale from the deep and he tells it not to
you but to the darkening sky and the world that
deserted him; a monologue, a cry to be heard and
seen and known. You heard.

"My diving company sent me to Agami, the Saint
Tropez of Egypt, and next to Agami there is a huge
Russian military base. Because of the military base

no one is allowed to come to enjoy this area. Our company rents a villa for us, with all the personnel necessary for our comfort like cooks, cleaners and housemaids. Our job is to prepare the seabed and destroy all the rocks which impede the way of the pipelines. We have to first survey the seabed and make a profile of the obstacles measuring their distance from the beach precisely to then decide which explosives we need to level the seabed and clear the way for the laying of the oil pipes.

I was about 400 metres from the beach when I recorded rocks at around eighteen to twenty metres depth. During my reconnaissance, I noticed on my right a huge pithos, one third of which is buried in the sand. It was one of those we used to trade wine or grain with the Phoenicians, and we used them to bury people. It will look like the amphora of Knossos if I can move it from its bed. But then I perceive a slight movement of what seems to be a misty dust. Like a cat I am curious in front of a mousehole and I swim close to the mouth of the amphora to look inside. With my hand I wave the mist away and to my astonishment I see a huge eye looking at me. I pull back, and then I realize it is a very very large octopus. This I confirm by the midden heap of empty shells around the opening. I am on duty and have no speargun, only a knife, so I return to complete my survey and then I swam back to the beach to give my report, recording the position of the pithos so I can return later to investigate. It is the secrecy of the military area that has protected the pithos from its removal by predatory collectors who are forbidden to enter all these years.

A few hours later I prepare my speargun and my diving gear with a single tank for lightness and I return to the sea. The sea is so clear and I can follow the line from the surface for at least three hundred metres. I dive to reach the pithos. Inside the pithos is dark and I prod the occupant of this dark interior with my speargun. The occupant objects to being disturbed after its long years of peaceful residence. One long tentacle suddenly appears, winding its chameleon way along my speargun towards my arm. I hesitate to shoot immediately, but suddenly a second tentacle appears and I no longer delay my decision. I shoot. Both tentacles rapidly withdraw into the darkness. I try to pull the line but the movement of the octopus inside the amphora creates a veil of dust and mud and I can see nothing. And nothing comes out no matter how hard I pull. I keep trying, without success. I make another decision. This amphora will be destroyed by our explosives later, and alas we have no permission to remove to safety such a beautiful piece. So my decision is to break the pithos. I pick up a piece of nearby rock. I smash the amphora easily as it was much cracked anyway. When the amphora fell open I was faced with the unbelievable. An octopus of such colossal dimensions I had never imagined before. It was too late to run away, for quick as lightning the octopus has me in its grip. My experience tells me I must immediately get the octopus away from anything solid that it can anchor itself to, for then I will drown, it imprisons me completely. Swiftly I walk backwards with the octopus attached to me. We are clear of the amphora and the rocks. It cannot anchor itself on sand to pinion me down. It begins to crush me and breathing is difficult.

My mind is racing, my predicament untenable. Both arms are pinioned to my side but with enormous effort I am able to wriggle my right hand down to reach the knife which is strapped to my right leg. One of the tentacles is around my neck. These octopuses are clever creatures. I manage to move my forearm enough to stab the tentacle around my neck. Slowly he slid this tentacle from my neck but another replaced its stranglehold. Yet another tentacle wraps itself around my face and rips off my mask. This time my response is to grab my mask, I had enough leverage with my right arm, but when I held it in front of my face I see that the power of the octopus's tentacle had squeezed the glass completely out of the mask. It is useless. My breathing is laboured; the life is being squeezed out of me. I am on the verge of panicking. In horror I feel another tentacle reach across my face. It rips off my regulator. I can no longer breathe. The pressure of the tentacles around my body causes the tank to turn over to the front of my body. Now I panic. I lift my head and look to the surface. I ask myself:

"Aristo can you reach the surface in five seconds, or will you die and be dinner for this monster?"

I choose to live and with all my power I begin to move what is free of my legs and use my flippers to propel me to the surface. The octopus comes with me; he has nothing to anchor himself on to impede my ascent. Once on the surface I lay back and fill my lungs with as much air as possible. The octopus is still around me but because of my own movement it is unable to position me to its mouth. Also I have my wetsuit on, which makes penetration more difficult. A curious fact of the octopus is that when its prey moves the current caused by such movement weakens the strength of its grip. I begin to swim with all my strength towards the shore, and some of the tentacles begin to float around me, unable to grip me securely. With superhuman effort and against the tremendous weight of the octopus on my back I swim for nearly thirty minutes to the shore. Many times I saw our team with the Zodiac, but I have no energy to scream for help. I continue to swim. After what seems an eternity I reach the beach, gasping. I try to call for help. Some of the divers look at me with this phenomena on my back and my tank on my front and instead of running towards me they run away! As I rise from the sea the octopus begins to slide from my body.

Oh no you don't, you bastard, I say to him, you wanted the ride, you come all the way!

And, exhausted as I am, it is now my turn to grip him and drag him with me with the help of the arrow I had originally shot him with. I am not a Scorpio for nothing! Then the other bastards come, laughing and joking with their bloody cameras. And to this day I still do not have a photograph. We kill the octopus; it weighs one hundred and twenty kilos, about two hundred and sixty pounds. I suffer with nightmares for weeks. Nicolette was not very sympathetic. She says to me: People die crossing the roads every day, why do I care?

You hardly know how to respond, you have never heard such a tale. At the airport the tension carries you through the goodbyes, until Aristo holds your hands and tells you he will wait with you no longer, it will break him. "Please, I have to go," he says softly, "but take this little souvenir. Do not open it until you are on the plane. And I will phone you tomorrow," he promises, pressing a tiny wrapped box into your hand. The lump in your throat tightens, you see the moisture in his eyes, you hold each other with an intensity that leaves you breathless and trembling as he turns and walks away. He does not look back.

On the plane you open the little package slowly. Inside is your shell, exquisitely set in gold, on a gold chain. In the little hole which countless aeons of tumbling in the blue waves and shingle of the Aegean had carved at the top of the shell is a cabochon sapphire, the same pure blue of the ocean. You hold it for a very long time, gazing at its sheer loveliness, then you clasp it around your neck.

CHAPTER EIGHT

The natural break in the narrative allowed Danaë time for reflection, time to feel her woman's knowing weave its way into the life of the woman whose very soul she was accessing. She wanted to continue in spite of the late hour, made herself a coffee to keep away the curtains of sleep, walked around the room for some minutes, re-positioned herself into the deeply upholstered *méridienne*, picked up the manuscript and continued reading Alexa's story:

One night Aristo phones, very late. You ask him teasingly if he has forgotten you. "No," he says firmly, "if I don't speak to you every day I will die." You will be at a seminar this weekend and he at once asks if you will meet a man. You will probably meet any number, but, you assure him, in the sense to which he is referring, that no, you are not going to meet a man; there is only room for him in your heart.

"If you do," he says, "I will ..." and there is a long pause so you offer: "kill him?" in true Greek form. "No!" he fairly roars, "I will kill *you!*"

Kill? For heaven's sake, you think to yourself. Aristo goes on to say he wants you forever.

No one has *ever* wanted you forever; your mother gave you a suitcase for your seventeenth birthday and has not made contact with you for over forty years; your father on the other side of the planet has not had you inside his home since you were seven years old, over *fifty* years! You've never known anyone who has wanted you *forever*. It is heady stuff and you can't think of anything more wonderful. You make plans to meet in Kos after the launching of your book's publication in July.

Before you plan for Kos your wardrobe undergoes a metamorphosis.

"Bring your strings" says your man on one of the many-a-day phone calls he makes from Rhodes.

Strings? The strains of the Air on a G drift through your puzzlement but you know the man isn't up on Mozart. "Strings?" you query, "what are strings?"

A warm chuckle responds: "Very little knickers ..."

You laugh. Thongs, you think, and say with much laughter that you don't have such things. The word itself conjures up childhood memories – growing up in Malaya and then Australia your feet were mostly bare or, to keep sensitive soles separated from burning sand, rocks, pavements or tarmac, were shod in soles of rubber held on by a V shaped strip of rubber – plenty of rubber plantations in Malaya then – with a thong between the first and second toe. Locals called them *thongs*. Years later on an English beach you hear them called flip-flops – you wonder at a flip-flop fetish.

Your *naïveté* causes a *frisson* of energy to centre itself somewhere in your body, somewhere you haven't been aware of in active memory. Time to expand your horizons. You phone your friend Atmadhara, who, like you, has long since left her swami army days and who, you learn with admiration and astonishment, has a *lover*. Goodness, you have some catching up to do – gone are the vows of renunciation, poverty and celibacy! Atmadhara is delighted you are re-entering the real world.

"Oh Sitadevi!" her light and lilting laughter warm in your ear, your old swami name sounding from a previous incarnation: "They're wonderful! Very sexy! Get some in animal print, leopard or snake – see the effect they have!" And after an hour of giggles and speculations you promise her you will.

For some minutes you sit, allowing this monumental change in your life to take root. You are slim at this moment in your usually plump life, very slim, as slender as the elegant Atmadhara; and yes, you can imagine such a garment might be possible without self-consciousness spoiling the seduction such a scene conjured up. Fired with enthusiasm you pick up your purse and car keys and head for Wells. Your confidence only dips a little when you, the age of a grandmother, are confronted with the super-confident sixteen year old salesgirl who coolly points you to the racks of *strings* at the rear of the store. Ah, no animal prints. Emboldened, you return to a seventeen year old who looks slightly more approachable: "Oh I'm sorry" she says, "they were last year, diamanté's are in this year."

And so they are. Bent on Big Cats you completely overlook the selection of diamanté numbers. Your eyes sparkle delightedly at the diamanté hearts (*for goodness sake!*) holding the thong at the triangle that looped precariously over the hips to settle – you suppose rightly – at the very apex of your delicious and hitherto unsung bum! *My goodness,* you giggle out loud, *you are learning so fast!*

You buy two in rose pink and another in black. The pink will go wondrously under the slender fitted black number with its slit mid thigh at the point of which you will pin the pink silk rose bought last week in Bath on a wicked shopping spree with a friend who encouraged you to buy a French black Chantilly lace top (half price, look what you save! even if the price is still three figures in the sale!) and pink and black polka dot kitten heeled shoes by a maker whose name goes straight to your newly awakened girlie heart: *When Too Much Is Not Enough.* Imagine such a name, such sheer indulgence, such wild extravagance. You love it. Your friend's comment reduces you and the sales assistant to tears of laughter as you trip around Russell and Bromley in pink and black polka dots and bows on your toes, winking and quoting Germaine Greer: *Fuck Me shoes.* "He just might!" you twinkle.

The sales in Bath benefit from your recent squirreling until you and your friend reach Jolly's, weak with hunger. You open your purse and panic pours out. Your friend, having been inspired by your sales philosophy (look at what we're *saving!*), has also let loose too many pounds. You settle for a glass of wine each and share a cheese scone to compensate for your profligacy; the bathos of your meal contrasts with the collection of glamorous bags and carriers and packages that surround you and you are each helpless with laughter not entirely influenced by the large glass of red sliding into your empty tums.

Sobriety descends later as you stroll down towards the Park and Ride bus, unable to carry another package between you. Almost too late you remember you need to buy loo rolls. More bathos indeed. You pass a Superdrug, call in, peer at the price and gasp "£1.59! I'm not paying *that* they're only a £1 in Glastonbury!"

Your friend, helpless with laughter, walks out of the shop trailed by an indignant you to sit on a Mall bench, wipes her eyes until she finally finds the words to say: "Alexa! You have just spent five *hundred* pounds on extravagances – what's fifty pence for necessities!"

"That's not the point," you say, all common-sense fled away in the flurry of such sheer folly and belated self-reproach at your fiscal frivolity. Your friend shakes her head, stands up, goes into an adjacent café and comes out with takeaways; two strong cappuccinos, handing one to you with the command: "drink this!"

Euphoria fades. Guilty pleasures. Damn it, you say, loo rolls can wait. Hyacinths for the soul are more in your mind at your great age. Your friend agrees, and three days later comes to spend the afternoon with you trawling through your wardrobe to help choose, coordinate, colour and code a week's worth of two changes of clothes a day all into a cabin case – you can't bear the thought of delays at the carousel to pack anything larger. She brings you two loo rolls.

The plane arrives late and to your dismay Ari is not there. Your heart skips twenty beats to land around your navel. Firmly you keep walking. No Ari. As you come abreast of the sliding doors leaving the terminal two arms suddenly enfold you – Ari had been hiding behind the exit doors, waiting. He lifts your tiny case, holds you so tightly you can barely walk in a straight line to his Vitara. He opens the door, you gasp to find the car full of roses. And, at the hotel, the room itself is filled with roses and candles and gifts and a tiny CD player playing the silvery songs you love so much. You collapse onto the double bed to discover, as you both fall through the centre to land laughing on the floor, it is two singles put together. Ari improvises with two of his belts to strap the base and head legs together as loving carries you through to breakfast.

The second evening is your choice for his surprise. Overwhelmed by the romance of Ari's roses and gifts and attention to the details of making your week together unforgettable you have kept the 'very little knickers' as the last of your gifts for him. You ask him to wait for you downstairs on the hotel terrace while you arrange the diamanté just so, pour your body into the slender black dress, pin the pale pink silk rose at the beginning of the split that goes from ankle to mid thigh, slip into the FM polka dots with the black toe bows, add a pair of pink feather earrings that your good friend insisted she buy you at the airport, having also insisted on driving you to because you were filled with last minute stage fright at flying off for an adventure with a man who, frankly, you barely know.

A dust of powder, another application of kohl, a spray of Côté Bastide *Rose*, and you pick up your tiny tapestry bag, turn twice in the mirror to make sure the long zipper at the back is closed to the top (such a contortion to reach) and step lightly into the hall to the elevator. Ari looks in wonder at the transformation of his Cinderella and fulsomely exclaims his appreciation. His admiration bodes well for the evening as he walks behind your rarely revealed slinky silhouette along the narrow lane to a renowned restaurant where he has booked the cosiest table in an alcove overlooking the harbour. Your mutual decorum in public – yours is innate, his cultural – which probably translates as innate too – keeps the chemistry between you incendiary. You are certain the meal is memorable but forget it as soon as you leave the table.

In your rose-filled bower of a room you lean into Ari as you take a few last moments on the balcony. The heat – is it from you or the night? Ari's hands move along your hips, and stop. He ruckles the smooth fabric of your so well-fitting black dress. You don't usually wear knickers large or small in the summer, or bras, he knows that, but here is something, *something* unexpected underneath.... You turn your face and smile, swaying into him as he perceives the invitation and slowly, slowly, slides the zipper down your back, following the insinuating curves of body and cloth. He stops. A faint intake of breath. You feel his hands have question marks all over them as they hold your hips. The dress falls over his wrist as it slithers down; you shrug its strap free and the dress parts company with your body, pools around your feet. His hands move across your belly, inside the minute pink triangle of silky fabric that holds the thongs that hold the diamanté. Breathing suspends itself into a silent pulsing on the edge of reason, and reason falls at your feet. Ari catches you before you both fall, fall onto the bed, you on your front, he grasping the diamanté heart in his teeth and pulling, tugging at the mock Swarovski, one hand still holding you, clasping your own blackness as you rise and wriggle for the thong to smooth itself down your legs. Ari turns you over as he looks up, eyes filled with laughter and mouth filled with diamanté. A quick toss of his head and whole snippet sails across the bed.

"My *phenomena!*" His laughter releases a moment of high tension, softens it to passion and the mutual pleasure of being lost in the joy of each other. Selene begins her night journey across the sky as your own potent mystery carries you both to uninhibited depths; playful, exploratory, initiatory – into the holy secret of your own sensuality. By dawn, warm in the fragrance of your bodies and still wakeful, you lay drowsily watching the pink and gold of sunrise over the turrets of the mediaeval castle of Neratzia.

CHAPTER NINE

Danaë rested the papers on her lap. *Swami, thongs, Cinderella* – she went to her computer to expand her understanding of references unfamiliar to her. Wikipedia gave her satisfactory answers without the need to go into much detail. *Swami*, she read, a term which applies to women or men who have taken the oath of renunciation and abandoned their social or worldly status to follow that path, undergoing disciplines of meditation or yogic practices or even scriptural studies which are distinct to India. The monastic name is a single word without a first or last name, ensuring non-attachment to the worldly personality. She supposed *Sitadevi* and *Atmadhara*, easily phonetic, were two such names. The life style is, surmised Danaë, equivalent to the nuns of her own tradition. But nuns, it seemed, without the religion, more a lifestyle choice to examine the deeper verities of life without worldly distractions getting in the way. This discovery added an interesting sideline to Alexa, one which explained her naïveté in the world of relationships, and also lent credence to her convent innocence. It must have taken up a significant portion of her life, mused Danaë, as she reflected on the chance of their not having met, a small regret.

Thongs took up pages of Wikipedia. But the moment Danaë saw the photograph on the webpage of the perfectly shaped golden buttocks barely exposing a minute thread of white fabric she smiled broadly – so *that's* what they're called in English. We've had them forever she thought, remembering athletes and amphitheatres. Fashion traded with the rise and fall of interest in our mythologies, she noted, though she had not owned a pair herself. She read further down and laughed aloud at the Australian term *G string*. Downunder, *thong* meant a pair of rubber sandals.

Danaë enjoyed diversion; using her computer this way provided a light relief from her usual day. She knew Cinderella as a character in a fairy story but failed to place her context in its English guise. But *of course*, she said to herself as Wikipedia loaded the page, she was Rhodopis, an ancient incarnation of the badly treated girl who lost a slipper and found a prince – or a king. In Rhodopis' case her prince was the King of Memphis no less. And she, poor captured slave girl, was freed by Charaxus the brother of Sappho herself.

Many stories, but she must continue to search for Alexa. She understood, as only a woman who has known a great love could, that between Alexa and Ari was a mystical bond, a union of spirit that would not be denied. The mundane world and their own mature personalities and all the attributes and experiences that formed them would make the smallness of daily life together impossible, but somewhere else there was a connection that would not be gainsaid.

She made a coffee, took some crescent almond biscuits, and stretched her legs by walking the room, putting down her tray, placing her hands on her hips and swaying from side to side. She grimaced only a little as she heard the slight grinding of cartilage in her neck, shoulders and lower back. Ah, she *ought* to be doing the yoga that she assumed Alexa has done for so many years.

CHAPTER TEN

Sea Change

The week on Kos becomes the watershed for his story; Ari had been born there, he takes you to his birthplace, tells you of his family's perilous escape from the Germans to Rhodes, the losses, the poverty, the hunger.

His reservoir of anguish flows into the sanctuary that your love holds open. He tells you then he wanted you with him, in Rhodes, forever; the next separation sparkles with promises – he will tell his wife she can stay in Paris. She had never really left, but he could now stop deluding himself he has a marriage, a wife yes, but not a marriage.

He takes you to the Sanctuary of Asclepius. You each sit on a fallen foundation stone of the high altar but after some moments something makes you turn to look at Ari – tears are pouring down his face. Aghast, you stand and walk to him, ask him: whatever is wrong?

"This place," he can barely speak, "I see too much. I feel too much. It makes me know I have lost you life after life and I do not want to lose you again."

His words pierce your heart. You assure him it is impossible to lose you: we are together now, you tell him, you will not leave.

Later as you both descend the vast stone stairway from the high altar he stops on the third step down and holds you close as tourists separate and flow past you with their endless chatter. The heat of the early afternoon is intense, you can feel it through your lime green raffia hat; he looks into your eyes, shadowed by the brim, and tells you his father was one of the stonemasons who restored these steps, these stones, this Sanctuary before the Germans came. You know the memory has released his memory of other lives in other centuries and you are silenced with the weight of it.

The week passes too quickly, Kos and Rhodes, trips to the icecream coloured Italian houses of Symi, a ferry trip to Turkey to eat a wondrous meal under fig trees and grape vines, not so stray cats and kittens, so loved by the Turks, having their own cushioned chairs to share while you eat. Titbits offered by your man fail to impress these almost pampered felines. Too soon you are boarding another plane to return to Bristol.

He phones twice, thrice daily on your landline and your mobile, the mobile heart that has become a permanent fixture dangling from your wrist now you are home. Can you live on love and bread and water with him, he says, for he can no longer live without you? His deep velvet voice purrs through the mobile heart. Yes, and yes again, you say. He adds that on Monday he will speak with Petros and afterwards he will be able to tell you "something solid". He reminds you once more of all the marvellous things you are in his eyes, that you are a unique creation, his *phenomena*, that you come from another planet. He loves you for your quality of "fire and truth" because, he says, he does not easily speak what he feels.

You have no family and do not understand the undercurrents that bind its members, but you can't see, no matter how hard you try, what possible business Aristo's divorce is to his son, a forty year old man who apparently harbours little good will towards his father's well being. Is it not to Nicolette that Aristo should be speaking?

Four hours pass. Aristo phones again, more drunk from happiness than from the two litres of wine he confesses to drinking during the talk with Petros. "I am free!" he tells you ecstatically, "you are free! We are free! I will come to you very soon, we have so much to organise and to talk about.. I will bring Crème de Framboise and coffee ouzo for your friends. I will tell everyone here *after* my trip to England that I love you Alexa *mou*, so that no one can blame you."

Another faint puzzle that you decide not to spend time puzzling over: Why would a man who has been separated from his wife for most of his marriage think anyone would apportion blame in your direction? Later you check your emails: "we are free Alexa *mou*, I phone Nicolette. I tell her. She does not mind, she loves Paris anyway. Tomorrow I go to the travel agent and I come to you, Alexa *mou*."

Aristo has bought his ticket, one way, for the 26th August. Emails and phone calls keep you at fever pitch but underneath you are just a touch concerned – it is so soon, what if you have made a mistake, Greece in the sun is so different to England in the rain? You smile at an old memory of Mike Williams proposing to Judi Dench on a glorious beach Downunder and being told to "ask me again on a rainy day in Battersea." You plan on a trip to Lyme Regis over the Bank Holiday – it will be guaranteed to rain ...

But doubts drift like whispering heads around your own: What if Ari changes his mind? You ask him this and he replies very firmly: even if you stop loving me Alexa *mou*, I will love you for two. You must never worry. You shake your head – your friend Glynis tells you comfortingly that she has known such things can happen.

He insists he will cook for all your friends, "just find me the house and tell me how many people, I bring everything with me," he assures you, confident your friends will have manor houses.

Karen, your friend in Townsville, who thinks your Divine Romance just the best thing that has happened for you in ages, emails you news that AIMS may be looking for consultants for their sponge aquaculture project on the Barrier Reef; "and bring me a Greek lover" she adds. The whole world glows with you.

Minutes before he is due to leave he calls from Rhodes airport, your man is nervous, you can tell. He is in Captain of the Ship mode and barks: *the airport! Be there!*

The plane is later than scheduled, you fret only because you want Aristo to see the Tor as the sun rises, it will be a rosy-veiled dawn this morning; later the sun will turn the rose to pale gold.

Your reverie in the Arrivals lounge is splintered by a peel of Beethoven's Ninth. Startled, you answer your mobile heart. "I'm here!" laughs Aristo standing at the luggage carousel behind the closed doors you have been focused on for the past forty minutes. Moments later you are in each other's arms.

Somerset is as pretty as a postcard, green fields dotted with cloud white sheep in the fading moonlight of morning, the hills rolling to the horizon as you swing left from the A38 and track across the Moors. You are still so in love with the West Country and you thrill to be sharing this earth, this blessed plot, this sceptr'd Isle of Avalon with the man you love. It seems incredibly important to you that these days blow fair for him, because for you to leave will be a move not taken lightly. You feel assured of his love and his intentions but he is still, after all, *married*, and a friend who knows these things has forewarned you of *those* perils when they are under the governance of French law. But, today, he is here, you are in love, and the sun is rising over the Tor.

Home. Your tiny studio is aglow at five o'clock in the morning when you arrive home and you fall into bed, unable to remain apart a moment longer. Later, at a more civilized breakfast time Aristo insists on getting up to make your coffee, with fresh ginger, bringing it to your bed and telling you to stay there while he unpacks. So many gifts he brings you, even a pair of beaded sandals. "How did you know my size?" you ask in surprise, and his eyes twinkle over his glasses: "I even remember your name!"

The days pass blissfully. A thousand plans have been aired and shared, your beloved loves the ocean and your recent life by the Great Barrier Reef gives him much to dream on. Aristo mumbles into your neck: *oh, my love, this is the life, in bed with the woman I love; do you have petrol in Australia?*

No sweetheart, you mumble back, fuelled by the colourful imagery of camel carts crawling down the Pacific Highway from Cairns to Coolangatta, *we fill our cars with kangaroo piss*. He shakes with silent laughter; you kiss, and drift into sleep.

The weather has been marvellous since Ari arrives and your plan to take him to Lyme Regis falls on Bank Holiday Saturday. You wake, the rain is falling in piano rods outside your window; *liquid carnage*, laughs your man, undeterred. He falls in love with Lyme, the wildest of winds and sheeting rain nearly blow you both off the Cobb and you head down into the gale to shelter in a fishing hide, complete with a bench inside painted Greek blue. You unpack your picnic and peer through the curtain of rain. Ari's gaze is fixed on a tiny homemade boat attempting to reach a mooring inside the safety of the mole. There is no evidence of human guidance. Ari keeps peering. Then to his astonishment and delight, once the virtual coracle stabilizes, up pops a tarpaulin and two people can be seen setting out a card table and a small gas burner, lighting it with difficulty against the wind, placing a kettle on top and settling themselves down for a nice cup of tea. Ari doubles up with laughter: "if you tell me this story of the English on their holiday I not believe you! This is a wonderful thing. These people are true islanders; I change their tea to ouzo and they are Greeks!"

The week passes as swiftly as the mists that rise around the Tor. All too soon you drive him to the airport and part again with many promises.

September the eighth is your fifty-eighth birthday. Cards tumble through your letterbox, well-wishers phone from all over the world, friends take you to lunch, to dinner. Aristo called in ship's captain mode again; he is returning in a few hours, another dawn landing, to help you pack and drive off into the setting sun to begin a new life on Rhodes.

Your reunion is charged with love and passion, but an undercurrent reveals a very different Aristo now in organizational mood. Now there is no time for laughter, he tells you, he must return to Lardos for his olives, his capers, his grapes, and October. He has only been gone a week but during that time has made the decision that you have a destiny to be together, and now he has returned to help you pack and move, to send everything to Rhodes.

You have not been able to think, for love has been a storm through your days, your tidy life, your thoughts, your known world. But, you confess to yourself, you have not a moment's doubt that this is perfect.

The relief of Ari's presence is considerable in the face of all the packing and sorting and planning and all that accompanies a move, even a small studio move, and when you arrive home Aristo sits you down with him on the sofa to say softly how good your friends are to help you with "all this". He waves his hand to indicate the mountains of boxes and bubble-wrap, and he says again how you will not find such friends like this, "not over all the world." He will definitely buy a bigger house in the country or by the sea so your friends must visit. Tears pool your eyes for some minutes. Then he gets up, steps over everything to reach his belt bag. He pulls out a small packet and hands it to you, wishing you happy birthday.

Inside the wrapping is a small red velvet jewellery box with Spiro's name impressed in gold. You open it, look inside, feel your heart somersault, shut the box again and momentarily lose consciousness. You actually faint, for heaven's sake and Aristo catches you, a delayed gasp puffs from your mouth, you open the box again and stare – at *those earrings. Those* earrings whose originals must have belonged to Empress Alexa herself. You look from them to him, from him to them and back to your beloved who is looking at you with the hugest smile on his face. You have never received anything so exquisitely beautiful in all your life. You are so overwhelmed you can't gather the words to even thank him, but, he assures you, your face says everything he needs to hear. You put them on, they are stunning. He reminds you to wear them carefully, not to lose them, they are special, for you, his *phenomena.*

"Cuddles," says Aristo, "are so *English*, the wild wind and rain creates them! Hugs are momentary, making love is another thing, but all-night cuddles are the most wonderful."

It is your final evening in Avalon. Goodbyes have been said, tears shed, banquets prepared and shared. The Man With A Van collected everything yesterday; you only need to pack the car, now named *Smaragathi*, emerald, an old Greek name Aristo wonders at your knowing. *Mermaid Madonna* you say, naming a much-loved Greek novel you've read in English, but he shrugs, none the wiser. Good name for a green car, he comments, *Smaragathi.*

Aristo has packed the car, you've bought fresh salads and fresh rye and spelt loaves from Burns the Bread, plus a couple of buttered buns for *smackerals* along the journey; you take a last look at your little hermitage, warmly hug your neighbour Glynis – how you will miss her – and drive away to Rhodes by way of Puddletown.

During the crossing from Portsmouth to Cherbourg Aristo is strangely uncommunicative. You take his cue and silently say goodbye to England, receiving grunts in response to your elopement elation since boarding the ferry. Cherbourg cheers him up. He, Aristo, had made the coring for the base of what is now Cherbourg Harbour thirty five years before. You are impressed. Yet back on the road his silence cloaks him from you. It is not a companionable silence; it is a silence that prohibits any communication at all, and it deepens and darkens like his face the further he drives you from all you know. For four days he drives, refusing you the pleasure of driving on the intelligent right as you had been taught in Europe more than thirty-five years before. His silence is a bulwark *against* you. On the ferry at night he holds you passionately, loves you to pieces, but come daybreak this silent stranger stonewalls any attempt at companionship. Perhaps, you think, exhausted from sleepless nights as he drives relentlessly on across France, Italy and down to Patras, he is just tired.

On the final ferry crossing from Piraeus to Rhodes, over another meal in frozen silence, touched by the beauty of the sea beyond the dining room, you are tempted to speak and say how good it will be to collapse into bed the moment you unpack the car. Aristo's face blotches purple across the table. His eyes bulge. Who is this man? Alarm bells toll. "The arrangements are made" he said icily, "for us to go to my son's restaurant."

You have already met his son. Aristo had taken you to his overpriced Moroccan restaurant during the conference. Father and son spoke not one word to each other throughout the worst evening you could remember. Spiro had refused to join you even though Aristo was paying – he had whispered to you he would *never* eat there, the son hates the father so much it poisons the food. A vast spread had been ordered and Aristo sat throughout in glacial silence, eating nothing. "I buy for you," were the only words he spoke. His son added to the surrealism by only speaking to his father as he handed him the bill, "special for you." There was no discount for his father whose fortune had purchased the restaurant and imported the furnishings. You vow in future to eat *fava* with a friend than a banquet with bile.

Aghast, you venture to appeal to his commonsense: "but, my love, we have been travelling since *Friday*, four days, I am exhausted beyond exhaustion, surely Petros will understand that? Is it possible to telephone him to put it off for a couple of days when we will have rested?"

You fail utterly to read the signs on the face of the stranger across the table. Laying down his cutlery Aristo looks at you without seeing, the purple flush on his face has deepened to puce. He erupts. "If you stop me seeing my son I will throw you away! We will separate! You should not have come! I do not say for you to come with me, *you* tell *me* you will come! You are disaster!"

There is an anomaly in the narrative somewhere but you have lost the script. His cruel words rend holes in the curtains of your dreams, hang in tatters. That night Aristo turns on his side away from you, ignoring your presence. You are numb with incomprehension. And thus you pass your fifth night away from all whose loss now compounds a grief incomprehensible, while the jagged edges of ends and beginnings rend the very fibres of your heart.

The Man With A Van arrives two days later. Aristo has not spoken to you once in the whole two days. He invites the Man With A Van and his co-driver to a meal during which he radiates *bonhomie* and good humour, proves a witty raconteur, and the whole evening is a delight, and for you a welcome safety valve releasing the claustrophobic tensions of the previous week. Aristo demands, however, before the meal, that the two men drive on down to a village twenty kilometres along the coast where the whole shipment of your possessions be offloaded in a cold, damp uninhabited village house which he owns. Nothing is to be brought to the townhouse where you live. The following day when the two men drive away something deep and terrible gnaws at you as you watch them go.

Friends from Glastonbury arrive for a holiday as planned and you have booked them into the Pan Hotel. You want to run down to welcome them, Aristo tells you to be very quick, and to invite them to dinner on Monday evening. He will put on his Feeding the Five Thousand performance to lull you into thinking you are, after all, imagining it *all*.

You have only been gone from Glastonbury a week yet both women immediately sense you are seriously *distrait*. You fight back tears, join them in a coffee on Mike's terrace, keenly conscious of time. How can you be this way? All three of you wonder this. You are at a loss to understand the *volte-face*; it is so sudden, so total, so *incomprehensible*. You say you will try and come again; these women are your *friends* for heaven's sake.

You learn to tread watchfully, the Monday dinner is difficult, his cruel barbs to you in front of your friends do not sit well with any of the company; he has included a French couple and his equally cruel asides about you in French are fenced and foiled by your English friends, who speak the language fluently. The evening leaves you tense and unhappy, and you are not permitted to see your friends again after walking them back through the Old Town after the meal while Ari cleaned up. As you hug each other goodnight the two women empty their purses of euros for you to top up your mobile phone, make you promise to keep your communication lines open. They are as disturbed by the Hyde as they had been previously charmed by the Jekyll.

Just as suddenly Aristo's mood swings again. Ari has become a stranger through every day, if only the nights would go on forever. He insists on doing all the shopping, all the cooking, all the cleaning which sounds wonderful on paper but the reality is that you are redundant. You learn the prescribed times of his drinking habits through any one day – beer at eleven, whisky anytime, ouzo before lunch, wine or retsina during lunch, whisky anytime, aperitifs before dinner, whisky anytime and television every waking hour with whisky anytime. Welcoming him home from shopping one day you offer to fetch him a beer. "Hi sweetheart," you greet him happily and normally, after all you adore the man. He may not be currently nice to be around, but your adoration verges on worship and you love him *so* much, *so* much that you left your friends, your home and your country for him, "would you like a beer?"

He snarls, he *really* snarls, that he will get it himself, and why do you ask, you have not asked before, he does not like talking to "create an *ambiance.* You are disaster," he spits, "I will take you back to Glastonbury."

The walls around you lurch in synchronism with your stomach and you reach out to steady yourself, stunned again by such gratuitous cruelty. You begin to walk away when he says in a low growl: "and your feet are so dirty, why you don't wear shoes in my house?" You kick up the sole of one foot to look at it and think how *can* it be dirty, Aristo bleaches the entire house *every second day*! Your feet are clean. But you will dig out the beaded sandals he gave you as soon as he allows you to bring some boxes from Kremasti.

Your hair comes in for a volley next, as he pointedly kisses a photograph of you which he had hung when he loved you – a lifetime ago. You have cut it yourself for decades. It is so fine that, since having your head shaved when you entered the equivalent of a nunnery a lifetime ago, you can't see the point of spending money where you can do the job to your own reasonable satisfaction. Except that suddenly it isn't to Ari's. You approach him and he elbows you away. That hurts, he is powerfully built, and his elbow, brought up sharply, thumps *intentionally* against your breast. You do not flinch but simply gaze at him in disbelief. He will not look at you, but then, you've noticed, he doesn't hold anyone's eye when he is looked at, only when he is telling a joke and becomes centre stage will he catch an eye during his story, but it is for effect. You *know* it is for effect, as sure as God made little apples.

It is difficult for your friends to reach you by phone. Aristo plays games with his complicated telephone set up, cancels the answering service so you cannot receive messages and switches the phone's reception to fax, refuses to allow you to pick up the phone during the six fax rings. The anguish you feel as the final ring tone ceases and no fax is delivered is not made easier by your intuitive knowledge that these calls are for *you*; no one calls Aristo. Trades people and real-estate agents use his mobile number. So do the women with whom he has gay and tonally sensual conversations with in French, sitting in the back courtyard for an hour at a time. "Ah," he says to you after one such call "but she was so *ugly*.... You have no need to worry Alexa *mou*, I will not spoil our dreams, dreams of me and you, Alexa *mou*." For you the dream has become a nightmare.

You are desperately lonely and have taken to going for walks now the weather is cooler. Aristo's moods are becoming predictable, no less destabilizing, no less punitive in his threats that you must leave, that he *never* asked you here, but you are slowly learning to live with the isolation within the home and without. You live each day, navigate moment-by-moment, cruise the fallouts. He will not allow you to bring anything you own to the house, the October rains are coming, the village house at Kremasti grows mould inside; your beloved books, artwork, clothes, mattress, sofa, shoes are growing mould. You beg to be able to put the heating on there once a week and Aristo's anger sears you. He visits it three times a week to slosh bleach over the floors and terrace to impress the real-estate agents and their clients. Sadly you prepare to relinquish all you own. You are merely camping in his townhouse, your life is in boxes and you cannot reach it, you have one hand on the door but cannot bring yourself to turn the handle for you do not know where to go. And the greatest anguish of all is that you *know* the man you love is in there somewhere, somewhere beyond your reach; perhaps, if he wasn't so godlike, his short-spoken cruel words would reveal him brutish, but you can't be sure, yet.

One night Aristo wakes shaking and you awake instantly. You have lived through weeks of abuse and raging tantrums, weeks of the most unjust accusations, nights of having your hand thrown back across your body when you have attempted a tender contact. For now he is frigid and wants nothing to do with you, chooses to sleep rigidly on his own adjacent mattress. You lay tense and still, he is moving, he is *moving* towards *you*. You daren't do something *normal* like turn to welcome your beloved and reach out to hold each other in your arms, yet all of a sudden he is on your mattress, clutching you, crushing you, speaking as if he loved you, as if he knew you, as if you were the woman he wanted and loved and pleaded with you to come and be in his life.

"Alexa *mou*, I have had the most terrible dream. I was in bed and I woke up and I could not reach you, there was a wall between us and I could not get through. Alexa *mou*, it was terrible, *you were not there!*"

You don't know whether to laugh or cry, but thankfully it is dark, as dark as Aristo will allow it, for he has night terrors and sleeps with soft lighting on all over the small house. You wriggle around, and you know you will love him forever because the Aristo you love will always be inside the Aristo whose cruelty you are only just beginning to know. Your loving, for the first time in weeks, is tender, powerful and indivisible, you both weep at the release of the past awful weeks.

He takes you to Lardos, to his olive grove. "This place is for me and you alone," he tells you. Later you learn what he means; it is the only piece of property he owns in the whole of Greece or France that his wife has not sewn up and stitched with her name across it. He pulls open the vast black wrought iron gates, with their central silver mock heraldic medallion, and turns to you proudly. His face drops all its tension; the Aristo you adore has taken residence. He is a man of his sea and his soil, this you understand and share. This piece of land, a pocket-handkerchief, is beautiful. Eleven ancient olive trees stand proud within a fence hung with grape vines and edged with well-established rose bushes, rose bushes he planted himself. There are salmon roses, deep pink roses, white roses and deepest red roses. You know old roses well, but these are all modern, mildly scented, and unknown to you. Their beauty is not of fragrance but of form and colour and Aristo tells you to pick what you like to place on the table in the shabby little caravan and enough to take back to Rhodes tomorrow. Artichokes line the southern fence; plums have ripened on the tree by the gates. He is blissfully *normal*.

The silence and the solitude and the wind of Lardos have a generosity, a beneficence that rests in your soul. You are happy here, and pick roses to fill the table. Aristo is overjoyed that you love his hideaway, tells you to remember always he loves you. "Remember," he repeats with passion, "I will always look after you. We will have a good life together."

Later that evening he asks plaintively over a meal in the village "How long will you love me?" Five years, you say without hesitation. "Why not six?" came his response. "Because," you answer, without missing a beat, "I will die then."

"Why? Do you have a problem?"

"Yes, my heart."

"What is wrong with your heart?"

"It is fragile and will break too many times with you."

He laughs, but his eyes fill with tears and he turns away.

This precious time you have together heals much of the past weeks' horrors and you broach the subject of his book. Perhaps you can begin if he feels he is ready to talk to you of his life? You think it may be a catharsis for him too; perhaps to speak the memories that weigh so heavily upon his heart would help you both. His smile pinions your heart like a butterfly to a board.

Two days later you begin his story. His facility for narrative delights your professionalism and you listen and type enthralled through the hours each day, pinioned now to the new office chair he purchased "just for you, Alexa *mou*." As you begin to learn more and more about this troubled, complex man you wonder if perhaps you are his unconsciousness repository for a lifetime of unspoken angers and anguishes. You recall how he admired your emotional honesty, he is unable to articulate his own.

CHAPTER ELEVEN

Danaë put down the manuscript. The intensity of the complete *volte face* of such a love story was alien to her long experience of life, her own marriage was so rich, so fulfilling. Absorbed, she sits cocooned in Alexa's love of Ari, of Rhodes, of life itself. The Ari he became shocked Danaë but she believes Alexa. She prepared herself more coffee, she had read until *wolf light, λύκος φως, lykóphos,* the dusk before sunrise. Whatever clues are to be gleaned as to Alexa's whereabouts must be found. Alexa's love for Aristo has taken Danaë back to that fullness within her own heart, a fullness whose name was Stavros, her own beloved husband whose amalgam of goodness together with what she hopes are her own finer qualities live on in their son, Pericles.

She took advantage of the natural break to drink her coffee and relax her eyes by gazing into the moonlit garden that has given family members for generations such pleasure within its walled sanctuary. The pause helped Danaë re-enter the essence of Alexa's world, for the next few pages of the story was extracted from her diaries, first person singular, hurriedly, as if Alexa knew that everything of each moment must be recorded. *As if knowing of something beyond her ken.* And through that deep knowing Alexa's voice changed, began to carry a weight, an integrity that supported her increasing self-belief and revealed a finely honed humour, a saltiness that carried with it pure sanity. She still wavered between first and second pronoun, but Danaë understood the contradictions; read between the lines and felt where the pain was too searing for first person acknowledgement, as she was forced to admit the man she loved had revealed himself. Above all, Danaë began to love this woman as a friend. They were, after all, fairly close in years, if only they had met, how different it might have been....

She read on:

Monday October 4th

He comes out of the sea with seven small fish and a young octopus. I watch him put his fingers into its head and rip out its ink sac, then methodically and with great power repeatedly beat it against a scraggy rock to tenderise it. The foam from the octopus bubbles like soap. He fillets the fish and washes them in the sea. I am conscious of having switched off my personal emotions while I watch him, the octopus looks at me from its bucket and there is intelligence in its eyes. I offer a prayer, even while knowing Aristo will cook one of his speciality dishes for me and I will enjoy the taste of the love he puts into the making of it.

Tuesday October 5th

We began Ari's book yesterday. He found it too painful to remember his earliest years and broke off many times, unable to speak against the tide of memories that came flooding up from his own depths. We worked for two hours and oh the change in him. His love for me has come back. The breaks he takes when emotion spills over means I can ponder deeply over the right words with which to construct his stories without losing the immediacy of its Greekness being expressed in his Englishness. He has a rare gift for storytelling.

Wednesday October 6th

Yesterday was a good day. Ari has stopped his litany of verbal persecution. Perhaps it is because I am engaged in doing his book. He took me to the hairdresser and the resulting coiffure is alright, rather Zizi Jeanmaire-ish. Aristo says this is why he loves me, because I am natural, he does not like hair dyed or *bouffant*.

Last night I dreamt of a tsunami. There was nothing, nothing of the world left. I called to Ari to hold my hand and we were plunged into the darkness of the curving wall of water together. We were Pyrrha and Deucalian after the Flood. They, alone of all humankind, prayed, and the gods spared them. I also prayed.

At lunch I share with Aristo my experiences of Delphi. His eyes fill with tears and he says again this is why he loves me, because I love Greece. He says he had looked for me for so many centuries and I ask how we would have met if he had not come into Spiro's shop that night. "No matter," he said "I would have found you somewhere in the streets in those days, we share the same dream, we belong together, I have always waited for you, Alexa *mou*." He tells me he will sell this house, but, "you

are home," he says, "in all of Greece you are home."
I want to believe it.

Thursday October 7th

We progress apace with the book. Ari is
warm and affectionate and relaxed. He brings some
boxes of my books here. I nearly cried to have some
with me again. Back to Lardos for the weekend. I
wash the caravan floor and lay down a brightly
woven mat I found in a cupboard in the townhouse.
Dictating his book is bringing terrible memories to
the surface; memories of his wife's fraudulent
expenditure of his considerable earnings while he
was down in the deep. I take them at face value but
know with a woman's sure instinct that should I
ever meet her she may well tell a different tale. For
me what is really gripping are his stories of
encounters with the denizens of the deep and of his
human courage; giant octopuses, massive sharks,
lethal Royal Rascass, heartbreaking deaths of fellow
divers.

I never understood before how not having
money, *really* not having money, is such a trap. I've
never had much, but what came to me was mine to
use as I wished. I am using Pamela's gift to eke out
for personal needs: stamps, paper, reprints of
photos of my beloved to share with friends in Oz, a
cup of coffee when I go out. This morning I will go
out and leave Zeus to his thunderbolts and
tantrums, they have begun again.

I am sitting with my muddle of thoughts
under the huge weeping fig at Aktaion in Mandraki
harbour for Ari exploded again with such violence I
was left reeling. I walked the harbour until the wind

dried my tears and I could see again the beauty of this island.

Wednesday October 13th

Aristo has cooked a special lunch of saganaki and stuffed squid, accompanied by broccoli and carrots. *I love you so much*, he says, *and I need you to love me. Since meeting you I have begun to take more care of myself. I am an old man of sixty-one, I do not want to go to fat so that you do not love me. I have waited forty years for you, alone, without love, without making love, only sex occasionally and this I can have every five minutes in Rhodes but I never want without love. I need your love. I must be patient while we adjust to our life; we have been separate so long.*

I gaze at him with more love than the whole world can hold. After a short silence he looks away and says wistfully, more to himself than to me, to some flicker of a memory unbidden: *perhaps I could have loved better in the past, but I didn't, and I didn't know how; she was so cold, so cold.*

Sitting there with him my heart is cleft in two. I know how painful the what-ifs of lost years and lost opportunities are. He says he can see how unhappy I am, but the moment is not the right moment for me to broach my increasing uneasiness over his anger, his rages and tantrums, let alone the spectre of my tenuous position in his life. But, and this needs be said, I have never been acquisitive or materialistic; I walked into life at the age of two and a half when I took my woollen pony and went beyond the garden gate, quite out of my knowing of things, into the wide world that called me. My passion for travel began then, and my passion for life, forfeiting all except, later, a few clothes, my various cats and my books. I knew I would always trust *le Bon Dieu* for His guidance of my future if only – if *only* Aristo was the loving, caring, funny and gorgeous man I had first met. Bread and water, love and roses actually suit me well. It is anger and fury that destabilizes me. Isn't love always ready to excuse, to trust, to hope and to endure? How long and how much does *endure* mean?

After love and what is left of siesta he suggests he takes me to look for a computer. Mine is terminally ill and I am, after all, sitting at it for six hours a day writing his book. He has a vested interest, but I am humbled when he buys a Toshiba Satellite laptop and a pen drive. And then later in the day explodes with anger so violent I lean right back against the wall for support.

Aristo swears he will never, *ever* touch you again; you have *insulted* him, he who is the *most* kind man; you are a *puttana*, a whore! I turn my head to see who he could be referring to.

And that night? *Alexa mou,* he says, *don't ever worry, I love you. I love you, and only you are in my heart. I am a unique man,* he continues, *I am unique in the world. I am unique and I am the most kind man.*

I am unsure of what he might mean, but, yes, he is unique and I manage to sigh in agreement.

November 1st

We go to Lardos for the weekend. Ari is untouchable but his face drops ten years when we get there though his temper is still on simmer and hard to bear. We have a picnic, I pick roses, he checks the fences around the property – and his face changes muscle by tortured muscle the closer we get to Rhodes on our return. This angry, scowling, tormented face is not one I ever saw in those heady halcyon days before he moved me here lock, stock and two smoking barrels.

I am becoming ill. My stomach can't face the food, his food, Greek food. It is a question of energetics, my body wisdom, its cellular intelligence, is rebelling against the abuse aimed at it, at me, at all of myself. Me, who can eat cardboard, and have done so in England where public food can be so wilfully bad and a oftentimes a wholly demeaning experience. My back is in pain. I, who never has backache. There is nothing for me to sit on here, only a wooden beach seat or my secretary chair – all day, every day. I have made a terrible mistake and I can see no way out. Aristo's intentions are in no way honourable to me. I am a peripheral passerine through his life; will I have to wait until Spring to migrate? But to where? Aristo makes his delicious fish soup. I nearly gag on it, force a little down.

I yearn for a break from his relentless anger, not just a few hours but weeks and billowing weeks filled with love and laughter. Even modest courtesy and meaningful conversation would do. Life is just so *bleak*. And when I look in the mirror I think I am dying. I don't mind death when it comes, but I do want to *live* until that moment. Life is being squeezed out of me.

My clothes, shoes, books, sofa, mattress, bedding, everything I own is growing spectacular furry mould down in Kremasti, the rain has been torrential and the house has creeping damp and sodden walls. Aristo refuses to put the heating on when we are there once or twice a week to clean the terrace. He has had the place on and off the market so often that no one goes to look at it now. I asked if I could put my summer clothes into the empty camphor wood chest by his mattress in the townhouse so that I could bring some warmer clothes here, could create a shelf by juggling the space of the one shelf allotted to me – NO! he roared, it is MINE!

Of course it's bloody yours, I think, *I only want to use the empty space inside,* but no, I wasn't allowed. Why, I wonder, or how, has he built up a reputation for generosity? He doesn't even share *empty space*. Christmas, I tell myself, I'll go at Christmas, somewhere, because by then I will have been here three months and of that three months if the ratio of his horrible behaviour continues as it has since September then even besotted me will have to admit defeat.

And *exactly* at the moment I wrote that he came to me and asked if I knew why he loved me. *Do tell,* I said, looking up from the Moleskine and attempting to keep one eyebrow from rising in withering disbelief. He almost took the wind from my sails by saying: *because you are so patient with me, I know I am terrible sometimes.* I press the advantage and agree, adding that all he has to do is to expand his capacity to include another person in his life, i.e. me. He says his 'capacity' gets 'overfull'.

I remind him he loves me, he knows I love him, and if we can remember humour it's the best medicine for survival but it has been in short supply around Kazerma Reggina lately.

Yet his cries of: "why does God make my life so bad, I am the kindest man, everyone all my life cheats me", are beginning to sound hollow and self-pitying. When he gets into his rages I am no longer crushed, my sad heart has grown a little membrane around it; it will dent and bruise but hopefully not pierce. One day he launches an attack so strange I struggled to fathom its source. *Look at you*, he rages, *how can I trust you, you are fifty-eight and have nothing, nothing!* I can only assume Nicolette must have called up for funds and he is reminded of what a *drain* on his wealth is my *eight* euros a week pocket money.

I am beginning to have nightmares. I recognise them as anxiety dreams. Christmas is coming, and I know I will have to leave. Death is the only other option, but I can't rely on that. I manage to track down a shipping agent with much difficulty as I don't read Greek phone books and I can hardly ask Aristo. I walk to the harbour and find a customs officer who confers with a colleague and they give me an address in the town.

After another lengthy walk I find myself sitting in front of Kyriakos, who speaks a most excellent English. "Where do you want to ship your things to," he asks, logically. Either of two places, I say and he raises an eyebrow just a tremor as I offer England or Australia.

Both eyebrows quiver then, and remain in his hairline while he shoots me a querying glance. I begin to explain that I was brought here by a Greek man I loved very much and – and I get no further as pent up emotions spill over in tears and blubbering apologies. He understands – *oh for goodness sake he's probably heard it all before*. As the relief of being heard overwhelms me, I recall somehow that I still have to tell this kindly man which direction I need the quote for. I settle for both, one for each side of the planet and guess at the five and half cubic metres.

Karen emails to say a mutual friend will offer me her house for three months if I choose a southern bound escape route. *Doxa to Theo.*

Thursday December 9th

Christine, the Belgian half of the French dinner guests who accompanied my Glastonbury friends *that* forgettable night has told me about an English group who meet on Thursdays at the Hotel Agla. I went this morning and was welcomed and invited to carol singing practice in the evening. I am so excited I rush back to tell Ari (who can't refuse me because it is *his* friends who urge me to go) I was going to the singing practice tonight. It was wonderful, I was shy, but this marvellous bouncy blonde Englishwoman introduces herself to me and I just love her on sight. Her name is Penelope and she has been happily married to a Greek forever, about thirty-five years. We have arranged to meet for coffee, she is all for doing that, it really must be a girlie thing because I just miss it so much. I am *soooooo* looking forward to speaking English, it will be like shooting a safety valve, and maybe if I can do that then I can see my relationship with Aristo more clearly, can gain some perspective, decide whether it is me who is out of sync or he who is completely off the wall.

Friday December 10th

I was so happy last evening I floated all the way home – to meet a leaden faced Aristo. And in the morning to face another tornado about his memoirs. We have completed the dictation but the whole thing needs editing and re-structuring and for that I need peace and a certain timetable of solitude. Ari asked how long that might take. Well, I say, thinking of other biographers I knew, it *could* take a year (*or two or three, thinking of some others*) and Ari went skywards. You have *lied*, he thundered, you have done nothing for 500 days (*how long is 500 days my beloved? I've only been here three months...*) *nothing*, and now you tell me a *year*. His face is purple-dark with rage. You must stop running to the church and this singing (*ahhh, so that's his problem*) you must stop going out every day (*ahhh, so there's the rub, once a fortnight, no less*) for coffee. This is stupidities (*really? I call it life*). You waste time, *my* time. For what? You don't paint (*where? how? you banished my materials to the village house*). You don't work (*you sabotaged the interviews I arranged with the translator, my dear one*). I will get another womans to do my book. You can go. You lie too much. I send you to Australia (*why? it's the last place I want to go at the moment*), go and come back (*why my dear one, have you another woman coming for Christmas?*) anywhere (*except back to Glastonbury because my*

friends whom you call shit just might think you are).
You lie too much!

"Did you just bring me here to fuck and write your book?" I ask quietly. He turned apoplectic. "We are finished, finished" he roared, "I promise you *nothing* when you come here, *nothing*, and we have no contract."

Well, in the face of such a non-sequitur, what can I do or say but *laugh*. I begin to pack. I take the few things I have here and I put them carefully in plastic bags. I plan to take them to Kremasti and repack them into the boxes there. Aristo looks on in silence while he computes what I am doing and then he explodes again and I am forced to stay.

Christmas Day

For the next days Aristo remains the man I fell in love with. I warm his nightshirt by wrapping it around my hot-water bottle, he thinks it quaint, but loves the gesture and expects it every night. He laughs when I tell him the old joke that French have sex and the English have hot water bottles and he lands on top of me to say the Greeks now have both.

Love is here when the postman brings so many Christmas cards for me in the so-welcome mail and letters from friends who still gather in the Persephone to ask of me. These are real graces. Jessica telephones to say my plea and prayers emailed to the Shrine of Our Lady of Glastonbury was upheld at Christmas Mass, the whole congregation of St Mary's are holding us both in love and prayer.

On Christmas morning I wake early, go downstairs to make coffee to bring to Aristo, reversing the morning habit. I light the kerosene heater, gather my gifts, take a rose from the vase to place by his coffee, lay everything on a tray and go back upstairs. I place everything by the side of his mattress and climb back into my side of the bed. The smell of coffee wakes him. I giggle excitedly and greet him good morning and wish him a happy Christmas, snuggling close.

He has *never* had such a loving Christmas, he says. There are tears in his eyes as he opens my gifts, especially when he sees my drawing of a bear, a rather good drawing if truth be known, for which I had found the perfect frame. Aristo is my grumbly, grizzly bear, his hands curl like bears paws, curl like those of many seamen and sailors. He shakes his head, his voice thick with unbidden emotion. It is beautiful, he says, clearing a space for it on the chest by his bed. He hands me a box, in it a gold ring, the ring of Rhodes commissioned from Spiro, with all the symbols carved on it: the Deer, the Rose of Rhodes, the minarets, the Cross of the Knights of Rhodes. It is too beautiful, I say, and he says I am like a child. I remind him of how long it takes to grow young, and I am glad to have finally come of age. And so the year ends, with love and with hope.

January 4th

There has been a terrible tsunami in Indonesia. It seems to have an echo here. I have a few English magazines, National Trust, Country Life and so on, precious because they are in English and I am starved for reading. Aristo grabbed the small pile, with only the strength of his own two hands screwed them up, shredded them and threw them on the floor in front of me. I look at the destruction sadly, but I leave them where they are, no longer mine. He finally stops bellowing. I am trembling, not least because of the force of such power.

I am meeting Penelope at two. She is just a joy. Come on, she said a day or so ago when we were sitting together over coffee and wondrous *galaktoboureko*, we'll go back down to Kremasti and I'll take your most important things home. She has a very large apartment in Ialyssos with a sunroom that spans the whole frontage, and has offered to let me move some of my more precious things there where they will be warm and dry. We spend three or more hours ferrying certain things; Ari is at Lardos for the afternoon, there has been strong winds and he wants to check his olive trees. The time without him is a balm, and, after we had locked up the village house, Penelope bought me strawberry tart and coffee at the Swedish Café. Divine. My spirit lifts immeasurably. She tells me of an iconographer in the Old Town though she doubts he will be there today, and even if he is she doubts he'll speak English, but she wants to take me to meet him. Penelope speaks Greek fluently.

We go anyway, and he is there and speaks English and he asks me pertinent questions of the methods I use for icons, asks me how I prepare my egg for the tempera, and we spoke of theology and of God. He listens to me, his grey blue eyes are sharp, I sense he is weighing me up. Half finished icons of every size and holy imagery fill the walls of his little studio, I am entranced. He speaks to Penelope in Greek and then turns to me and invites me to come to his studio class in Apolona on Saturday evenings. It will not cost me anything he says; he can see I have been taught correctly and he will help me.

It is a marvellous encounter; my soul is engaged once more. Penelope will take me there, join in with the class and I am so happy for the extra hours in her company. Before we leave that corner of the Old Town she takes me to the little chapel of St Panteleimon the Healer. It is one of the oldest shrines on Rhodes and I light the customary beeswax tapers to place in the candle-stand. Penelope does not know of my affection for the third century saint, or of the very old icon of him that I have resurrected from Ari's dusty collection and hung near on my side of the bedroom. I take it as an omen of better days to come. At home I was enormously happy, and Aristo said he missed me, he had gone from Lardos to his son's restaurant having picked capers from his land. When I shared my lovely day and Vasilis' offer for me to go to his studio in Apolona and paint icons under his tuition Ari snarled savagely and said: *well go and live there.*

Well, I just might.

January 26th

How am I to interpret his anger? Penelope names it control. She and I have been talking together of how I can leave and not lose everything I own. "And you *are* taking that computer," she said. Yes, I agree, and Bob's painting.

Later. Aristo still very explosive. I long for normal verbal intercourse, for a non-threatening co-existence. My friends have proved their salt and I would rather their salt on bread than Ari's *cordon bleu* peppered with anger. Behind closed doors he is a very damaged and cruel man. Is this really me saying this? Are my glasses no longer so rose coloured?

Penelope's husband doesn't bat an eyelid at the growing hill of my possessions in their sunroom.

Good grief! I came home and Ari's face curdled purple as I enter the house. "I am sending you to Kremasti!" he fairly bellows at me. Now *I* am being banished to the village house! I am so exhausted, depleted by fear, I can only feel a wan pity for the man.

As I am being banished to the village house I can lay claim to the hours in my day, and so I begin by going to visit Father Luke, the local Franciscan priest, whose assessment of Greek men is bleak. Yet there must be at least eight Greek men on Rhodes who are loving, appreciative and affectionate husbands because Penelope's husband is most definitely one of them.

I am banished but Ari insists I return for lunch each day so he can launch into a litany of my unacceptable behaviours. How I ache for this difficult, damaged, turbulent, contradictory, irrational man. He is relentless. I weep. Ari pushes away his chair from the table, gets up, and looks down at me scornfully. His whole demeanour alters as he grins and says: "I think I'll have a nice little drink." He walks past me to the bar, pours himself a large tumbler of whisky, with glee, no ice. Ice-cold dread coalesces in the pit of my soul – *the man is demented.* What will he not do? This is psychopathic behaviour, no wonder he is so intent on keeping me isolated. Penelope will be alert to anything amiss should I disappear.

February 12th

"I will break your mind to obedience" filters like the ancient whisper from a Greek Chorus through my sorrow; he said this once to me, I couldn't even write it down it seemed so shocking to me, yet indeed, that is what he is doing. I will survive until Thursday when Penelope and I meet and I rescue more boxes to give to her for safekeeping.

Perversely Ari responds to the beauty that unfolds as I progress with various icons. He buys me timber, boils the rabbit skin glue to the correct temperature to secure the linen over the finely sanded wooden panels, stirring slowly, very slowly, to avoid air bubbles, criss-crossing the brush strokes in the iconographer's traditional imitation of the Cross. For the gesso he is even more meticulous; reheats the glue to 40 degrees celcius in a bain-marie, sifts coffee cups of fine natural gypsum from Sienna into the glue, lets it settle into a pyramid. This may take him an hour, not one air bubble – the mark of haste and a frame of mind unworthy of the sacred – must there be. He stirs this pyramid with a stick, slowly, gently to form the pure *sotile* gesso that will feel like ivory when he finally applies nine coats, each sanded smooth, each application criss-crossed in the way of the Cross, over a week, refining the sandpaper with each successive sanding.

I stand and watch in awe, but have to swallow my frustration because he will not permit *me* to learn! Vasilis remarks on the perfection of Ari's preparation. Perhaps I can persuade him to share this special gift with me, become part of the class? Then one evening he begins to copy my work; in the class we are using sketchbooks first to draw the icon prior to pricking it out on the panels. Ari is, not surprisingly, very gifted, and obsessive. I will bid him goodnight at nine-thirty, leave him absorbed in his new discovery, and he will come and shake me awake at one in the morning to show me his drawings. They are beautiful, as if the saints and angels themselves are appearing through this window of calm to grace us with normality.

One morning he calls me to look at his favourite drawing of mine which he has framed and placed on the wall: "you know, Alexa *mou*, when I shout at you sometimes afterwards I feel very bad. I stand and look at your drawing of the *Panaghia* on the wall. She is so beautiful. And once She came off the wall to comfort me, She came from out of the drawing. It is very special what you do."

I am moved. Perhaps there is hope. If love was here I would stay. And he fast-forwards to a fantasy where something as fragile as our relationship has endured beyond pain and disappointments. A *place bathed only in the pure clear light of love and sanctified desire*; I read the words somewhere, they remained with me, never did I think they would describe me.

We go to Lardos in the Spring, which is early here. The fields are carpeted with bright red and purple anemones, glisten with yellow buttercups and kingcups, sweet celandine, coltsfoot and oxeye daisies under silver grey-green olive trees. The ephemeral beauty of this early Grecian spring lands in the hurt places of my heart and I find myself standing alone in the field behind the olive grove with tears bathing my face, wrung out of me by the sheer beauty of the place…

Friday February 18th

We go beachcombing after the storms. I find a tiny turtle shell, the body still attached but decomposing. I do not want to separate it so place the pretty thing on a pebble at the littoral and the tide takes it back to the deep. But the tide turns, and when we arrive home Aristo is again the violently angry man I am becoming afraid of. He erupts over something I cannot recall and in the fallout of my mute gaze he bellows: *What is the solution?*

Easily and quietly the words I have been afraid to voice even to myself fall from my lips: *help me pack, help me to go home.*

"Where will you go," comes his thunderous response "you have nowhere to go anymore." I agree, and say I don't know, but that it doesn't matter, I have to go somewhere.

"Am I wrong," he shouts, "to shout at you?"

"Yes, you are my love, there is a way to speak gently," I say, "shouting and roaring about me, or about my different ways, is never acceptable. We need to sit as adults and talk about how we can accept or modify our differences. You shout that I have destroyed your life. I have been in your life for five months. Your life is sixty-one years and four months long, and you tell me it has been a terrible life. I don't think I am really to blame, do you?"

I continue, the walls that have imprisoned me, the words of his that have bound me to him, all roll away as I unmake them: "I want to laugh again, you loved me laughing before I came here; I want to feel the sparkle of joy in my eyes again; you loved the teasing sparkle of happiness in my eyes before I came here; I want to feel that inner smile of happiness at just being alive again – I lost Alexa somewhere between Portsmouth and Cherbourg."

He spent the evening in his cups, whisky and tears.

Slowly slowly his tears became less and he can see me more clearly, but my eyes are full of tears that refuse to fall. He touches my neck, my cheek, "you have become so thin" he says softly. "Tomorrow I buy our tickets for Australia."

But in a body blow that leaves me reeling he changes his mind at the travel agents desk the following morning, shocks the staff by thundering "why I go to Australia, I live in paradise," and storms out. I think I am trapped forever.

My days in Kremasti are *liberating*. I deliberately leave my mobile in the house and go for long vivifying walks along the beach. I fall in love with Greece for itself; love the craggy lilac mountains in the distance, the scent of thyme and oregano as I walk the waste ground on the way to the sea, marvel at the marvellous church in Kremasti and so look forward to seeing Penelope whenever she turns up. I am so really happy which just proves to me that it is Ari who is barking mad, not *me*. Happiness fairly radiates from me but for the nagging reality of my situation – and penury. Penelope feeds me coffee and cake, Ari insists I drive to Rhodes for lunch with the good man, but – suddenly my happiness evaporates as the good man misses me so much he will come to Kremasti to be with me!

My heart plummets. Penelope and I have been smuggling all my stuff back there from her sunroom. Panos puffs on his pipe good naturedly watching the farce. I am working out how to get Kyriakos and the shippers there without Ari foiling the escape plan. It isn't a major plan, just a moment by moment step by cautious step development. I'll tell Ari when everything has gone, and I will spend the last days with Penelope before following the container. The *last* thing I want is for Ari to move in. Penelope continues to lift my spirits, she's always a step ahead. We decide that the safer of the two options is for me to be ultra-attentive after lunch, stay for siestas, and lull the good man into remaining amongst his own home comforts. Anything to keep him from coming to Kremasti.

I promise myself I will buy a one-way ticket to Australia on my unused credit card as it is now the plan, not my chosen plan, but a home for three months on one side of the planet is a goal to aim for. I'll take whatever escape route is open for me. Once Kyriakos has taken everything, *everything*, I will go to Penelope's and leave Rhodes from there.

For three days Penelope and I pack, dismantle canvas wardrobes and the recently assembled bed for my occupancy of the village house; the fiendishly well-assembled icon table so lovingly made for me by my so contradictory lover takes almost a whole day. On Thursday the pair of us pack the last of thirty-two small boxes, prop the queen size mattress against the wall. I phone Aristo and ask if I can spend that evening in the townhouse as I want to go into town on Friday. He has, in fact, not been near Kremasti since his brutal volte-face over the tickets to Oz but it would be too ironical if he rolled up unannounced, and it is safer that I sleep in the townhouse with him on Thursday night. Kyriakos has arranged to pick up everything at eight-thirty on Friday morning.

My mind is completely blank about *how* I am going to be in Kremasti at eight-thirty on Friday morning without incurring the slightest suspicion that would alert Aristo to follow or accompany me. I am on red alert and frankly, *terrified*. Penelope cruises, she still has a trick or two up her sleeve.

On Thursday evening, exhausted, I drive back to Rhodes via the home of a young woman I have met to whom I will bequeath Smaragathi once I have left. Penelope and I have packed and sorted and dismantled and listed and labelled thirty-two boxes, trunks, cupboards, flat-packs of assorted furniture parts over the past two and a half days. My sleep has been fitful, I am so nervous I could eat chalk and not know it. I pray Aristo does not decide to visit, he disappeared on his bike in such high dudgeon on Tuesday after his tantrum at the travel agent and I haven't in fact seen him since. Unbeknown to me Holy Mary is keeping Aristo on his toes. Unbeknown to me Petros and Nicolette, in the light of my continued association with their inheritance and source of wealth, have been putting enormous pressure on Aristo over the past few days to sign the remaining French properties over to Nicolette to insure that I, in my role of usurper of pocket-money, do not stand to gain so much as a door latch. I continue to pray that Ari continues to stay away until Thursday so he doesn't see every last belonging of mine assembled and sorted as if for a long journey on the high seas.

Miracles are mine for the whole week. He is busy in town, will make a special meal for when I arrive. One more night and then Kyriakos will launch my escape.

CHAPTER TWELVE

Pericles, meanwhile, had been swallowing in chunks the story of the island hero written by Alexa. A skein of unease underlay the text, unease at the consummate self-pity of its hero, giving Pericles the uncomfortable sense that Aristo Theohalis was not only a highly trained cold blooded killer but might, just might, be capable of killing in hot blood under provocation. Wherever he might be now Pericles could only hope Aristo was not with Alexa, that each is alive and well and apart. The pages he had read left him in no doubt that the man loved her in his way, but the more he read a deep sense of dread surfaced that refused to be gainsaid.

A taxi spun the gravel, Danaë and Maria walked in together, "Lunch will be ready in an hour," smiled Maria. Pericles nodded, looked at his mother, placed an affectionate arm around her shoulder and led her away,

"Mama," he spoke quietly, "this is a very difficult story. The man loved her, and when I read his story I cannot help but feel great pity for him. Maybe we'll never know the truth, but I think the man has struggled with the wrong thing all his life – he has struggled with perfection, not truth. Alexa loved him, he loved Alexa, but perfection can be a shallow bedfellow. There is something, I can't put my finger there, but something almost *inhuman* about that kind of perfection."

Danaë walked across the room to where her son had now positioned himself on the arm of a chair. She stood behind him, placing her hands on his shoulders, looked out of the window. She spoke as a woman still finely tuned to the archetypes of her own mythology, with words that carry a parallel power: "Crimes of passion are the true tragedy. Tragedies are like our old myths, they have the power to move us to the core of our being. Alexa was ravished by a dark god; there is no *cold* blood in an *affaire d'amour*. No, of course I am not justifying any end result, even of our own myths, I am only seeing the vagrancy of the heart. *Love*, my dear Pericles, is the story we tell ourselves."

Danaë bent to place a gentle kiss on her son's thick wavy silver-grey hair as she continued, almost as a reverie of her own spoken thoughts: "Alexa saw beyond the surfaces of things, I would imagine it might discomfort some people, like cats do. I think she walked on air, even against her better judgment. Our Tragedies allow us to live through the unbearable; they incarnate betrayal, incest, murder, infanticide. Our audiences – the readers of Tragedy – are confronted, confounded, forced to live through the terrible story played out before them. And, my dear, these pantheons of the possible – and even the impossible – strengthen us, we buy their power to live through our own lives with the smaller coin of our own lot."

Maria called them to lunch. They ate their meal quietly until Danaë was inspired to suggest Pericles take a trip to the Old Town, to idle away an hour or two, clear his mind. The tourists are few now and he could walk freely through the ancient alleyways. She knows how he loved the winter months there amongst the cobbled ways surrounded by the old songs that can be heard from the ancient stones that still sing in the quiet hours. He could walk the old walls, or along the moat. She would take Alexa's Moleskine and drive up to Philerimos to sit in the herb scented gardens amongst the ruins of the old monastery and read.

A fugitive thought played at the periphery of Pericles' mind: the Old Town ... *those* earrings ... the jeweller who introduced Aristo and Alexa ... there were still enough tourists to warrant keeping a jewellery shop open ... but an atelier? Could he trace who it might have been? Spiro was a common name, but a *working* jeweller would be easier to trace amongst the gold filled shops of the mediaeval alleys. His whole demeanour lifted; his mother didn't know he had one of Alexa's earrings, but maybe he could share the knowledge later. Pericles slipped upstairs to collect his jacket – in a pocket of which was the precious piece of singular jewellery.

Pericles parked the Spider in Fileninon Street and entered the Old Town through San Francisco Gate, the simplest way to walk to Sofokleous Street, where Alexa had met her *moirae*, those ancient Weavers of Destiny. Finding the jeweller was simple – there it was, half shuttered as Alexa had seen it, dimly lit, a handful of exquisite pieces in the window to indicate it was an *atelier*. Inside sat a young woman at her working bench. She looked up, greeted him, apologised for the shop's gloom but she was finishing a commission and didn't want to encourage browsing tourists to enter and interrupt her: "How can I help you?" she smiled up at him.

Pericles introduced himself, hesitant to reveal too much. "Well," he began, "we have just received a report to say an English woman is missing, not from here, but she came here, she lived here for a little time in fact, and she has not returned to her home in England. The reason I am here, and it may be a wild goose chase, is that a photo came through with the report and the lady is wearing rather spectacular earrings. We Rhodians are known for our craftsmanship. It's because she had associations with Rodos that I'm approaching *ateliers* not retailers."

He took out Alexa's photograph instead of the Interpol fax, which he was also carrying, and passed it to the young woman.

"Oh!" exclaimed the young woman, "of course I know this work! It's my father's, they are gorgeous aren't they! But what's this about Alexa missing?"

Pericles recalled that it was right here where Alexa had met Aristo; the daughter of the jeweller worked beside her father and Aristo was probably a family friend.

"Here, here is my card, I am Detective Inspector Pericles Kostakides. I know it's Sunday, and this is an unofficial call, but I am trying to keep a low profile on all this, keeping it from the media if I can, because Kyrios Theohalis is connected with her – and he's a local hero." He shrugged, "if you can tell me anything I will be most grateful."

"I'm Sofia," said the young woman, "my parents are divorced, my mother still comes here every summer. She is not Greek. I know the difficulties some foreigners have when they marry Greeks. When my mother couldn't take more of my father's temper she had to leave. He has mellowed a lot, that's why they can rub along through the summers together. I know Ari's wife, she is French, she used to escape from *his* temper. And I know it never got better. Finally she refused to live here." She paused, and led the conversation back to Alexa.

"My father introduced them, he felt their meeting was pre-ordained in some way, they looked so perfect together. He is an artist to his marrow, my father, and he told me how the two blended on the first day they met. He couldn't help but see a story! I saw it for myself later – that first day she was wearing a swirling silk skirt in dove grey with all the colours of the sunset washed across it. I laughed later when she told me she christened it her Camargue – the description was sublime! He was wearing dove grey linen trousers, French of course. And they were each wearing black knitted tops – French, *of course*! They're both small and neat and you'd have thought they were the perfect couple, but ..." she looked away for a moment, brought her attention back, sighed and continued: ... "but it all went sour very quickly once he brought her to Rhodes. She came in once and pleaded with my father to talk to Ari. He did have words with him actually, but Ari couldn't see what he was doing wrong. We all lost touch and then I heard she had gone back to Australia and Ari moved away, down the coast. There was a terrible scene just before they left, my father's telling of it seemed a bit garbled but whatever its basis I didn't see them together again. Here, take our card, you are welcome to call my father."

Pericles thanked her, admired the gold piece the young woman was working on, bid her good day, walked thoughtfully back to his car and drove to the promontory to sit on a shoreline boulder watching the sea, sifting his thoughts as small waves sift sand on a littoral.

Really, he thought, *what do I have to go on?* Leaning into the breeze he rested his elbows on his knees, cupped his chin into his hands, squinted into the horizon's glare and considered what he knew – almost nothing in the way of facts that might illumine the whereabouts of two missing people. Hearsay suggested they were together, but the only verifiable fact he has is that they were known to each other. Sitting, just sitting, brings flickerings of submerged images to the fore. No words, nothing tangible, but something kept prompting him to look sideways, under the shadows and beyond his growing assumptions: *what if,* a thought catches him, *what if Alexa had perpetrated a crime when she could take no more?* His myths were full of these women as the conversation with his mother reminded him – but they were Greek of course. Do English myths have a Medea? a Tethys? an Artemis? He could only recall the Roman viewpoint of Boadicea and she burnt an entire city in revenge for their brutality to her daughters. He had to think in mythological terms, would not consider common or garden murderesses. He would choose his moment, and his clarity, before sharing such thoughts with his mother.

CHAPTER THIRTEEN

Settled in the sun, Danaë absorbed herself once more into Alexa's rich narrative, a 'voice' so immediate she felt a minor shock as:

"Did you miss me?" asks Aristo in a voice that would melt chocolate. As if he was looking over Danaë's own shoulder – as if she too could echo Alexa's wit:

Do you have amnesia, I want to reply, *no I didn't miss you at all* but I smile my sweetest smile and assure him I have. I still have no escape plan for tomorrow morning. I eat, compliment him for his cooking as always, and hurry to bed. He follows; he has been alone for three nights. Can I bear it? Think, think, *think*! Only tomorrow and my things will have gone, I only have to live one more night and get through tomorrow.

He missed me sooooooo much. Lying in his arms (as sweet as vines, the scent of his skin after decades of marine therapy sweeter than all the perfumes of Arabia) he says how happy he is that I have come home. My forbearance stands me in good stead and I don't remind him it was *he* who banished me. "Oh Alexa *mou*," he says sleepily, satiated, "I may be a leetle late to prepare lunch tomorrow; I have to go to a lawyer very early in the morning. Be patient if you come home first, we will go out to eat."

He doesn't notice my whole body floating right out of his arms and up up up through that wretched mezzanine ceiling to Holy Mary on Her Throne of Wisdom to prostrate myself at Her feet as She looks down at me with laughing eyes. I smile back at Her and tell Her that living at stress o'clock is beyond my coping mechanism at the present moment, but oh, I am so so *so* grateful. I thank Her with all my heart and slip back to the arms of the man I still, incredible though it seems to me, love.

Friday March 11th.

I wake. I am trembling with nervousness. Aristo brings my coffee and ginger. I let him use the bathroom first so he can get ready to go to his lawyer; I dare not show any alacrity by also wanting to leave so early so I concentrate on writing in my Moleskine. After all, where am *I* going in such a hurry? Aristo dresses in his most sartorial. I have no idea why he is seeing his solicitor, but it must be serious for him to spend more than usual attention on his appearance. I am dying for him to leave. Penelope promises she will be at Kremasti to meet the truck by eight o'clock, not that Greeks are ever early, but you never know. Finally Aristo leaves, with a curt goodbye. His meeting *must* be serious.

As soon as he shuts the front door I belt downstairs to watch him get in his car and drive away. White tornadoes have nothing on my movements now as I shower, dress, grab a banana, clean my teeth, lock up, race to *Smaragathi*, throw up a prayer for a clear road all the kilometres to Kremasti. It is seven minutes past eight. The road is clear all the many kilometres south. I fall out of *Smaragathi*, trembling with nervous tension. Dear Penelope! She is already there; I had given her the key to the village house just in case she alone had to oversee the removal of all I possess, just in case I couldn't get away from the house on my own. She has brought buns for breakfast, the kettle is on, tea at the ready. I love this woman.

The sky is black, ominous, threatening a deluge. The only thing that would stop the operation, warned Kyriakos, is rain. I puzzle my brain only a second over that one, what difference can it make? I'll soon see why.

Aghast, I stare at the antediluvian *camion* pulling to a shaky stop by the gate. It has no top, just a tray with a metal bar along three sides and barely eighteen inches up from the tray base. I rue my all too fertile gift of imagination and look on in horror. The rain! My precious belongings! The *mattress* which I have entrusted to Kyriakos to cover!

"This is Rhodes," says Penelope firmly "Sit down. Sit *down!*" and she positions herself in front of the kitchen window so I hear, but cannot see, my treasures being dragged up and across the filthy corrugated floor of the truck. I only have to endure the sound of things being cracked against door frames, scraped across the terrace and the road. Nothing is lifted, positioned, thought out; all is just hurled in to this infested little camion. No wonder the removal process will only take an hour. My antique leather topped desk, the painted Indian cupboard – oh my heart aches for these lovely pieces made by craftsmen who would turn in their graves at this crudity of handling. The clouds grow blacker; my face bleaches to a paler shade of white. Penelope tells me to have another cigarette, those slender harmless French menthol *Vogue* numbers that make her smile as I smoke such an apology. The orthopaedic mattress – these peasants had never *seen* such a mattress, could not conceive such a one was worth more than their entire flock of scrawny sheep – is thrown, *thrown*, on top of everything else; the black sea-trunk suspends over the open flap of the tray base at the rear, jamming its sharp metal corners into the soft wood of the painted Indian cabinet and the pine bedside cupboard. I let out a squawk as torn, *torn* as in huge gaping holes, and filthy plastic sheeting, is flung over the lot. Not a tarp in sight. The camion drives away and the heavens open.

Overwhelmed that everything has gone, even in such dreadful conditions, huge and helpless sobs shake my whole body. Penelope holds me for long moments until they subside, pours a fresh cup of tea. I light up another Vogue. Calm slowly steals over me – *I've done it!*

The pair of us sweep and mop the floors, put the two empty mugs in the sink to wash later, fold up the wooden chairs. I need to drive to Kyriakos in town to give a delivery address, passport details, pay by credit card.

"You are Australian?" he asks quizzically as I hand over said passport, I have my European one tucked in the other pocket of the antique beaded and embroidered wallet. "But," he says for the second time in our acquaintance, "you speak such a perfect Queen's English." The hearing of my fine-tuned English friends might debate that point on the occasions that my vowels slide south to the Antipodes.

"You must write a book," he tells me warmly, "write a book about your story, we are not all like this, you know, write your book and make some money and begin again."

Numbness is stealing over me, a veil of amnesia that protects me from anything but the present moment. I thank him, offer well wishes for the imminent labour of his wife in hospital as we sit there, and walk into the bright sun. The world looks the same. It is my world, well met after the longest winter I have ever lived through.

Penelope takes me back to her home to leave my flight suitcases with her. She has lent me a coat; mine, not needed for tropical Townsville, has gone on the high seas. So has Aristo's blue travel bag, also filled with my clothes which he has not permitted me to unpack since leaving England. I am quaking too much to drive, anticipating Aristo's wrath, so *Smaragathi* will remain parked outside Penelope's home for the time being and she will drive me back to the townhouse after the panacea of good English tea and her full-hearted company. Almost reluctantly I suggest we leave in time for Ari's lunch hour of noon.

At three minutes to midday my mobile phone rings. Penelope's eyebrows shoot into her fringe: "twelve o'clock" she mouths, "lunchtime! Where are you!" she mimes Ari as he echoes the same words into my other ear. We are, in fact, on a narrow road not four minutes from Ari's house, blocked behind a shit truck attempting a three-point turn in front of us. Penelope and I are watching with increasing interest, sensing the driver's increasing frustration. Finally he doesn't give a shit about anything as the inconvenient wall to his rear cracks at the concerted and repeated impact of his truck attempting to negotiate the seventh three-point turn. We watch in astonishment as the ancient wall silently folds in slow motion and crumbles to the ground in front of our very eyes.

Penelope grabs my arm and her little car rocks with great gales of her wonderful laughter. Mine borders on hysteria. *Doxa to Theo* for the pantomime I can present to Aristo of the shit truck and the wall, it's all good *boys* stuff and he loves it.

"You are so beautiful when you tell these stories" he says, laughing at the scenario I share. Swallowing hard, not missing a cue, I add "oh, and my stuff was taken from Kremasti this morning, it's *en route* to Australia." I tell him the shipper had called to say it had to be today (white lie) his wife was going into hospital this afternoon (truth) to have a baby (boy) tonight or tomorrow morning (truth).

"Your things have *gone*?" asks Ari, incredulous. He then lifts the large and ancient icon of Saint Panteleimon from the floor by the table where he had obviously placed it having brought it down from the bedroom you no longer share. I love this icon, not just for the courage it has bequeathed me during the months I slept close to it, but for itself, and I have never seen its like. "I make you a present," says Aristo, "my icon of Saint Panteleimon."

I am lost for words; he has shouted about "his" icon so many times: why do you like it? it is *mine* he would thunder, why are you so interested in this things? Do I have interest in your things? Don't think you can have it (I don't at all, even though I rescued it from its dark obscurity where it had been ignored for years) and more besides. To be presented with it now, now that I have only two hands to carry two suitcases, my computer, a bag with my hat that can't be packed and a pair of sandals to the other side of the planet, and now a very large icon, leaves me mute. I manage to thank him without tears in my eyes.

Go upstairs, he tells me after lunch of baked salmon fillets, Greek salad and baked carrots, I will follow you. Loving is tender, but Aristo is listing starboard with contradictions.

The following morning Ari goes to Kremasti to check my story – and returns to savage me about the two mugs Penelope and I had left in the sink. While he is away Penelope and I shuffle our cars back to their rightful driveways. I listen to Ari's outburst and then I walk right out, Saint Panteleimon under my arm, barely able to contain my laughter over such trivia and drive to Penelope's for a late breakfast – tea and toast, sunlight and sanity. I spend the morning with her repacking my case with the icon safely protected.

"And what will you wear tonight?" inquires Aristo, reminding me that the evening with Vasilis in the sanctuary of his studio at Apolona had been cancelled for some reason and therefore he is taking me to dine with the dreaded son. I confess that what I am standing in is all I have. Everything, *everything* has gone to Australia. Aristo stares uncomprehendingly for long moments. He then crosses himself before erupting: "are you *crazy*? You have nothing else to wear? I cannot support this!"

"Have you ever seen this coat before?" I laugh, "of course not, it belongs to Penelope. You want to take me out, I go like this." The truth is I don't want to go at all. Aristo is not amused. In fact he is almost apoplectic with disbelief and anger, though what it has to do with him now I don't know. But I *do* know that one more outburst and I'll be on the next plane.

Tonight is Carnival and Petros is preparing a 'special menu' of fish that his own father has caught, capers that his own father has picked, olive oil that comes from Lardos, and much else on the 'special menu' that he will be charging his own father a 'special' price for the privilege of eating in the restaurant his own father bought for him. However, this is the last time I will have to appease *anyone*. The evening is grim. The American woman who bought his hotel is back from America, dressed like a drag queen for the Carnival. Aristo refuses to allow me to wear my pixie ears, which I had kept from packing, and I am really miffed at looking so *dull*. He can't take his eyes off the American who plays to the gallery. I sing across the bar that next week I will return her packet of 'very little knickers' she left at our dinner table, after a day's shopping spree, in January. Aristo looks murderous and I smile my finest minx.

The following day Aristo tells me the reason he went to the lawyer on Friday was to sign all his French properties over to Nicolette. Petros and she have been threatening dire deeds with his retirement papers in the bureau in Paris that represent his French pension three years hence. That accounts, I think, for the spectacular tirade on Sunday afternoon, before his showdown on Tuesday over going to Australia at all, about how *I* will work in Australia, how all *his* money will remain in Greece. When I suggest that what he lives on *here* would give him a good standard of living *there* his reaction is hot enough to fuel a rocket. "It is *my* money," he roars, "you want me to use *my* money? I support you for a year and you give nothing, *nothing,* you do *nothing* for me! I bring €100,000 to Australia for me, *me.*"

I go hot and cold at the revelation of such sums, and swallow wormwood and bitter aloes over my seven or eight euros a week for the whole six months I've been with him. I swiftly calculate in-house courtesan rates for the six months, and settle an account for ghost-writing eighty thousand words and reckon €100,000 might just cover it. The bastard. On Tuesday, I'll buy my ticket to Australia on my credit card and leave.

But Clean Monday comes first. Clean Monday is one of the Mondays put aside for fasting before Easter. It is shared with friends and families, is a national holiday. Aristo is taking me to Spiro's where other friends from the village will gather to celebrate the day. Aristo is particularly vile that morning, but the travel agents are closed for the holiday so I accompany him to Salakos as he insists that I do; saving face and all that machismo schmaltz, and swearing silently in my heart and soul that tomorrow, *tomorrow*, I will go and get my single ticket to Australia.

Spiro greets us warmly, offers me a glass of his own Muscat which is superbly easy to down in my present mood. Funny how my brain clears and my tongue loosens. I hold the words that are forming, keep them just there on the tip of my tongue. We all sit to eat and Aristo's phone rings. Some heightened sixth sense tells me exactly who it is even before he gets up to go outside to answer it. He comes back in to excuse himself, he must go to the road, the American needs him to direct her to Spiro's hidden country retreat. Ah! With what delicious freedom I declare in tones caustic enough to strip varnish: "Good! then I shall be able to ask her *exactly* what she thought she was doing last year, it's a unfinished score, Aristo, by leaving those 'very little knickers' of hers under *your* chair, wrapped in tissue and ribbons, at a dinner party in a restaurant. I'd like to know these things before I leave Rhodes, then they won't take up space in my memoires." I am in fine fettle, and by the devil it feels good. The memory of the woman's lacy thong, gift wrapped and slid under Ari's chair, hit the personal nerve endings of the potent, but denied, possibility that my first foray into the titillating may have been the fifth or fifty-fifth for Ari. The

American's deal over his hotel may have *strings* attached to it.... *strings like very little knickers ...*

Aristo is speechless and rage turns his face its familiar puce. *This is Spiro's house* he hisses, *you cannot behave like this*! My lightening riposte echoes first his own favourite expression: "I don't give a shit!" before I continue: "I shall do exactly as I please, and if you bring her here that is *exactly* what will happen."

The man I almost no longer love looks like he will have cardiac arrest. He grabs me roughly, spits at Spiro to go and meet the American in his stead and tells him he is taking me home. I smile at Spiro and add: "that Muscat is *wonderful* Spiro, thank you *so* much! I feel better than I have felt in the whole of the past six months – and you know why." And he does. That is when light creeps through the cracks in my brain and I begin, just begin, to see *insane* spelt a.r.i.s.t.o. Spiro picks up his car keys and leaves.

Suddenly I see Aristo, like all bullies, is afraid of my mood, my truth and my absolute lack of fear. I continue, in case anyone sitting at the table thinks otherwise, to queen over this situation and add, at approximately seven decibels: "and we'll stop as we pass Spiro on the road going in the opposite direction so that I can tell both parties why we are leaving." Aristo, frankly, does not know what to do, either with me or the situation which is more out of hand than a mutiny on his barge. I *am* mutinous. With a lead foot he forces his car over potholes and ruts and deep gullies and the corrugations of the many kilometre track that leads from Spiro's country house to the asphalt road when I see the other two cars approaching. I jump up and down in the passenger seat waving madly for them to pull over. Aristo applies more lead to escape confrontation and nearly runs into a goat minding its goat business on the edge of the track. I settle down, smirking cat-contentedly. Point made.

Neither of us speak a word all the thirty-five kilometres back to Rhodes. I am coiled like a cat watching, watching. As Aristo swings into Kazerma Reggina he pulls up in front of the house to let me out as he drives on to turn the car round in the cul-de-sac for parking. I have thirty seconds. Thirty seconds and two of them have already gone while I dither. Then I run. I run with all the Eumenides behind me, run and run and run down to *Smaragathi*. I dare not pause to see if he has turned the car and seen me running, as long as I can round the other bend before he parks he will assume I have entered the house. That will give me another twenty seconds until he realises the house is still locked and – well, where am I? That twenty seconds will give me, please Holy Mary, enough time to unlock the car door, get in, switch on the ignition, drive up to the turning circle (where he will see me if he chooses that four seconds to look down the road) turn and race to the gates of this small private road to turn right into the main traffic flow of Democratus Street. I can then swing right to go up to Monte Smith past the Acropolis, turn left and I'll be gone. He will never know the direction I have taken to be able to follow.

My fear has taken flight. I feel unbelievably light. *I've done it!* I am cool, calm and certain. I drive slowly now, along the cliffs of Monte Smith, looking down at the heart-stoppingly beautiful turquoise sea of this lovely island whose magic could have graced the rest of the lives of two people who could have had everything and paradise too. Problem one, only one of the two wanted it that way – I didn't know what the other wanted. Problem two was that I loved Aristo, and Aristo loved Aristo. We both loved Aristo and there wasn't room for me in that equation.

Before I go to Penelope, and I know she won't be at all surprised, I take the long winding road to Philerimos, the ancient monastery and crypt where Aristo photographed me on our first day together. The gates are locked when I get there and I stand waif like in front of them. An elderly Greek man approaches me, asks where am I from. *Australia* is always the magic word in Greece as the population of Greeks in Australia is second only to the homeland and like all magic words it has an immediate effect: "ah, my brother is in Melbourne," no surprise, "if you wait a moment I will get the key and let you in."

He locks the gate behind me. I am alone in this blessed place, the path ahead winds up to the sanctuary and the crypt, and I begin my ascent up the ancient flower filled stone walkway, bathed in the silence. There, the archways, the chapel of the Virgin, the cloisters, the icons, beckon me. I am right to have come here. Within the darkened crypt I pray in front of the ancient icons of the *Panaghia*. I light two candles in front of one, one each for me and Aristo, but with separate intentions: me, for the courage to go forward alone; and he to find the happiness that thus far eludes his troubled nature.

Coming back into the clear bright sun after the darkness of the crypt I walk the ancient gardens of daisies and camomile, artemisia and campion, butterbur and corncockles and all the descendants of the monastery herb gardens of the Knights Hospitallers of long, long ago. A wave of nostalgia floods over me; these are the flowers of my South Down childhood, those chalk downs of long warm summers and bumble bees, granny's homemade jams and fresh mint sauce, of helping grandfather bottle feed day old lambs; of honeysuckle hedgerows; of putting milk out for the hedgehog and milk-soaked bread for the farm cats who live in the huge barn and protect the hay from mice through the winter. I feel the pain of the human loneliness of my life, and choose to fill my heart instead with the fullness that is all around me, has ever been all around me, and of which I am an infinitesimal and integral part. For now, it is enough.

The brother of the man in Melbourne is waiting for me, he smiles, lets me back through the gate. The feeling of having stepped over a threshold pervades me and I do not want to leave its protective balm, I sit on the low stone wall and wait for a sign that tells me it is okay to carry the pain and keep on walking.

I reach Penelope's with the inestimable shock that my glasses are not on my face. I cannot read a thing without them, they live permanently on various attractive chains or beaded cords around my neck,

French style. For some inexplicable reason ... fate? forgetfulness? stress? I am aghast at the loss. I will have to return to that hateful house ... Kremasti was emptied, nothing, but surely nothing was left in the townhouse either? My passport is with Penelope, I have only the clothes on my back and my toothbrush in my handbag, how could I, oh how *could* I have mislaid my eyes.

Penelope welcomes me, she has sensed I will turn up anytime, tells me she will drive me to fetch my glasses, I am not to go there alone, not to go in *Smaragathi*.

It takes more courage than I have ever imagined I have to stand by that door and knock. Aristo has been crying. My heart ... Penelope diplomatically ignores his distress and is as gay and bright as ever as I say, *my glasses, I left my glasses*. I head for the bathroom and there they are. Penelope and I wave goodbye and walk down to her car waiting in the space where *Smaragathi* once was. We get in – and I break down completely, sobbing into her arms. *I can't walk out like this*, I cry, *no matter what he has done, I cannot simply walk away.*

Wise friend that she is, she agrees: "go back up there and tell him you'll meet him for coffee tomorrow so you can say your goodbyes."

Ari is distraught when I return. I hold him as he sobs, "please come home Alexa *mou*, please come home, there is nothing of you here, tomorrow we will buy the tickets for Australia ..." and I believe him, *again*. So, with reservation, does Penelope.

"Okay," she says, "but leave everything with me. I'll text your passport number through to you for the ticket."

My flight for freedom embraces our loving. It has been a very long Monday. And we *do* go to the travel agent the following day and Ari *does* buy two tickets. We leave in one week. The drama will play out to the end. English friends are dumbfounded when I tell them I am going to Australia.

Two days to go. After bringing my ginger coffee Aristo goes downstairs to make kitchen noises; soon delicious smells of baking drift upstairs; five minutes later up rushes my man with a tray of freshly baked miniature *spanakopita*, crisp and golden and sizzling hot. Oh how I love this mad and unpredictable man. But I write in my Moleskine: *never forget Alexa mou, never forget the anger, the fear, the banishment, the abuse, the days of Coventry, the rejection, the sheer cruelty – never forget these when you are far away and overwhelmed with loss of him.* For I know now, in the stillest smallest corner of my heart that loss is inevitable, whether from design or from death, loss is inevitable.

Monday 28th March.
"I am going for a little trip with my Alexa." Aristo prances panther like around me, showered and perfumed and gorgeous. He goes to the kitchen to prepare a picnic lunch for the hours we will wait in the airport in Athens for the Thai flight to Bangkok later in the afternoon. Penelope is

collecting me at eight-thirty to pick up my bags which we decided would remain in her home until the day of my departure. Petros is taking Aristo's car and will drop him at the airport. Aristo goes to put his bag into his car. I take Bob's painting from where I have hidden it in the wardrobe, run upstairs, roll it carefully in a sheet which I cut to size a couple of days before, rush downstairs, put it diagonally inside my bag, grab the now bare frame, run down the terrace stairs to the road and hurl the empty stretcher over the university wall into the rubbish area. With pounding heart I run back up and inside before Aristo turns back from the car just metres away. I am shaking so much I can barely stand up, so I flop gratefully for the last time into the dreadful secretary chair. Aristo may have bought the painting from my friend but Robert Sisson is a tessera in *my* tapestry and his painting is my shared history. "And you *are* taking it," said Penelope, brooking no emotional equivocation.

I don *those* earrings just as Penelope arrives: "see you at the airport sweetheart," I say, hugging my true love. I make the most of Penelope's rich and generous company over tea and toast and blackberry jam as I pick up my bag and passport for her to drive me on to the airport. She adores the sight of the rolled up painting sticking alarmingly and obviously out of my bag, a large French carry-on that includes the computer with the manuscript of Ari's life that was written in blood on its C drive.

Ari is waiting at the airport already, sitting alone, looking forlorn. I am happy, sad and everything in between, but I fix on happy and remain that way. Spiro arrives with a bunch of freesias from his fields; their perfume fills the air around us. Penelope tells wicked jokes in Greek, Aristo perks up delightedly, adds a few of his own and everyone is happy. Our flight is called; hugs all round, moist eyes, so many goodbyes.

CHAPTER FOURTEEN

The flight is hell. Aristo's temper plummets from Athens onward. From Bangkok to Brisbane he prods and pokes me relentlessly to prevent me sinking into the blessed release of sleep. But I hug a story to myself that keeps me buoyant, reduces me to billows of muffled laughter and an affinity with the goddess Nemesis who placed the thought in my numbed mind in that awful hotel room in Bangkok as my terminally miserable savage went for his shower.

A few days prior to leaving Rhodes, and in line with Ari's impossible scene over *his* money and therefore *I* must work to support us both in Australia, he had brought home wads of euros which he packed in envelopes each containing up to 1000€. Reminded of the thousands the Man with the Van had charged me for taking all I owned to be incarcerated in Kremasti; the thousands that the shipping company is charging me for releasing all I owned to the high seas; knowing that whatever rapidly diminishing funds are to go to releasing my goods from Australian customs (goods from England, deemed to be infection-free are exempt, goods from anywhere *foreign* are, like the refugees Australian Immigration deloused with kerosene on arrival, contaminated – releasing my goods will prove a costly procedure) I see enough red to clothe a cavalry. I set about re-calculating in-house rates for the previous six months as a courtesan and ghost-writer; shipping costs *and* compensation for premature aging. I reckoned a hundred thousand any currency might do it but seeing an arrow slot of opportunity I will settle for any one of those envelopes just to maintain a modicum of integrity over the worsening situation. It is Bangkok or bust.

He is in the shower. His money belt, with at least ten envelopes in it, is on the dresser. It is now or never. The envelopes are numbered. When will he miss one? As long as it is in Australia I will be able to cruise the fallout amongst friends.

The water is still running, I can hear the changes in sound as his body slips in and out and around the flow, can just make out the slap of soap, the squeak of a foot on the ceramic shower base. My mind spins as my heart pounds thick into my mouth; my fingers slide the zipper back, my hand reaches in to one of the thinner envelopes, but too late to locate a thicker one now, the water pressure is running slower, *oh my God, zip that belt up, take the money to your carryon, quick, inside the back panel, push it down below the plastic sleeve with all the flight printouts and hotel bookings.* Thank heavens I have already showered and can remain glued to the carryon for the last wearisome leg of the flight.

Bizarrely there is a hold up through the x-ray as we pass through the Bangkok departure; Ari's money belt is held in the x-ray cube while the rest of our bags pass through. I feel a mite nervous that the delay will trigger Ari's own nerves about carrying so much cash but the belt finally comes through and he replaces it around his girth.

Australia is condemned sight unseen by Ari from the arrivals lounge for not being permitted to take his muesli bars with him, and for their paranoia over his Greek passport. Then we are seriously confronted by the Woman in Uniform whom Aristo mistook for a man (they are all so *ungly*, he said of Australians from that moment on) who brings sniffer dogs to our luggage with a vengeance. No, I don't have a hidden Mars bar, muesli or marijuana plant on me – but Penelope's terrier did insist on sitting on my suitcase when I left it with her for safekeeping. Harriet's doggy odour must have attracted the sniffer beagles. The anger on Ari's face almost spelt guilt as we were both forced to unpack everything to the last bootstrap. The sniffer dogs got bored before the envelope in the side pocket was revealed.

But I am home, I can speak my own wonderful language, I can laugh and I am safe.

The room at the Astor on Wickham Terrace is perfect. Modest, that's the budget, but perfect. Everything is perfect. Ari has developed a cold which is even more perfect as he decides to collapse on the bed. I can run, skip, hop down the hundred steps of Wickham Terrace to Edward Street alone to find the first Westpac bank I come across and count my well-gotten gains over the counter and in to my still nominally extant bank account.

And that's exactly what I do. I am delirious with freedom, find a Westpac, flop the paper currency on the counter – and feel thoroughly pissed off that after all that adrenalin I really did pick the thinnest envelope – only 800€. It translates as a reasonable number of dollars though, enough to bring my goods and chattels up from Brisbane to Townsville by rail when they arrive.

Back in the hotel Ari is murderous. "Those bastards!" he fumes, "those bastards in Bangkok they hold my money belt and they steal all my moneys, *all my moneys!*"

I look suitably shocked and the right words fall consolingly from my lips as I think: *silly man, it was only one envelope and I know exactly what was in it, I wish I'd taken more!*

"You look *dreadful*," says Karen who meets us at the airport in Townsville. "as if you have been exhumed from the grave!" I think it an apt metaphor. Lines no friends have ever seen before are etched on my face as deep as lithographers' acid on stone. I have aged ten years.

Aristo alters his opinion of Australians again, daily, hourly. I am so tired. Suddenly he can stand it no longer and three weeks later he returns to Rhodes. At the airport I don't cry, but Ari does.

"I will go back to Rodos, resolve my problems there and I will come back to help you pack up and we go back to England," he says and I know his life is a tragedy of his own making. "I love you, Alexa *mou*, always remember this." He turns, tears sparkling on his face under the cold neon lighting of the departure lounge, walks down the long corridor to disappear, leaving me with the ashes of my life to rake over for some semblance of flicker to fan into flame, again. Yet I hurry too quickly back to my faithful Alfasud to drive along the curling road to pause, park, jump out and watch as his plane banks to rise swinging up over the ocean and back over Castle Hill; my prayers and love for this impossible man visible in the slipstream.

La Strada is showing at the local arts cinema, Hélène and Karen will meet me there on Thursday evening. The finely nuanced performances of Giulietta Masina bewitching, Anthony Quinn, demoniacal, but as the film unfolds my recognition of where I am dissolves – this is no film, this is reality. I have just lived it, every whiplash of it. As the credits roll and the lights come on the two women beside me see my ashen face. I am unable to move. Hélène brings me a strong sweetened cup of tea; Karen puts her arm around me. When I can speak, tears rolling silently down my face, I manage to whisper: *"it's too close for comfort."* By then each woman has glimpsed the schizophrenic face of my so beloved, so tormented, man – and they understand.

The home I have been loaned is fifteen minutes from the centre of town, fifteen minutes from the edge of the town in fact, because as sprawling Australian cities go Townsville is one of the sprawliest. The flat brown plain out toward Black River was subdivided years before to be sold as housing blocks advertised as close to the river. There was a river, some distance, which made its appearance in a good Wet; the barren housing blocks were never able to boast alluvial soil, or even much soil at all. Baked hard and pale beige it held no promises, other than for the collectives of wallabies whose ancestral homes are now subordinate to the encroaching fibro and tin-roofed dwellings spreading rash-like across the flatlands. For now, though, I am home and the deluge of laughter from the kookaburra that greets me each dawn leaves an aftershock of delicious sound. Moments later a second kookaburra laughs through the whole joke again.

Gradually word gets out that I am back and friends call. Karen, or my historian friend James, who comes regularly with picnics and treats, and a pattern of life, long since left behind, resumes. Karen offers me tickets, as part of her voluntary position with the Australian Festival of Chamber Music and as part of my healing therapy, for whatever concerts I wish to hear. I choose every one of the performances by Piers Lane, and a selection of quartets. These are grand affairs, the highlights of the Townsville cultural year, and a far cry from Zeus's thunderbolts.

James, alone again after an amicable divorce, brings picnic hampers each Saturday filled with strawberries and quiche and baguettes and champagne, chequered tablecloths and real cutlery and glasses – and best of all erudite company, his own love for England – he has transplanted tolerably well – and books of poetry. We drive to the nearest sea and walk for miles, talk for hours. I wonder how we can be so compatible yet share no chemistry. His presence is the greatest blessing, and his affectionate memories of student holidays hopping the Greek islands and his passion for the Classics makes for the closeness I need as defence against the criticisms of some Australians still harbouring the illusion that all Greeks are little better than immigrant peasant wops and wogs and what on *earth* could I have been thinking of?

I am about to take my turn at the checkout in the nearest supermarket to my rural retreat when my mobile phone peels its Beethoven's Fifth as I wait in the queue. I thought only Ari knew this number but the screen shows the code for Far North Queensland. Joy, delight and a dozen exclamations in between colour my delighted response: "Diane!"

The following week I take time to drive the amaranthine coastline north into a different world. I love the territory north of Ingham, and Ingham itself is always a pleasure, an Italian world in miniature. Its annual four day Italian Festival fed me for months with the most delectable regional Italian specialities as each small community vies with another to produce the finest flavours originally brought there by the women as they followed the immigrant labourers, or were sent for as brides-to-be, to the far northern sugarcane fields to live lives of utmost privation in those early years of settlement and sugarcane. Now the tables had turned – the original landowners and growers were slowly, slowly being bought out by the wiser, older, blood of the Mediterranean whose life source knew the true value of a "block of dirt" and a vegetable patch. The huge swathes of sugarcane that run from the sea to the darkly forested mountains of the

Hinterland, like Van Gogh's patchwork wheat fields around Arles, are owned now by once impoverished workers, risen to prosperous growers themselves.

I pull in to the Olive Tree Café to have Mario's famous bruschetta and cappuccino. He greets me with astonishment. I had driven up to say goodbye when I had left for England a lifetime ago; had spent many hours listening to Mario's Sicilian reminiscences, and promised I would send postcards when I visited Sicily. I never quite made it there, but Greek history was evident all over the now Italian island so I had sent postcards from Rhodes as the nearest equivalent.

"Where are you headed now?" he asks, and you are thrilled to say Karnak! He whistles, and grins. "Ahhhh," he says, "she is one of us of course, *Cilento*, the second most beaudiful place in Italy. 'Ow you know Diane?"

The first most 'beaudiful' place for Mario isn't really in Italy, it's still an autonomous Sicily, whose history comes down from the Phoenicians as *Magna Graecia*. The postcard from Rhodes met his approval apparently, and my slender association with Diane Cilento brings me up another four notches of his ladder of esteem.

Mario is delighted to see me. I spare him every detail except: "Greek tragedy Mario, I'm back for a while," and he smiles good naturedly: "*whaddya expect from a Greek?*" written along the bushy lines of eyebrows raised above the usual shoreline of rich wrinkles on a forehead that has known hard field work, the blistering heat of cane fires and tropical sun. I catch up on his kids' weddings, local funerals, the new play written especially for the Festival with the delicious title *The World Comes to Ingham,* "and so it should Mario, so it should!" We part warmly, and I agree to drop in on the way home in a 'coupla days'.

I savour the next part of the journey, driving up and over the Hinchinbrook Range to stop and gaze, as everyone does, at the jewelled islands in the Hinchinbrook channel, feel a *frisson* of regret that the four day trek to Zoé Bay is beyond my current stamina, and pocket. The road swings back down to the plain, hugs the pellucid coastline along Cardwell and on to Tully, the wettest town in Australia, and the doorway to the magical world of the now endangered Cassowary, that astonishing bird from a primeval world.

I skirt right from the highway to follow the slip road along Mission Beach and before I come out again at El Arish I drive a short detour into the licuala rainforest on the off chance of seeing a wandering cassowary. I park and walk deeper into the forest to a stout wooden corral built for the intrepid to sit in while they eat their sandwiches, for the six foot bird will not stop at bowling humans over for easy food; their three-toed feet have sharp claws, fearsome when it can kick with legs powerful enough to eviscerate. I sit, the only human present, ears attentive to the rustles of the rainforest creatures around me.

The rustling increases. I hear the familiar very low frequency *boom* that heralds the approach of this shy, rare and magnificent creature. Its sound is the lowest known bird call, close to the edge of human hearing. I sit, my anticipation mounts, and there through the forest clearing steps with delicate precision the most spectacular female cassowary in full colour, taller than me. She comes forward, I wish I had a gift for her, but instead gaze at her with a heart full of admiration and gratitude that she should bother coming to look at *me*.

She stands at the corral, sizes me up with one huge eye, head tilted to one side, before trundling off the way she came. I send a prayer in her wake that she survive to her natural life-span the threats from dog packs and motor bikes – killers of these last great flightless and so ancient birds. She leaves by a different path and I quietly close the corral gate to walk elated back to my car, cool under the licuala *ramsayi* canopy which closes fanlike, twenty feet above.

All these towns have memories for me and I love the Tropics. Beyond Innisfail I come to the sign for Babinda Boulders; the boulders are massive and spherical, half submerged in clear tropical pools or waterfall cascades; the rushing waters smoothing and shaping their granite mass.

The Dreamtime myths draw me; I park once more, taking time to walk, breathing the damp rainforest air, silken soft on my bare arms. How good it feels and how restorative. The legend of the Boulders tells of drowning lovers; Oolana, it is said, still guards her waters, waters whose tumbling and gurgling echo her lament and loss. And mine.

On the road again Mt Bartle Frere looms to my left, its towering dark form a benediction that accompanies my drive along the low coast road. Bellenden Ker, Walsh's Pyramid ... I can, now, by this strange twist of fate, say farewell to them with love. Will I ever pass their way again?

I drive straight through Cairns, pass by the luscious Port Douglas to the tacky hotel in Mossman where I have booked to stay a couple of nights to take full advantage of whatever time in her busy days the gorgeous Diane Cilento can spare for tea and gossip.

The following day I check directions with the hotel staff to Whyanbeel Road and leave plenty of time to take in the tropical scenery as I meander up to Karnak. The sight of the famous Playhouse set in a tropical paradise, sloping down to a lake, enchants me, so does the white cat who appears as I explore the theatre. A good omen, like the silver moon cat of the book so recently published. The sound of a car motor alerts me to Diane's arrival and I am charmed to see that face to face we share a similar height, or lack of. Broad smiles link us both, she ushers me into a room filled with books and posters and: "I see you've met Miss Prism," she says of the white cat who follows her in to jump on her lap the moment she sits down.

"I'm a cat woman," she said, "but then most Sufis are, Mohammed certainly loved cats. You know the story of his love for his favourite cat I suppose?"

I do, but deny it so I can hear the story told in Diane's throaty purr: "he was resting one afternoon with his favourite cat asleep on his robe when his Grand Vizier came to wake him for prayers. Looking down at his beloved cat Mohammed ordered the Grand Vizier to bring his knife, with which he cut his robe in a complete semi-circle around the sleeping cat so not to disturb it."

We both spoke of mysteries and of Mecca, from where Diane had just returned: "Bennett," she said of the man who became her spiritual teacher après life with Sean Connery, "always said that we all have a religion in our essence. He became Catholic in spite of his closest association with Gurdjieff; I would say I am a Muslim," she shrugs and waves her hand at the brown *jellabiya* she is wearing: "I've just returned from Mecca," she says, inviting my surprise that a foreign woman, with such a well known face, could reach the Ka'aba and the Holy of holies. "Ah well," she twinkles, "you have to know someone with the right connections!"

And thus we spend the rest of the day speaking of the deeper verities of shared connections – "yes," nodded Diane, "I met Mrs Tweedie a couple of times, but Bulent Rauf was my teacher." She said she would be in England to promote her book soon, and she would come to Glastonbury for she had a special duty to perform for Bennett who was buried at Sparkford in Somerset, close by. We exchanged emails and she gave me a splendid photograph of herself in a cage of lions, a publicity shot of the bright young star fifty years before. "Being with those remarkable cats was a high point of my life," she said, "though I confess there was a sheet of glass separating me from them! I adore cats, so *My Nine Lives* is an obvious title for my own book of many *alter egos*."

Then the phone calls from Ari begin, at first loving and conciliatory, then accusative and promissory. Where are you? he almost shouts at two in the afternoon, a time when I escape the pain and have gone into town to see friends, take in a concert, go to the dentist or enjoy reading John Julian Norwich with James. He keeps up a barrage of calls which, oh foolish me, I interpret as love, that great deceiver. I should not be enjoying life when he is so lonely and misses me so much. I am not enjoying anything, but I do have the rare gift of living moment by moment and the cumulative moments without him are pleasurable, and normal, and I just might believe that I could live without Byzantium.

Out of the blue, just as my travelling friends have phoned to say they will be home in a fortnight, Ari phones to say he is coming back – in a fortnight. And so he returns. He will take me to England. Once more my belongings are on the high seas. Once more I say goodbye to dear and loved friends in FNQ and once again set my sails toward sleepy, sheepy Somerset – and home.

My friends: suddenly I realise what I am leaving; love has made me an exile and my heart breaks into shards whose serrated edges leave wounds wherever I turn, there is no turning back; yesterday is another country.

During the long flight home Aristo's abuse again becomes so public, so intense, his vilification of me so virulent, that my capacity for thought is stretched beyond dysfunction. He delivers his *coup de grace* on landing: and by the carousel at Heathrow *I sat down and wept*. He *never* wants to stay in England, he *never* wants to see my friends again, I make such a *scandal*, I meet "the English" (Penelope) and "she controls your thoughts and make you run away. I give you *everything*! Why you leave! I will go back to Rhodes," he shouts, demented, "as soon as I collect my bag!"

A still small voice deep in my heart reminds me that I can also pick up my bag from this same carousel if I can see through my throbbing tired tear-filled eyes and I can walk outside and down to the coach station, catch a coach to Bristol, change to the local bus and swing my way down along the green hills of the Mendips to Glastonbury where nothing will have changed and I have been offered a room for a few days.

"I wish you love, Aristo," I say. I am sick with grief and sorrow, but deep inside me, like the sap rising from winter dormancy there is a stirring of something light and once familiar – hope and love and ... *I am home.*

For weeks I hear nothing from my feckless lover, but each morning I wake and he wakes in me, in my mind and in my heart as a living part of me, like a breath or a pulse. We were so beautiful in the beginning, was it a dream? "Evil," said a friend, fixing her clear eyes on mine, and referring to Aristo's disarmingly lovely smile, "comes beautifully packaged. As a commando Aristo belonged to that army of walking dead, psychologically too brutalized to ever be helped or think he needs help. Sad man; I shuddered when I read your first email."

The day before my birthday Aristo phones. A friend of his has died of a heart attack at sixty-seven. I know it is Ari's own fear of a lonely death that has prompted his call, yet it is joyous to hear his voice, he wants to send me an airline ticket to anywhere I choose and he will meet me there, he wants to talk. Hesitantly I say I *am* where I want to be, England in such warm weather is idyllic and I have fallen in love with the West Country all over again. He phones back, and four times the following day, *four times*, to wish me happy birthday, to tell me how he loves me and misses me and my heart opens all over again to let him in.

"What are you doing about a house," he asks. Nothing; in my poverty I am at the mercy of trusts and councils and housing associations. Aristo proposes to send me a month's rent: "I cannot leave here until I sell ... I propose you we have time together ... I send the airfare ... we must talk ... I love you, I miss you."

"I am happy in England," I say cautiously, tending my re-opened wound, and his reply sharp as a knife:

"You are supposed to live with me in Rodos," allows me to whisper the only real truth:

"But you broke my heart Ari my dear, I had to leave."

> *When empty seas and winds and distance divide us*
> *I still could turn my face to where you were*
> *and say: that way is he for whom I wait.*
> *I have no compass now to tell me where you are.*
> *And I have lost the key to our Paradise.*

How important money is if you do not have it: it brings lovely things like independence and dignity and learning and travelling; beauty and good health and good dentistry, the last three so influenced by good food, a good environment – and above all the peace of mind a *home* can give. I am *homeless*.

After nine long homeless months the local housing association offers me a bungalow in Glastonbury, in a tiny mews tucked into the old Abbey wall. It is a malevolent little hovel and has been trashed by the leaving tenant. I am overwhelmed with horror as I stand in the bleak room. I reach for the housing officer's arm, whisper: I do not think I (or even a herd of piglings) could live in this, this *bothie,* and she unofficially agrees with me, but tells me the official stance: if I refuse it I will be struck off the housing list for a year. The filthy concrete floors; the walls dripping with soot and grease from an illegal wood stove, now removed; the heap of bricks where a separating wall once stood between the corner holding a kitchen and the lounge; the squalor, the darkness of the bathroom and kitchen devoid of window or door or fanlight – how can I live in a place like this? Just two tiny rooms? I sign the tenancy because I have no choice. As I record my despair in my diary I am struck by a distant memory, the voice of Mrs Tweedie coming through *Chasm of Fire*: "Two tiny rooms, a flat. Took it in a flash, I had no choice." I laugh; her circumstances echo my own sense of the absurd.

Aristo telephones. I am not to worry, he will wash my little hovel, paint it, fix it, put shelves up, help me unpack, buy a stove, make sure I have a fridge freezer. I borrow money to buy carpet to cover the filthy concrete floor. Neither Councils not Housing Associations are to blame for their minimalist approach, having seen with my own eyes a perfectly dear little cottage turned into a broken derelict filthy slum I can only agree with their decisions. Such wanton vandalism must break taxpayers' hearts.

True to his contradictory self Aristo flies in from Rhodes – with welding gear, drills, paintbrushes, spices for his cooking, whisky for his drinking. In three weeks he transforms the place, but pulverises me in the process. Now he has gone and I will sleep and sleep and sleep will grant me the sovereign remedy of healing. Friends welcome me again, even people I hardly know welcome me home as a familiar sight along the harlequin streets of this affectionate town. I spend long hours under Geoffrey Ashe's blossoming magnolia in the Abbey grounds. Connecting after all this time with the person, the place, the legends and the myths, the magnitude of these realities add their own magic to my healing. It is Spring, my own sap rises and I am changed, and changed forever. There is a body wisdom that I have never known before. I welcome my *womanness*. My life's narratives of nothings re-assemble themselves with all the interest of somethings. The world is mine once more.

CHAPTER FIFTEEN

Late now, Danaë closes the notebook, collects her belongings, drives home, her mind more in the Moleskine than her own skin. A hasty tisane of peppermint and, unresisting to its lure, folds herself into a large armchair to continue reading without breaking the spell:

"It is our anniversary Alexa *mou*," he says, oblivious of the anguish he has caused, but then, that is the nature of the beast: "I have been so busy on this new house (what new house?) and I want to share it with you. Please come."

I doubt, yet I go. Knowing the shelf life of my beloved's happiness gene is approximately ten days I stipulate he sends a return ticket for that period. On the drive from the airport to Phanes Aristo cannot contain that happiness: "I never thought you would be here with me again," he says, kissing my fingers as he lifts my hands to his lips. "You keep coming back," I say gently, "it makes me broken." And I know again that Love hides in the limen between finding and losing, knowing and not knowing. It is an eternal thing that belongs to the mysteries of the heart.

I insist on being with Penelope for a whole day, her beneficent company a joy and delight. We splash around the bays of Kalithea, dine royally, lie soaking up the sun before and after. She has, however, no illusions about Aristo's character, and reminds me crisply that he is controlling, cruel, contradictory and charming. And, no, she says, you cannot live with that combination. No one can.

I don't meet with Penelope again – Aristo launches into tirades about my friendship with "the terrible English who control your thoughts and make you run away to Australia".

I return to my Glastonbury dollshouse wiser, stronger and smile to myself. The first week with Ari was bliss, but logic suggests maybe the ten day shelf life will naturally shrink as I determine life without him; a wholly restorative thought. Ari had spoken to me of my sixtieth birthday not many weeks hence. He would take me all around Greece if I would choreograph our journey with my knowledge of contemporary Greek history *and* the classical world of goddesses, gods and heroes. I couldn't think of a more exhilarating gift – and September is the most marvellous month. Would his temper survive a fortnight? Should I plan for ten days? Eight days? Oh, go for it Alexa, go share your Greece with your Greek. It is too good an opportunity to ignore.

...his affections dark as Erebus: Let no such man be trusted. Mark the music.

Danaë looks up, reflective, momentarily remembering, with Alexa, how even Shakespeare knew:

Shakespeare knew something there, continued Alexa's journal, no wonder the Greek myths tell of so many men whose excessive pride sets them apart from the mortals around them. They considered themselves godlings, perfect and above the common lot. Ah, the gods do not like that! Tantalus, Sisyphus, Oedipus, Icharus, Jason to name but few – each man had noble qualities, mostly they were attractive, well-liked, even loved, but they shared the tragedy of hubris and each suffered a terrible fate. It is Narcissus whose name most symbolises the tragedy of a pathological self-obsession and one which I would slowly come to recognise in Aristo. Aristo's gifts are many; he was favoured by the gods in every sense; handsome, gifted as a person. Nicolette once phoned the house when Ari was out, before I had met Penelope. I answered the phone and actually cried with relief that I was speaking to a woman *and* speaking English. I felt deeply indebted for Nicolette's words:

"Alexa be careful, behind that beautiful face is a very sick mind."

It was so late. Early, actually, for Danaë had read through the night. Her eyes felt it, but her mind was awake. Travelling through Alexa's love for Ari was like wandering through a shadowy moonscape of shattered things. By reading Alexa's *memento mori* Danaë had entered the anguished world of a woman struggling for self-knowledge, and one who, she sensed, had achieved it to an honourable degree. The decision to stop reading at the point of the reference to Erebus caused Danaë considerable pause. Erebus was the primordial deity of darkness, one of the five beings to come into existence from

Chaos. Erebus is also a region of the Underworld through which the dead pass after dying.

She laid the papers on the small intarsia table she and Stavros had brought from Sienna on one of many holidays and pulling her shawl closer over her shoulders she rose and walked to the long window bay of the old room, stood looking across the garden as the *wolflight* lifted the night's shadows. She sighed for Alexa, she had felt her many sorrows as she followed the story. The ephemeral acquaintance of Stavros with Aristo many years before had barely left a memory, the merest echo of his name, and Stavros' short-lived disappointment with that particular project, a project hadn't even got off the ground, had not extended to an ongoing acquaintance between the two men. If it had then Aristo may have become a friend. Stavros made friends easily with people whose skills he respected and whose life meshed in any way through his work as a financier. His sideline interests as a benefactor of theatre, museums, salvaging wrecks and setting up bursaries and grants for the young and talented meant Stavros met a colourful cross-section of the community. Alexa, once she had arrived into Aristo's story, would have found a warm welcome with us, reflected Danaë.

She understood deeply that a woman like Alexa could, would, once she had vouchsafed her heart, be foolish enough to return to the profoundly disturbed and psychologically damaged man she had been led to believe she knew. She *had* returned again, and again. Danaë was loathe to conclude that

Aristo's need to possess Alexa was irrefutably linked to her disappearance; however....

Her meandering thoughts came to an abrupt stop. A stiller, darker voice intruded, a voice hardly familiar as her own: *Erebus ... but what a strange reference for Alexa to make. Just as she was gaining her own integrity and strength ...* Danaë's eyes widened involuntarily as the thought presented itself full-blown into her mind – what if they had all been following an *incorrect* assumption based on their personal emotion? *What if Alexa had murdered Ari?*

The draft manuscript may have ended months before, and following as it developed and transferred itself into the vigour of a strong, first person, narrative comforted Danaë deeply, but it stopped well short of any real clue. The Moleskine diary was current. Pericles was not yet aware of the contents of Alexa's draft manuscript, nor was he quite yet convinced of the dual nature of the man locals referred to as a hero.

Danaë went to the bathroom, splashed her face, applied moisturizer, picked up a handful of small change and slipped out to the corner *fourno* for a loaf of fresh bread the fragrance of which had filled her mornings for as long as memory. Returning with the still hot loaf she tore herself two wide chunks, put them with a scoop of olives on a plate, poured the nut flavoured oil provided from the first pressing of her in-law's olives into a small bowl, sprinkled it with sea salt, made a cafetière of coffee and turned just as Pericles walked in. She calmed her expression, offered him coffee and a share of her breakfast.

"Mama," greeted Pericles, kissing her on both cheeks, "you look as if you didn't sleep."

"I will tonight," she returned his smile, "Alexa's story was not exactly a lullaby. I want to read the last pages of the Moleskine. I am full of unformed apprehensions, two missing people, too strange for coincidence now we know they know each other. I want to avoid galloping assumptions."

Pericles' usually still expression lit up in warm appreciation with the leitmotif of his mother's pet irritations known so well from his childhood: galloping assumptions – her name for sloppy or falsely associative thinking – categorical syllogisms, platitudes. She had honed her son's own use of language to a fine edge which benefitted his choice of profession immensely. Affectation, he knew, was outside her province and she had no patience with it in others. Danaë ended with a sigh: "I don't want to waste time, or set ourselves false trails."

Pericles looked carefully at his mother, she had that *don't ask me now* look which held his surprise at bay.

"It's Sunday, I'm going to Ayios Panteleimon to light a candle for Alexa ... and Ari," added Danaë as an afterthought. "They need it. He loved her you know; in his tortured way he loved her. I have no doubts that he was as confounded by the depths of his own feelings as by his inability to deal with them when they erupted so insanely."

"You think he's insane, Mama?"

"Perhaps, but not in a way the word is usually prescribed. Violence is never sane, and by default the training of the human heart to close down in order to perpetrate violence is the ultimate insanity. We call it military intelligence and accept it. Correction – men accept it. I don't think we women want the babies we birth to ... *oh, never mind*, I don't need to explain, you had no love for your national service did you, even though you felt it 'right'. The older I get the more I feel the rights themselves chiaroscuro to become the very wrongs they set out to right. Remember Metaxes' telegram to Italy: *Ohi!* It was the proudest moment of our lives back then, and still we say it: No! to war with Iraq, to Palestine, *we* are their neighbours, America must grow up. *War* is insane, any war, anywhere, yet it remains 'acceptable'."

Pericles' special gift was *sensus communis*, sheer common sense, that rare ability to cut through the persiflage of dialectic; he was always able to sift out specious reasoning from the most ordinary of fallacies. He had a heightened faculty through which instinct and memory made random sense-impressions cohere and he readily acknowledged his mother's modest outburst on the accepted ideologies of war. He took a different tack: "Alexa's story's really touched, you hasn't it" he agreed, "and you've made me see how urgent this all is, how little time we have to make our own resolutions before the investigation gets taken over and reduced to facts without feelings. I'm going to call that Australian woman now."

"Hullo," came a voice, her greeting rising with the characteristically Australian question mark, "hullo, Karen speaking." Pericles responded, slipped into his attractive accented English, introduced himself, explained his purpose.

"I expected you to phone," said Karen. "Nanette gave me the rundown of her aunt's call, it gave *me* the shivers. I haven't heard from Alexa for over a month, we're pretty close y'know. I knew Ari was taking her on this trip for her sixtieth birthday, but in my bones I felt really bad about it. How would we ever know if anything happened to her?"

Pericles listened carefully, allowing Karen to speak as much as she wished before asking her opinion of Aristo Theohalis when they had met.

"I picked them up at the airport, she looked like death, he just looked like a fat little Greek. I couldn't compute what I saw with the photos she had sent me of when they first met – he was like a god in those! But then she always did take photos of her friends through the eyes of love and not the lens. I knew all she had been through, and as I saw more of him I could see what she had seen. He could charm the gold from his grandmother's teeth."

Pericles hesitated: "Do you believe he was capable of *killing*?"

"Yes, I do," said Karen, too firmly for argument. "I knew his story, he had been *trained* to kill, and the training destroyed his capacity for human relationship. I'm afraid for Alexa. I could see how attractive he was, I was affected by it myself. It wasn't a simple question of her telling him to piss off. He had turned her life upside down, removed all the knowns, all the goalposts, broken every promise, she had no place to fall, and she didn't want to be here even though she loved the Tropics. *Culturally* she ached for France, Italy, England, and Greece of course. They're her soulscapes. She belongs there. When they finally left here to drive down to Brisbane in her old Alfa, oh," Karen veered right from her monologue, "that was such a *classy* little car with its polished wooden Momo steering wheel, so *her!* A real little icon. She used to drive up to Ingham each May to the Italian Festival, said she felt reincarnated in Little Italy."

"Anyway," she swung a left to return to her monologue, "driving down the Coast was his idea, but as *he* wasn't going to spend *his* money they stayed with *her* friends along the way. All of them, every one of them, warned her, could see the reality, and one of them, a doctor she had known in Glastonbury, laid it on the line. I happen to have his phone number, she gave it to me – or I might have asked for it. Here, it's a Gold Coast number, the first one's private the other two are surgery. Name's Jeremy Venter. But she didn't tell me she had gone back to Ari the following July until after the event. I thought she was mad, but it worked for the ten days, so maybe small increments of Ari would work for them both. We made her promise she would tell all her friends both sides of the planet whenever she was going to Rhodes in future. So we all knew how much she was looking forward to the Grand Greek Tour for her 6oth."

Karen steered the conversation to Alexa's time in the Tropics; "she was uncommonly self-contained you know, spent her life in a suitcase, in transit or in storage – if you get my drift. She's a true passerine," and, at Pericles' questioning monosyllable, she added, "a perching bird. Poor by most standards, but rich in ways we couldn't quite fathom, not having her depths. She had a wilful vulgarity that people of faultless taste use to protect themselves from faultless taste! When she returned from Karnak she bought with her an astonishing fruitbowl by a local artist. I loved it! The fruitbowl sat on the head of a long-necked negro woman with huge bunches of strawberries as earrings! Almost gross, but then Alexa could serve Moët Chandon in a teacup - it would be finest bone china of course, and probably missing a saucer and no one would bat an eye. She said yes to love, yes to life, yes to loss – she'd had so much loss in her life – and ..." Karen's sigh stilled the distance between them.

"D'you mind if I share a few memories with you?" Karen asked Pericles, who said he would enjoy hearing the three-dimensional side of the woman whose two-dimensional diary lacked, by its very nature, the requisite depth or range that an outsider's view could bring.

Karen paused, gathering memories: "You know, the last time Alexa phoned me was to share something really special. A few weeks before she was to go on the Grand Tour with Ari in September Diane Cilento emailed her to say she was going to be in England for August. Alexa was thrilled, emailed back to say she had returned to Glastonbury and Diane was welcome to stay with her. Actually," Karen chuckled, "she gave up her own bed and slept on the sofa. I had a blow by blow account of the two days – they went to Sparkford and Alexa was really moved to see Diane sit on the grass alongside the simplest of graves where John Godolphin Bennett, her spiritual teacher – a successor of Gurdjieff you know, a Greek from Kars who had a very strange effect on people – was buried."

Pericles registered the reference to the unknown Greek and resolved to look up the name; Karen's voice resonated back into his consciousness: "... she said Diane had prayed, laid flowers, and just sat there in silence. Alexa said she felt like an intruder and went some way off to wait. On the way home they bought some salmon which Diane insisted on cooking. But not before a visit to the Abbey where to Alexa's amusement Diane helped herself to handfuls, *armfuls*, of herbs from the old monastery herb garden. Alexa laughed hugely as she told me the story, said she thought that if anyone could smile her way through the gate on the way out under the watchful eye of the ticket seller Diane would. And the ticket seller turned away just as Diane came into view so both women walked right past him into the street! Herb coated salmon was delicious apparently, and Diane thoroughly approved of the olives Ari had sent a week earlier, from his own grove; "the man has the right values." The words probably came from the ancestral marrow of Diane's own Italian bones. This was Alexa living normally, attracting experiences that just seemed to happen along the way. I suppose Ari was one of those experiences too, but I am afraid ... I *am* afraid, you know, it isn't like her not to phone."

The line went quiet. Pericles digested the colourful narrative until Karen spoke again, this time in more sombre tones: "Alexa had been beset for some time with recurring periodontal infection. It became chronic, would flare up to the acute stage and she'd be unable to eat or speak from the pain. Oh, and don't think she was *laissez-faire* about treatment, she hounded the dental clinic for repeat appointments with hygienists – but dental treatment is only for the wealthier here, clinics are the last resort for the poor and only annual appointments are permitted. End of story really. When she went back to England she found a good dentist and a good hygienist on their National Health system, but it was too late to reverse the damage. I got quite interested after hearing a radio interview with Diane Cilento, she mentioned that husband Tony Shaffer had to return to England when he developed serious periodontal disease. She said he reckoned the dentists' here couldn't deal with it. Imagine that! Anyway I paid attention to the programme because I knew Alexa suffered the same thing but I admit I was shocked when Diane said straight out that Tony's condition was so bad that back in London he had to have all his teeth removed – and he died of a heart attack! I did some research – and found that periodontal disease is directly connected to heart failure. Nothing at all to do with poor dental hygiene, which is the popular embarrassment of bad press, it's systemic, and directly linked with stress and the body's coping mechanism. Different bodies, different stress points. Alexa's childhood pre-disposed her to the problem, having a mother who should have been committed and all that. Truly ...," Karen was on another roll and could sense Pericles' open astonishment half way across the planet urging her on, "... she still had food issues when I met her. Her mother shut her in her bedroom every Sunday for years during the Reign of Stepfathers to fudge their discomfort that little Alexa could see through their games and deceits. No Sunday lunch for her, no afternoon excursions either, locked in her room while the current family unit was out and about. No wonder she loved travelling as an adult, it echoed a need to escape. The point *is*" Karen drew breath, "that when Diane stayed with her it was during one of those perio flare-ups and Diane detected it at once, and identified it, made her speak of it. Diane knew about it so well, it had killed her husband. Only, for Alexa by then, it had gone so far it was beyond normal hygienists' ability to halt and the NHS didn't cover the only treatment that could alleviate her considerable pain. The warm-hearted Diane made Alexa phone her dentist to ask the cost of the treatment and then wrote a cheque for the whole amount, telling Alexa to have the work done over the next four weeks, *before* she went to Greece. She did, and it was painful" added Karen, "I know; I had a blow by blow account because I asked her."

Pericles' brain was in overdrive, he remembered Eve's comment about Ari refusing Alexa the treatment his own dentist said she must have.

"Karen" he asked briskly, "if Alexa had this so seriously, well, would it be possible she may have experienced heart failure? Somewhere, along the last journey? I have no idea how we begin the search, but I could alert Interpol of this, they would then make exhaustive hospital checks which could bring Alexa to light. But Ari ... disappearing too ... this is another conundrum ..."

"Ah!" said Karen, "it *is* possible, and then Ari's disappearance ... well, he did love her in his weird way, what if she *did* have a heart attack? What if she'd died in the car and he left her body in a forest somewhere," - Karen looked for the romance - "and then," she warmed her imagination, "he went and jumped off a cliff in despair! A sort of reverse Sappho."

Pericles' thought it a bizarre concept but had to concede the idea of heart failure was a distinct possibility. He knew people died of stress cardiomyopathy, his gods and myths had always known that, Zethus himself had died of a broken heart. How like modern science to take three thousand years to acknowledge something so humanly basic.

Karen's sigh returned his attention to the present: "She used to laugh and say fools didn't suffer her gladly, but love makes fools of us all – even Alexa."

And, thought Pericles, enough stress will kill anyone.

Common considerations had reached a natural hiatus. Conversation brought the events to the moment, their shared concerns, their relief at Alexa's good fortune in meeting Penelope whose own generous passion for life gave Pericles a tenuous cause for optimism, perhaps there was, after all, a natural conclusion to the connection between their missing persons, yet why the distances? Pericles' gave Karen his phone numbers; they promised to keep each other informed as they hung up their respective phones.

Pericles turned to his mother: "Mama, there is a thought pressing the back of my head, it doesn't want to speak, but ... does Alexa's manuscript take you to Australia and back?"

"Yes," replied Danaë, "it ends with her having settled back in Glastonbury, Aristo renovating her bungalow, and her coming, rather tentatively, to him in July for ten days. I want to finish her Moleskine because I am certain that will lead us up to September. We may not want to go there but it's the only way we'll find any clues. It's beyond a puzzle, almost sinister, that Ari has gone missing too."

Pericles' silence suggested to Danaë that he might be sifting through other scenarios. She held back the fugitive thought now sitting on the threshold of *her* consciousness that maybe, just maybe, Alexa herself was *responsible* for Ari's disappearance. A suspicion had found sanctuary in a distant quarter of her mind; a shadow, an insubstantial thing. It lodged itself, claimed a solidity of its own. A shadow has no substance of its own and yet ... and yet is cast by something that has. Danaë narrowed her hazel eyes, attempted to peer inward at the suspicion taking form in the shadows of her mind.

CHAPTER SIXTEEN

Pericles heard his mother out. He sensed an edge to her conversation that for all his years with her, and all their closeness, he couldn't quite place a finger on. The thought that didn't wish to be spoken would need probing; time for that soon enough. He kept to his current focus: "I don't need to tell you what the Australian lady said, you will have read much of it already. When they arrived in Townsville Alexa was apparently unrecognizable. Reading *his* story adds to the possibility that he might, I'm not saying he is, but he *might* be capable of doing anything. I'll call the doctor Karen spoke of, the one who knew Alexa in Glastonbury, see if he can add anything to our patchwork of possibilities. But, and this is something Karen said, Alexa had a problem that too much stress just might prove fatal. Let me make the phone call first and I'll tell you all."

It was also possible, just a slender window of possibility, that Dr Jeremy Venter would lift the doubts circling his head and say, medically speaking from his recent knowledge of Alexa, that heart failure may account for her temporary disappearance. Only temporary – her whereabouts or her body still had to turn up.

The phone only rang twice before: "Jeremy Venter here," answered a crisp South African accent as Pericles introduced himself. Responding immediately to the professional manner of the medic Pericles first gave his own credentials before saying he was investigating the disappearance of a woman whom the doctor may have known: Alexa Buddicom. Indeed, the doctor confirmed, she had been a patient at the practice when he lived in Glastonbury.

Pericles briefed the doctor on Interpol's involvement with the missing Alexa. Jeremy's long low whistle hummed in Pericles' eardrum. Lifting the phone away from his ringing ear he turned the receiver towards him and spoke into it like a microphone. Posing the obvious question he took in an imaginary breath, a pause just enough to phrase the question: "can you tell me anything you might know that will help us?"

Pericles waited while Jeremy gathered his thoughts before speaking: "Alexa and I met when she came into the surgery for some trivial reason and we hit it off at once. Pix and I had left South Africa after a number of friends were murdered; we thought England would give us the life we wanted. We hated it. Alexa told us to come to Springbrook, her book was set there, we loved her book and we took a reccy during my holidays and fell in love with the place. She was right; Australia gave us the lifestyle we were used to without the fear and racial instability. When she met Aristo we thought she'd found real happiness. We met him, he seemed okay, not what I'd expected, but she was blissed out. Love made her beautiful. When Pix and I saw her here a year later she had aged ten years. Ari was with her, they stayed with us overnight. He had brutality balled in every muscle. I took her aside and told her she was risking her life – one drink too many and he would kill her. I also told her it was none of my business ...but... now you're telling *me* ...?"

Pericles swallowed; the conversation was sobering and wasn't going in the direction he had hoped. No question of systemic potential for heart failure here. Jeremy Venter's knowledge of her medical history did not assume other possibilities.

"Frankly," Pericles said, speaking slowly, "I can't tell you anything at this minute, but you have told me what I need to know. Neither body nor person has turned up, but we believe she didn't come back to Rhodes with him after their trip around Greece ..."

"Their *what!*" exploded Jeremy, "are you telling me she went *back* to Greece after all she went through? You'd better hunt down the whole fucking country for him – and her. I can't believe I'm hearing this." Pericles wished he wasn't having to tell the story.

There was little else to say. Pericles promised to keep Jeremy informed, and reluctantly he put down the phone. Reluctant because he had run out of alibis, excuses, explanations. The words of Penelope drifted into his mind, he smiled when she said them but they held more than a grain of truth; he had known of many dramas over the years with holiday romances gone awry: *the road to the airport,* Penelope had laughed, *is littered with foreign fallouts from marriages to Greek men!*

Pericles' usually quiet face spoke volumes as he set the phone back on its base.

Across the room Danaë sat still, she knew in her bones what her son had just been told. She had already read it, knew the enormity they were faced with – one way or the other. She waited for her son to untangle his thoughts, think of his next move. For all the stillness in his face Pericles' mind ran razor-tracked from Apollo's silver bow.

"I'll go in to the office, let me give you the Moleskine diary now, read it through to the end, see what you can make of it," said Pericles handing over the Moleskine. "I'm going to have to skip-read Aristo's story to the end too; somewhere the stories may cross enough to give us a clue. I don't think time is on our side. When I send copies to Athens in response to Eve's report they may well expect me to hand over the diary, I can't recall if I said I had it – but Ilias knows anyway. The pencil's too fine to photocopy – we'll have to read it today. Tomorrow we'll have no excuse to keep it."

Pericles drove to the office, photocopied the Interpol report, slipped it into a plastic sleeve and was about to leave when he noticed the red light blinking on the answering machine. An Athens number appeared on the window; he let out a groan and made an executive decision to ignore it until tomorrow. It was Sunday after all, what could anyone do? Alexa Buddicom and Aristo Theohalis are alive or they are dead, either way they don't need him. He had a different imperative.

He drove back home slowly, settled himself in three different positions in his favourite generous armchair before feeling comfortable enough to skip-read Ari's story. He found his taste for boy's stuff had waned since the first chapters, the sombre reality that had descended since his conversations with Karen and Jeremy had shut down his edge for the hero tactics as he flipped through chapters on white sharks, fatal attacks, leopard sharks and other variously grim and gruesome swimming-with-shark-stories more swiftly than usual. He found himself appalled by accounts of burning oilfields and burning barges, burning seas and burning men. Terrible reiterations of tetanus and severed limbs, drunken captains and exploding cargo, Kuwait and cadillacs, classy dinners and grisly murders. The recitative of drama would keep film scriptwriters in outpourings of horror scenes for a decade. All through it Aristo's heroism was genuine, and his fearlessness. His career soared; he was headhunted for the largest barge in the world, until his life turned upside down over a point of pride. He left his ocean and returned to Rhodes. That chapter moved Pericles deeply, Alexa's writing of it so poignant stones would weep.

Pericles felt compassion for this man who had fallen through every flaw of his own character. He had tried so hard, this was apparent in every situation, every story, every sentence. The flaw was in his need for perfection. His life, as Pericles read the change of it, a paean of farewell to the ocean, cast him in the mould of Odysseus. He was a true Greek, with all the passions and failings the ancients were heir to. But, and the *but* did not come readily, there ran a *leitmotiv* of – could he say it? *self-regard?* and more than a touch of self-pity in the landlocked future of Aristo's transition to terra firma when his life in the ocean he loved was over.

Valiantly Pericles read on, and on. Close to reaching the end of the manuscript he struck gold – *here was Alexa.* Pericles' attention was honed to every word.

CHAPTER FIFTEEN

Danaë collected her shawl, her photo chromatic reading glasses, water, a low folding chair and the Moleskine. She drove back to Philerimos. The tranquil ruins of the old monastery of the Knights Hospitallers was a favoured place, beset with remembrances of things past and ever-present. She had come here often after the death of Stavros, finding the calm of the *Deus loci* a peaceful presence. The slow sad susurrus of wind fingering the Calabrian pines bequeathed its balm and the anemones, rare white peony cyclamens and tiny purple orchids, reminded her of the fragility and beauty of life; at best an ephemeral bequest from the gods.

Setting her seat down on a grassy knoll in the clear but cooler sunlight of early October Danaë watched a honey buzzard lazily spiralling on the late summer thermals above the high woodlands before turning her eyes to the small black pocket diary that she had drawn from her bag. The silence from the old ruins enveloped her, expanded her sense that she did not end at her skin, that she could slip through the veil of centuries and stand in another place as real as where she sat now. She reflected over her arcane understanding, always held dear, that Angels live in the oxygen of God, the only reality that kept her alive during her own grieving. The wind played with the corners of her shawl, in animate affirmation of her thoughts: *the wind force of the Divine Mind, the spiritual intelligences that connect all planes of existence – these were the Grigori, the Shining Ones. They will know, or they will know not.* She wrapped her shawl around her shoulders for comfort and began to read the final entries:

August 29th

Ari phoned, will be there to pick me up at the airport. I did tell everyone that this is Ari's 60th birthday gift to me, a trip around Greece, with me coordinating the ancient, classical and more contemporary places of mutual historical interest. Penelope and Panos are coming to Phanes on the last night before I fly back to celebrate my 60th at Ari's favourite taverna.

August 30th

Ah my man I love him so! I am almost won over once more by the gifts all over the bedroom; my photograph on his side of the bedroom wall, handpicked roses on the dressing table at my side of the bed, bowls of figs, *saganaki* ready for lunch, a silent fan blowing cool to my side of the bed as I dislike air conditioning through the night, new padding and quilting on the head board for me to lean against when I write my journal in the mornings, a two sided mirror, one magnifying, for which to apply my kohl, an icon varnished on a piece of slate and a truly and spectacularly bling new handbag, gift-wrapped in silver tissue. A flask of chilled water sits on my bedside table along with 'my' mobile phone, charged and ready for use. He has bought new towels just for me, yellow with orange daisies embroidered on one, and the other orange with yellow daisies. Aristo says over and over how much he misses me. I ache with the fairytale perfection of it all. And close my ears to Cassandra's whisper to beware of Greeks bearing gifts.

August 31st

Alas this morning Ari changed like the wind and the old familiar combat returns. I sigh, keep myself busy and silent as we drive to the harbour to pick up the dawn sailing of the Blue Star to Piraeus. I adore adventures, and settle down to enjoy every moment of the next twelve hours, the next days. Aristo sits away from me, scowling and sullen. I ignore him. Fortunately while we are away from our seats having lunch the ferry docks at one of the islands and a well to do family, with an enormous sense of entitlement, move Aristo's bags and mine to assume possession of our very good seats. Aristo is absolutely livid. Even I am astonished. A hair-raising scene follows with abuse ricocheting around the lounge and gathering steam from observers, passersby and anyone else who wants to air their own opinion. I play my part by quietly sitting down on the lap of the woman taking my seat. It is her turn to be astonished, but I sit firm. She has to ignominiously wriggle her way out of that one. The contretemps unites us for the rest of the trip and we disembark and drive away across the Isthmus of Corinth to our first stopping place.

September 1st - 4th

Epidaurus for healing. I stand astonished on the little centre stone and hear my voice echo to the fifty-fifth tier. The history as I re-tell it to Aristo should make his Greek blood proud. But it doesn't. It makes him angrier and angrier and he refuses to stop at Argos and drives right past Mycenae. However, I know this is a trip of a lifetime, his *and* mine, and nothing, *nothing* short of death is going to dissuade me from loving every moment.

September 5th

We fall into delightful hotels each evening, the days are heaven sent, the sky cloudlessly blue, nights cool and sleep is easy: but for my beloved's bad temper. I have only marked one place on the whole itinerary specifically for me – Missalonghi, I want to send a postcard to Colleen McCullough. Aristo loathes the town on sight. He turns so savage that he drives right out again. He is a terrible navigator, would lose himself in a lift, and turns left to find himself back in the town. His anger reaches Olympia and he leaves the low lying swampy town once more, turns left and ends up back in the same town, different street. I know better than to laugh. I know better even than to speak, but it is obvious to me that I am meant to find a postcard for Ms McCullough so I sit back and watch the drama unfold.

I know that Ari hasn't an atom of interest in Byron, *Vironos,* who died of malaria it is kindly said, in this town and I haven't his ghost of a chance in Ari's present health and temper of finding the Byron museum or much else – but there, not two metres from the passenger car window, are two empty chairs and a small round table upon which lie two mosquito coils and a blister pack of two aspirin. As a metaphor for Byron, malaria and Missalonghi, it is perfect. I take photos just as Aristo returns and bellows at me to get back in the car; he now has a town map and he *will* find a way out of this pestilent town. He is such a *difficult* man, when life could be so easy.

September 6th

Arta and the infamous packhorse bridge fail to interest him. Hardly surprising. It is Turkish, but the Greek stonemason buried his wife alive, tying her in a sack and sinking her, to ensure the foundations held. Her lament, it is said, may still be heard. Mine almost joined hers right then and there: Aristo is *bored* with his Greece.

From Arta we travel to the River Acheron with its icy fast flowing aquamarine waters over which departed souls must pass on their way to the Underworld. The ancients named it the River of Woe. Too apt, I think, and flippantly consider the possibility of joining the hovering shades as I fill a bottle from a spouting tap directing the flow of its icy water through the cut of stone millennia before. The water has an exquisite taste, I am surprised. We lunched at Glyki and, surviving Acheron, I asked directions for Suli and Zalongo. Surely these will interest Aristo. We find Kassope and wander for a while, I take notes and photographs enough for a whole travelogue, linger by the ancient theatre to gaze at the views of the Ambracian Gulf and distant mountains. The silent landscape is thick with presences and the high-pitched *zzzzzzzz* of the occasional cicada. We leave the quiet ruins, paths of dense pine needles buffering the sound of our footfalls as we walk.

Coming out of the forest we look up to Mount Zalongo and see something vast and astonishing.

This is the one place I feel certain Aristo will resonate to if all else fails, and all else did fail. This place, which he knew only vaguely from his history, is the mountain from which jumped sixty women and children to terrible deaths on the granite rocks below to avoid capture by the troups of Ali Pasha in 1803. Their men, to the last young boy, had already been killed. The women had walked for days across the bleak mountain passes, tracked by soldiers unfamiliar with the landscape. Reaching the ultimate escarpment they formed a circle and danced, these women of Suli, a pavane of quiet, desperate dignity. As each one came to the edge of the precipice she threw her baby, or her child, or her children into the chasm of death and then, not faltering one dance step, followed them to the jagged rocks below. Their plangent voices resonate on the restless winds, remain in the stones. I hear them.

In honour of these women we walk the four hundred and sixty seven steps up to the top of the mountain and stand in awe of the vast monument commemorating the women's story. Aristo confesses he is amazed at my research, my knowledge and my navigation. And he stands moved at the colossal memorial of women dancing, a final funerary liturgy.

We continue on to Suli itself. It is hidden along mountain passes so breathtakingly beautiful the twenty kilometre journey takes an hour and a half as we snake around these mournful mountains. The village is deserted. Not one Suliote was left alive after Ali Pasha and even now I am aware of its haunting loneliness. Ari is quiet. The impact of the not so distant history is tangible in the deserted village, the silent homes, the eerie half fallen roofs. Not even a chicken scratches the dry soil, the light extinguished from the soul of Suli. We drive away silently.

From Suli we continue on to Dodona, ancient theatre of Zeus, and bed down in a charming hotel in Ioannina with a dovecote balcony for our breakfast room, glassed in against the fierce winters. The next morning, horror of horrors, a million wasps wake with us having slipped in through cracks in the dovecote. Aristo retreats to the bathroom and I phone for help. He is seriously allergic to wasp and bee stings. The wasps sense his fear and crowd the door. Great consternation. We are given another room, we are even given another fridge at my request, and the hotel staff assures us the wasps *are* dangerous.

Aristo's ill temper returns apace. I have choreographed our trip to arrive at Meteora on the 7th as I want to visit the heaven-pointed rock monasteries built by ancient hermits who hauled themselves, workmen, mortar and donkeys up each sheer cliff face in baskets to the pinnacles. Meteora is a moonscape from mythology. Then on to my beloved Delphi, where I will wake on the 8th to celebrate two birthdays – Hers and mine.

And there the Moleskine ended. Danaë broke out in goose bumps. Ioannina! Those mountains. Those lonely roads by Metsova... The loneliness of the landscape...

Danaë sat, thought denied, for some minutes before she gathered her things, shook out her shawl to drape over one arm, reached her car and drove on autopilot down the steep curving road home. She pulled in through the tall gates just as Pericles was entering the house.

Following him inside Danaë greeted her son as he turned to the sound of her footfall, her frown showing unusual concern: "*paidi mou,* this is more terrible than we can think. I finished the diary, there were only a few pages, we must talk now about what I think we must do before tomorrow."

Pericles was taken aback by the imperative tone in his mother's voice. The impulse to tell her of the earring went on the back burner. As she talked his skin prickled, thoughts buzzed in the very air around his brain; his mother recited the wasp incident, his own adrenalin stung by such a clue: "*wasps! Theo mou,* every hotel in Ioannina must be called, there is no way the one they stayed in would forget that little incident."

Danaë nodded, echoing the obvious: "wherever they stayed the staff will remember it. The computer's on standby, bring up Hotels in

Ioannina now, phone them all. My stomach is a valley of butterflies."

Pericles began at the top of the list. On the fourth call the receptionist remembered the incident clearly. "Kyria Theohalis, she came to us speaking in English and saying that the room is full of wasps. Alas, we know she is right, it's a problem here and we know they are dangerous. My manager is called and they are given another room immediately. We close off the room so we can fumigate it. Quite early next morning Kyrios Theohalis checked out, and Kyria Theohalis tells to me they are going to Meteroa. I smile and say they must not miss seeing Metsova then, it is exactly on the same road to Meteora, and it is one of our most unusual villages. She smiled, he didn't, but I think they will go there. She asks me to post a couple of postcards for her, to *Avustralia* and *Angglia*."

Pericles thanked her for her help, assured her again that he will call her manager tomorrow, Monday, to confirm that her confidences were a police request.

Pericles turned to Danaë, his face pale, expression strained: "the diary stops at Ioannina, Alexa never wrote anything of Metsova, or of Meteora, whatever did happen on that last day happened before they reached Meteora. And she didn't come back to Rhodes. Yet how fast must he have driven to get from Ioannina to Piraeus, it's three hundred kilometres at least. The Blue Star leaves at seven each evening, if they left the hotel at nine in the morning, stopped in Metsova, even from there ... well I suppose it *could* be done. He would have to drive slowly over the mountains but once past Kalampaka the plains of Thessaly make for a fast road, until Parnassus, but over that range is another fast road to Piraeus. It could *just* be done. I'm going to make another call to Blue Star, I'll be two minutes."

Pericles returned, his expression spoke more than words: "my hunch was right, Aristo changed his booking."

He spoke more to himself than to Danaë, the clutch of thoughts running like chickens in a coop around his head: *a search party has to be coordinated along the road to Meteora, I should call Athens right away, no Alexa, no Aristo, after all this time I feel less and less certain they are alive.*

"There was nothing suspicious about Ari's disappearance, apart from the disappearance itself," Danaë spoke softly, "We know Alexa ... well, *what* do we know about Alexa really? She became a different woman once she returned to her own familiar environments, whether Australia or England. We think we won't see Alexa again and you can let Angelos deal with that, but I still have a fugitive doubt on the threshold of my consciousness that Alexa is alive, and it is Ari who is dead. You can tell your Angelos I spent the weekend reading the manuscripts, and skipped through Alexa's journals, and that the full stop as far as the reality of her presence is concerned takes her to Ioannina. But .." and again the thought chilled her, even exhilarated her if she allowed it to, "there is a *frisson* at the edge of my mind that sees her returning because she is now stronger, and who's to say ..." she sighed a breath filled with unthought knowns which were no more known than any other unthinkable – "just supposing Alexa, the stronger Alexa, is responsible for the missing Ari?"

Pericles, never loquacious at the best of times, turned his head to one side, looking, thought Danaë, as if the weight of her words were pulling his whole brain sideways. She knew instinctively that she was giving voice to his own thought, the one he had denied, had pushed aside in preference to the hope that Alexa might still be in a hospital somewhere, death recorded comfortably as heart failure.

"What if ..." Pericles continued the thread slowly unravelling and found his voice somewhere at the edge of his tongue: "Mama, could she? Was she capable ...?" He answered his own question mark by raising his left eyebrow as a reel of powerful women passed in front of his eyes – Medea, Artemis, Tethys, Atalanta, the treacherous Queen of the Goths, Tamora; images of a fearsome feminine power that brooked no argument when pushed beyond their givens – "yes," he answered himself quietly, "I suppose she was."

Danaë's smile reciprocated his thoughts, spiced by a gaze both rueful and piquant. "I think we have come to care for Alexa. She loved her Greek so much, and he loved her but didn't know how to love *anyone*. He was a lonely man. I hope," said Danaë finally, "that we find both of them in whatever circumstances so we can lay this to rest. There is still a chance that she may have gone completely to ground having done what she may have been pushed to the edge to do – *perhaps*. I can't imagine doing anything like it myself, and yet in the marrow of my bones perhaps I can – it becomes a survival of primal intention."

Kai tou poulion to gala, mumbled Pericles into the phone as he dialled Interpol; *and there's even bird's milk...* He stopped short as a voice answered his call. Without embellishment he spoke to the night officer manning the weekend shift, half dictating a request for a memo to be left for his superior, telling him Pericles had located their missing person's last known whereabouts. He also requested the whole area be tooth-combed from Ioannina to Meteora urgently and left his office, home and mobile numbers – a short conversation in the morning would take the case from his care, but not his concern. Nor from Danaë's.

CHAPTER SIXTEEN

Ioannina:

Bloody hotel, bloody wasps, bloody trip. Why she want to take me here, I cannot support this anymore, I should be at home, I need to prepare for picking my olives, finish my house, I am not interesting in looking at my Greece with this woman now. This hotel, they say the wasps are a problem. They know the wasps are a problem and they do not seal the rooms against them. I nearly died from these things; I cannot believe after all my life and all the dangers I lived through I am in this kind of situation.

Oh, Ari ... he is so angry this morning. So what's new Alexa, even the receptionist blinked at his surly behaviour as we were checking out. What can I do? We've seen such beauty; everywhere we've been has gifted us with unexpected pleasures. I don't suppose any of them have even penetrated his clouds of anger.

"Here's Metsova, you want me to turn, you want to go and look at this place?" Surly, angry words hurl themselves around the car, the first Ari has spoken since leaving the Hotel.

I can't read him, I really can't read him. Does he want to or not? Do I say yes or no? I'm damned either way. Goodness, his face is darker than I've ever seen it before; he's really brewing up a storm. I hope to God the bars or at least a good kafenion's open. He has gone ahead, looking for a bar. Oh here he comes ...

"There's nothing in this fucking town, they're all bloody Albanians anyway, we're leaving, get in the car."

Daren't speak or attempt small talk – his mood's more poisonous than the Dior Poison he sprays all over himself. Thank heavens we've reached the top of the road, oh good grief he's turning left instead of right, back to Ioannina!

"Ari, sweetheart, we turn right, not left."

This stupid woman – "how you know we turn right, you are not Greek, this is not your bloody country, there's no signpost to say where is Meteora, no signpost for anything! You think you know these things? WHY IS THERE NO SIGNPOST?"

"I am holding the map ... we turned right onto the road down to Metsova, we must now turn right again to continue in the direction we were travelling; I don't know why there are no sign posts, and I don't need to be Greek to be able to read a map but if you really want to know why there are no signposts why don't you ask your own fucking government and get them to put one there."

I groan inwardly at my own silly reasoning but my happiness gene is wearing ever so slightly thin. I didn't raise my voice, but oh dear ... here we are still stopped at the T junction. I don't believe I am seeing this – he has got out of the car, flagged down a huge semi trailer with a Bulgarian number plate and he's shouting Meteora! Meteora! The driver points ahead – so we have to turn right. Oh oh! He's going to want to kill me for being right about turning right! Stay calm Alexa, stop scribbling notes as he drives – and get that darn grin off your face, you <u>know</u> his rage! Here we go, turning right. What's he pulling over for? Oh my God Ari, Ari, don't do this, let go of my scarf. I mustn't struggle, must stay very relaxed, he'll realize what he's doing, Ari ... oh ... Ari ... don't do this. Oh Ari, my dear, you are so foolish to do this ...

"I kill you, you stupid woman, why you are right? You think you can say these things to me, with a wasp in your voice. "Den ftaio ego", it's not my fault, you make me crazy, the stupidities on this trip, I never want to do this, it's for you I leave my island. Why you don't speak, why you let me do this? Why you don't struggle, it makes me more crazy, you are like a toy, I can do anything with you ..."

Darkness descended over Alexa. She hasn't struggled once, like the caught prey of a cat she relaxed completely into his stranglehold, felt the pressure on the sides of her neck. There is no pain, only blackness, flickering lightness and darkness swimming in her brain. Her body slumps down the seat, the Moleskine diary slides from her lap, forgotten, by her bag on the floor.

Aristo loosened his grip, letting go of Alexa's scarf. Darkness descends. He is left with the blinding, terrifying clarity of Alexa's immovably inert body where moments ago sat the woman he loved more than anything in the world except his beloved ocean. Stricken, he pulled her body to him, *Alexa, Alexa mou, Alexa, listen to me, hear me, wake up! wake up!* His experience of first aid kicked in – but her warm has gone, *she has gone. Alexa*, he sobbed into her neck, her perfume filling his breath, his memories, his blind rage. Why was he blind, what happened? Was it the wasps? What made him so blind? His anguish found voice and he roared into the thick silence: *What makes me so blind!*

    The gods remain silent. No one answered. The silence was absolute. Only the sound of his pounding heart filled the car; hers was still.

Aristo sat for an eternity, holding Alexa. Slowly the awful clarity, fugitive on the threshold of consciousness, flooded his thoughts. Alexa! Alexa was *dead*. He could not speak the unspeakable – that in his own blind rage he had killed her – but he knew she was dead and he could not drive round with a dead body in his car; *Theo mou*, but he wanted to get home, *now*, as fast as he could, he must think, *think*, how could this happen?

    The road here was so lonely, the truck he had stopped was the only traffic in the past ten minutes, he could see for miles left and right. He was alone. The village of Metsova was so far below he couldn't even see the chimneys. The forests over the precipice – ah, the forests over the precipice, perhaps she had fallen, his thoughts were sending him crazy again, yes, she must have fallen, someone would find her and say that. He would go home and no one would know, he would tell the interfering English that Alexa had flown home from Athens.

Ari climbed out of the car and walked around to the passenger door, he was parked right on the edge of the precipice. He looked around, the ground fell some thirty metres right there at his feet, the gulf yawned below him where the mountains fell away to their very roots, the first outcrop of thin firs far below. He would lay Alexa down, sit with her, tell her how much he loved her, she knew that, he knew she knew that, he would not question anymore, then he would let her body go down, down into the trees ... He pulled her bag from the floor and threw it, in a wide arc it flew over the canopy and disappeared – somewhere, beyond his caring.

Oh Panaghia there's a car coming, I must make like I am doing *pipi* then they'll take no notice of me parking here. He pulls at his jeans as the car speeds past. I am becoming nervous, I must go, I must get back, I must catch the Blue Star *tonight*.

Urgency lent wings to his wheels, even on the mountain road. As the pinnacles of Meteora came in to view many kilometres further on he failed to register their unearthly appearance. Knowing that most of the next 200 kilometres across the Thessalian plain and the E65 fast until he reached Lamia and Route 1 to the foothills of Parnassus, his foot sat leaden on the accelerator. He had no time to think, reaction had not set in, he played the CD's Alexa loved to make sure she was still beside him, but too loud. Why wasn't she telling him of the great battles between the Titans and the Olympians, here alongside them? On these very plains. Even he knew *those* stories. She was quiet, she was not complaining. *Oh my Alexa, my Alexa, what can I do?*

Ari sped across the Thessalian plains, south, south ... too fast to think. For hours he drove, driven from within, over the Parnassus range, the single road through Delphi forcing him to slow, forcing him to use force to keep back the threatening flood of tears dammed behind eyes seared with sorrow. He would *not* stop ... he would get on that ferry ... tomorrow in his own bed he would wonder why Alexa had not come as she promised she would. They were going to have such a beautiful time together again. Why did she always leave him? He drove and drove and drove the thoughts away.

He was home; *le bon Dieu* was with him all the way ... he had reached Piraeus and Gate E to board the Blue Star in time ... was able to access the ticket office to buy a new ticket, forgetting he already had a return for a few days hence in his jacket. Unable to sleep Ari sat in a single seat along the corridor, too numb to walk to the bar, too numb to numb himself with a few hours of whisky. Dawn ... and he walked on auto pilot to the lower deck, got in the Vitara which drove itself back to Phanes. In the familiarity of place the day ahead hung in hideous clarity; whisky heightened the horror, failing him when he needed oblivion most.

Ari, oh Ari, why are you doing this? He can hear her, her voice is with him, her face is with him, in front of him when he looks into his own mirror to shave, she is with him, but where does she go at night when he turns to hold her and she is not there? Alexa, Alexa *mou*, your Ari misses you, so much he is missing you.

Every day the nightmare drove deeper into his mind ... he had hardly touched her ... his thumbs had only pressed ... that nerve ... it was so long ago ... this was ... not a commando course ... where is Alexa, my Alexa ...?

I will go back to my ocean, I was happy in my ocean, never never does my ocean make my life a hell, we have a *rapport* my ocean and me. The book, I take my book with me, who will read it now? Who is there to know I am Aristo Theohalis; but who is Aristo Theohalis ... now he has ... no ... Alexa?

I will leave my story in the car ... it must be found ... someone must find it and know Aristo Theohalis ... even if my son and my wife they care nothing ... nothing for me ... my Alexa must know who I am.

Alexa? *Alexa mou?* Where are you? You are waiting me ... I know you are waiting me ... in my deep ocean ... and this time we will not separate ... this time ...

CHAPTER SEVENTEEN

Ilias was already in the office inserting the manuscripts into a padded envelope when Pericles arrived. "*Kalimera* Ilias," he greeted his friend, reaching into his jacket pocket and pulling out the Moleskine, "slip this into the packet too; I have read everything I need to read. Inspector Apostolakis can have it now."

"*Phew*," Ilias expelled his signature whistle, his calm and ordered mind speeding up from its usual *andante*. "If she didn't come back, and if he's gone missing, and ... *po, po*, I am seeing a picture that isn't what I like to see. Kyrios, what *else* do you know?"

Pericles raised an eyebrow, preparatory to telling all. His narrative spanned continents and seas: "He followed her across galaxies, Ilias, he loved her, but he was crazy. Whether from the life, or from the loneliness, or from the gases, or from ... who knows what, but ... I am very much afraid to ask any more questions, but we must."

Ilias sat all the while, steady as a metronome, absorbing with a calm eye and ear the words and pictorial images coming at him. After the monologue he remained silent, sealing the packet he had been attending to when Pericles came in. Satisfied it was secure, with additional sellotape along the seams and flap, he held it to his chest with his left hand and made a swift sign of the cross with his right. "I'll go and post this now," he said, "I need a walk."

Angelos Apostolakis would receive the manuscripts and the diary by special courier later that day. The trail had been set in place, and Interpol were, as they spoke, calling upon the police forces of the Prefecture of Ioannina and those of Epirus to stage a massive search along the roads to Meteora for any sign of the body of the woman named Alexa Buddicom. Pericles had tracked down her last known whereabouts. He would read about it in the papers, and now he, Pericles, was praying that Aristo Theohalis would walk through his door and solve the mystery by saying Alexa had decided to return to Glastonbury by way of Kanchipuram and that her appearance was merely delayed.

The next three days brought early winter storms to the south eastern part of the island, the coastline along Gennadi Bay would be ripe picking for beachcombers through the heaped up flotsam and jetsam the churning ocean bed coughed up from its depths. Pericles needed the wild wind to clear his mind; he had never lost the habit of kicking through the miles of debris along the littoral, a pastime loved and remembered from his childhood when he and Danaë would look for little turtle shells and three thousand year old amphorae handles and other treasures from the great sea gods. He climbed into the Spider, hit the pedal with the sense of exhilaration that air thick with the scintilla of negative ions always gave him, and drove a mite too fast down the eastern coastline. The sea still churned but the wind had dropped and the rain stopped. The drive blew away the cobwebs of his confusion, the road was his own all the way south. He parked, ran his hand through his hair, breathing in deeply the clean clear air, pulled off his shoes and socks to walk the wet sand. An hour later, brushing the sand from his feet and letting them dry before putting on socks and shoes, he was heading back to Rhodes Town.

He barely recognised the expression on the face in front of him as the normally inscrutable Ilias. "What happened ... you had bad news?"

"Bad news? Maybe. Some tourist beachcombers phoned, they found a body down by the rocks at Plimiri, they are in Yiorgos' taverna and wait you there. You want me to come with you?"

"No, Ilias, stay here, man the phones ..."

Whatever happened Pericles did not want that body found by anyone else. Fifty flying minutes later Pericles returned to where he had been previously paddling and pulled up in the driveway of the modest taverna belonging to Yiorgos. He knew it well, leapt from his car, slamming the door behind him, took two stairs in each stride to come face to face with a middle aged foreign couple looking like they'd seen a ghost, which, under the circumstances was a fair comment.

Reaching out his hand he introduced himself without waiting for any emotional rhetoric that would delay him, and asked crisply for directions to the body. The man, who seemed even more shaken by evidence of his own mortality than his wife, described accurately the precise rocky outcrop where the body had been wedged, "on the right of the ruined peer where the army firing range extends to the seashore."

"Yiorgos, give these people anything they want, drinks, coffees, food – I'll settle up later, if they want a doctor or something to calm the nerves, fix it for them, I'll be back."

In English he thanked the couple profusely for their presence of mind in going straight to the taverna, and in his natural tongue thanked Yiorgos for his rapid call, raced back to his car and drove furiously along the corrugated tracks of the firing range that led to the sea.

Scrambling over the low rocks with the agility of a goat he landed on wet sand, scooted swiftly along the littoral until he came to the shallow rock bed that formed a still pool and there, ahead of him, one free arm waving like giant fingers of kelp, was an unmistakably human body.

Pericles bounded over the rocks, careless of the lack of purchase his shoes had on the slippery wet surface, and came to a shaky halt beside a not too badly decomposing body of a well muscled mature male. He paused, gathering his thoughts before bending down and turning the mottled body face to the sun. First, he must get the body to the mortuary; he dialled the hospital; he would wait for them. Then he called Kosta – was he was willing to identify the body?

The most powerful impulse welled up as Pericles had turned the body up to the light. The face ... the face held an expression of hierarchic calm, the eyes had gone, eaten by fishes, but for the rest Pericles felt he was in the presence of a god, a god whose vacant marble eyes gazed beyond the onlooker to a place where only the soul might go. Aristo Theohalis had returned to his beloved ocean, the body may have been brought back by the wind and the waves, but his soul ... the ocean had claimed that. The man who knew little happiness on terra firma was for all time where he belonged. That he was there was a tragedy of Sophoclean poignancy. Around the neck of the corpse was a heavy gold chain bearing a crucifix so ornate it could only have come from the same hand as Alexa's earrings. Two rings, of similar craftsmanship, heavy and gold and Byzantine jewelled were on each of two fingers. These Pericles would leave for ease of identification, but the cross ... he would take the cross, now, before anyone came, it was an impulse from the clear blue light of those heavens which Aristo Theohalis would not see again in this life.

The ambulance brought three men, stretchers, cloths and a body bag ready to dissemble and collect the mortal remains to take them back to the mortuary for forensic examination. Pericles drove back to the tavern, the couple had already left, settled up for a Metaxa and two cups of tea (they must have been British), thanked Yiorgos and drove lead footed back to Rhodes.

"Thanks to God you are back Kyrios, the phone call when you left, it was Interpol, from Athens. Their English officer wants to speak to you. The Epiros police found a body. A woman's body. Not even much covered up. There was no sign of struggle but they want to talk to you *now*. I tell them you are interviewing beachcombers about a

268

missing body and your mobile is off, but you must call them *now*, Kyrios. Sit, I bring you coffee, you look like you need one."

Two bodies in one day. Even if they are connected there is still 1000 kilometres between them. Pericles put his head in his hands, elbows on his desk, as he willed his thoughts to coalesce into a single stream. A thousand kilometres? Who is he kidding? He knows when he returns Zafira Middleton's call she will tell him only what he already knows. Icicles drip fed the very marrow of his spine as he picked up into the phone:

"Kyria Zafira? Pericles Kostakides here, you found her then? Where? Fifty metres from the Metsova turnoff? Well, I can complete the story ... the body of Aristo Theohalis was washed up after the storms ... no, it hasn't been conclusively identified yet, but it is ..."

The crisp voice of Zafira Middleton cut across his conclusion, launching his thought pattern into another weave:

"You are certain it is Alexa? Yes, yes, you can get dental records, I'm so sorry this ... we found manuscripts, diaries, here, I've sent them to HQ in Athens ..." Pericles mentally applauded himself that he could use the past tense – this was serious stuff: "... connection between the two, you mean ... perhaps, but not cold blooded, there is a story ... perhaps you might read ... I know, I *know* murder is murder in England ... *what's that*, can you say that again ... an *earring* ... no, of course, there wouldn't be much left of an *ear* after, what, three weeks on open ground ... under the head you say?"

Pericles hesitated, the warp and weft of this tapestry begging the question, the seamless stitching of the whole, *what would they do with it?* He remained silent. The crisp English voice of Zafira Middleton continued:

"And you need to know that although it appears she didn't struggle her scarf was partly used to strangle the woman," pause, "but that didn't kill her. What killed her outright was a trained killer's knowledge of the pressure points under the jawbone. Her murderer," Pericles wished she would stop applying pressure to the word so heavily, *"was trained to kill."*

Pericles spoke slowly while his thoughts unravelled: "Thank you," he responded, still resistant to acknowledging the obvious slant of her accusation, which was almost audible. "I suppose the case is closed. Can we keep it *in curia*? Theohalis was one of our war heroes you know, first man down in a diving bell, won the Pentathlon when he was in training, had a troubled life, loved this woman ... if it's not impossible I would like to preserve the better side of his integrity, nothing is to be gained by the gutter press getting hold of it; we can't actually prove he did it despite all the circumstantial evidence; we can hardly bring a corpse to trial for murder, even *in absentia*."

Zafira Middleton put the phone down first. Very loudly.

Pericles mentally closed the case; it was out of his hands. There would be a funeral for Theohalis of course, people would gather together and reminisce over his being such a *good* man, reminisce over his cooking, his jokes, his stories of life under the ocean waves. Maybe some would recall the Cyprus affair – some of the older Greeks still blame Turks for the time of day, the hero's life of Aristo Theohalis was all grist to their mill. The Inspector sat sipping his coffee to its grainy sludge, chasing the strong bitter taste with the sweet water from the mountain springs.

Danaë was putting finishing touches to a large vase of flowers as Pericles came in. It would come as no surprise to her, much as she had hoped otherwise, and hoped other conclusions; she knew Alexa would be found. Pericles told Danaë the facts, came directly to the point, which was the discovery of one earring, one of the earrings that Alexa was wearing in the photo, with the body; he spared his mother the description of the mortal remains of one ear.

"And I have the other earring here, it was caught on the seat belt clip in the car of Aristo's" he said, holding it out to her.

Danaë took it in her hand, "but it is *beautiful*," she sighed, as Pericles continued, telling her of Ari's body being washed up after the storms. Hesitantly, he pulled the heavy gold chain from his pocket ... "and I could not let this go with him, there was other jewellery to identify his body."

Danaë looked up, smiling her most mysterious smile, the one his father had loved so much: "and, my dear Pericles, you are going to keep *both* these pieces because I am going to tell you what must be done. This earring, it was made with love and it was a gift of love. We will honour the essence. Aristo was a damaged man; no one would know this but someone who could 'see through the cracks'. His gold cross touched his own essence. Love is always good. It was a doomed love but we can honour it. We know Alexa wanted to reach Delphi – well, *paidaki mou*, we will go to Delphi for them, *we* will take these symbols with us and *we* will find a place to lay them together in the sanctuary she loved so much. He called her his *phenomena.* You know my *penchant* for making connections: *Phemonoé* was the name of the first priestess of Delphi. Remember when they were together on Kos and Aristo knew he and Alexa had been together before, and had parted many times? Well they had. I have no doubt of that. I don't need to spell out what I am thinking, you can follow it. *We* are going to Delphi."

Across Pericles' calm features superlatives of the emotional register were liminal at best, its normal range resisted surprise, highly impressed or plain astonished. At this revelation of his mother's however, his left eyebrow rippled, the corners of his well-shaped mouth, still closed, resembled the upward curves of the archer's bow on the pediment of the Temple of Aphaea. His mother, he acknowledged, was a phenomena. It was high time he said it: "Mama! You are a phenomenon yourself! Oh, how Alice will *love* this story, it's the perfect conclusion. Let the law render unto Caesar, *we* will attend to the gods!"

"The *goddesses*," reminded Danaë, speaking with a regency he was unfamiliar with, "Alexa loved Delphi because she knew it of old when the Python guarded the Oracle for old Mother Earth, oh she *knew* it ... were you told of what state of decomposition her body was found? The earring may not have been *in* her ear after so many weeks ... remember our word for python, *pythein,* πύθειν? It means "to rot". Rot is the decomposition necessary for growth. After Apollo killed it he left the body of the Python, the great dragon who guarded the Oracle of Old Mother Earth, to *rot*. From that comes growth, as darkness and light are equal and necessary. Seeds grow in darkness, light alone is barren. Pythagoras took his name from the Pythia, descended into the Underworld, the dark, to bring back the light of wisdom, *enlightenment*. The Oracle of Delphi was his final teacher, he may have been her messenger, but *She* was his source of wisdom."

Danaë settled herself more comfortably into the cushions of her favourite armchair before continuing in a softer voice, a voice redolent with meaning, "how you loved our myths when you were at school. *We* are going to Delphi, to acknowledge the mysteries of the deep past, and we will go mindful of all we know and all we carry in our blood, in our collective memories.

Let's drink something my dear, a libation to give our words truth and meaning, and I will continue my trail of thoughts, yes, what a lovely idea, a little retsina, nectar from the gods, it will do us well," she added as Pericles stood to fetch a small bottle of pale golden liquid from the fridge.

"Alexa was a worthy inheritor of this ancient chain of succession. She had studied our ancients, knew their depths and truths, by all accounts she was a true artist, not as a writer or painter or iconographer, but she knew the *art of living*, isn't that what you heard in Glastonbury? Aristo sensed something special about her. We don't need to grieve; she *knew* the Old Wisdom of the mother Goddess." Danaë's eyes twinkled as her discourse gained a slight momentum ... "*Glastonbury*, dear boy, where Alexa came from, is the ancient Isle of Avalon. It is a place where at certain times of the year, solstice, the equinoxes and so on, the veils between the worlds are thin. The veil hides the ancient secrets of Avalon. And our Delphi hides ours."

Pericles sat, enthralled. He had never seen his mother as she looked now, had never heard her speak like this, and with such authority. She was so full of surprises, no wonder she had held his father's heart and respect and love. Had he, Pericles, ever really known his mother as a *woman*? She was always his mother. How had his father seen her?

Suddenly an image from long ago sat fully in front of his vision. On the ninth day after the burial of his father came *mnemosyna*, remembrance, when the family gathered around the grave. Danaë had made *koliva*, the traditional offering of wheat kernels boiled until they were soft, wheat for Demeter in her loss; sweetened with honey and flavoured with pomegranate seeds for Persephone in her darkness as Queen of the Underworld. Half the seeds belong to the Queen of the Dead and half to the King of the Dead. The pomegranate seeds mediate between life and death, the fruit is neither of death or life, but the inseparability of the two. Almonds were for Aphrodite who gave his parents her gift of Love, raisins were added, sacred to Dionysis and sesame seeds – said to open the doors of consciousness. *Koliva* was shared and with the living and the dead. His mother had shared this richness with him, ensuring its continuation.

At the graveside there were four that day: Danaë and Pericles, elderly Aunty Zozo and her daughter, Ariadne, a first cousin a little younger than his mother.

When the others had left, Pericles had said again the arcane words of farewell: *antio, patera – sto kalo. Kalo taxidi: Go, father, toward the good. We wish you a good journey*. He walked away and turned to wait for his mother. She had remained standing by the grave. He watched her from the distance. She was wearing a long black dress, the lowering sun behind her glowing aureole through her hair. She was a small woman, though plumper than she appeared in her linen shift. Her whole image struck him as a candlewick, on whom grief burnt like a flame. He saw her lean slightly, into the bitter winds of fate; sensed a storm hidden in every fold and sweep of the cloth she wore. In that instant she was no longer his mother but a woman enveloped in a world he could not enter, would not enter, until love introduced him to Dimitra, and death took her away. A fierce protecting surge of emotion swept over him as other images of Love and Death kaleidoscoped and he knew then that pain stalked them both silently, and silently each had borne their own griefs. *Thanatos* was a shared bedfellow. The force of human loneliness exacted its own memory before Pericles returned to the scene around him now, in which his own dear mother was just that – his own dear mother.

"Mama ... you ... are a true ... *phenomenon* ... you would have loved Alexa wouldn't you, you resonate with her ... and Alexa, she was more Greek than Greek. I feel a great weight has lifted from me; we are doing absolutely the right thing."

Danaë's expression was unreadable. The curl of her mouth at its corners sent a measured thrill through Pericles. Not something he would associate with a *mother*. More the kind of look she would cat-glance at his *father*. He watched as she curled back into the curve of her chair, the lines of age around her mouth, her eyes, playing, creating a force field of magical synthesis, giving to her usually hierarchic mien a glimpse of something *other,* something of the fée, impish perhaps, though far from ethereal.

"I haven't told you many things I learnt of Alexa." Danaë's eyes matched the impish smile on her face, a *flirting* mirror. Pericles sat, vaguely aware that something was in the air. And it wasn't ions. This was his *mother* he was about to meet.

Danaë took in a breath and continued: "She and I would have laughed at much together. The question of not wearing knickers for example, she wrote in her story that she never cross-dressed! How I laughed at that. And I couldn't tell *you, paidi mou*. I am with her for this! She wrote: "we are spirits on a human journey." She spoke, wrote, of water cleansing our energy field; and of fabric, clothing, taking from or giving to that energy field. She refused anything counterfeit, affectation of any kind, creed or colour. Even in her clothes she knew that synthetic fibres built up a charge that short-circuited the pathways necessary for energy to function. She only wore natural fibres in resonance with the low frequency field of Earth, our Gaea. She wrote in her journal something that so made me smile: *I never wear clothes louder than myself, it's such an insult to the landscape. Even the fabric must be from the natural world.*

We knew this too; our Mysteries forbad anything but flax, garments of new linen, gold, leather to be worn in our sacred sanctuaries. They knew, the ancients, that energy will flow through these, will resonate, will create pathways to the holy, through to the Mysteries that imbibing potencies of *ergot*, *amanita* or *acacia* enhanced." Pericles sat, entranced. Danaë was enjoying herself.

"The purity of the soul's clothing, the body; and the purity of the body's clothing, the clothes – were, and are, essential. This is when natural magic bleeds through into daily life. How many people know this? Few. Most would think a woman like Alexa a little left of field, wouldn't see how she moved to a different rhythm, a consonance of calling no formal education can offer. Alexa didn't wear underwear because I suspect she knew instinctively that the electric charge of polyester threads and elastic increased, even when used with cotton, and inhibited energy flow, and with that the polarity of the body's cells change. Where are we taught such things now? Nowhere. Those moguls of advertising have anaesthetised our ancient commonplace knowing. I don't suppose she left the washing up, an argument, or an untidy desk for the morrow either. It's nothing to do with tidiness;

chaos simply creates an energy drain. And that's before you begin to cope with the up and coming distractions of a new day."

Pericles sat shaking his head ever so slightly as his mouth curled into a rare smile, enchanting when he wanted to give it. His loving expression, directed at his mother, confirmed her rightness in inviting him in to her interior rooms, part of the many mansions that made her who she was.

His mother, said his smile, was proving a true hierophant, filled with light and mysterious insights. He allowed himself pause... Eve! Her face now claimed his thought, that bookshop, how his mother would love it. The titles to which he had paid no more than a cursory glance were floating now at the forefront of his mind. How had he missed this aspect of his mother? Had his father known her this way? With all these hidden eddies and depths going on underneath the surface of all he thought he knew of her, did he really *know* her?

"When would you like to go to Delphi?" he asked, when he finally found his voice and knew there was nothing else to say. And: "when we've bought new linen to wear!" was the reply, her words tinged with the gold of her smile.

CHAPTER EIGHTEEN

I am at the Beginning as I am at the End. I am the
sacred circle of Life, the Spinner of Space and the
Weaver of Time. I am the Cosmic AND: Life and
Death, Order and Chaos, Eternal and Finite. Why did
you make me either/or? Flesh or spirit? Body or soul?
Thinking or feeling?
You insult Me, defame Me, devalue Me, neglect Me –
but I remain. I wait in my sacred places. I live in your
dreams. As Nightmare I call you to task. As Nemesis
I remind you of Truth. I am the Great Goddess. And I
AM.

Danaë and Pericles flew to Athens on the earliest
morning flight from Rhodes and hired a car for the
hour and a half drive to the ancient centre of the
known world. After booking in to a hotel the pair
began their reconnaissance. They ignored the
museum and temples and treasuries, knowing the
Deus loci had long flown with the shades who no
longer sang there, and continued out of the town to
the Kastalian Spring, undeterred by the sign that
said, for the benefit of tourists, *Entry Forbidden*.
"This is *our* heritage," said Danaë, lifting her skirt
and climbing over the low barrier, "the hoof of
Pegasus himself struck this rock to birth this sacred

spring, muses and priestesses and women have bathed in its water since before time; we are walking in a sacred manner. Follow me."

Her voice had a new edge that Pericles had only learnt of in these last days. Obedience to its dictates overrode any doubts his official reaction to the intrusive sign might have given him. Yet, once within the boundary, for all its sanctity, its solitude, its silence the Kastalian Spring whose waters purified countless priestesses three millennia ago did not whisper to either of them: "*stay, it is here*".

They climbed back over the barrier, crossed over, and continued along the road to the Tholos itself, the sight of the three remaining Corinthian columns, sentinels standing like prayers below them, amplified a *frisson* each of them acknowledged. *This* was the place. No tourists were present, too late in the day and too late in the year, and the caretaker was preparing to leave. He greeted them, suggested they stay until sunset when the atmosphere became particularly charged.

Pericles walked the site, Danaë sat and felt the stories. Later, leaving the site as the sun slipped behind the towering Parnassus mountains, she whispered: "we'll return tomorrow at *lykóphos.*"

Danaë and Pericles bid each other good night and went to their respective rooms, set their alarms for the morning, stepped onto their adjacent balconies to breathe in the moonlight, spoke quietly for a minute or two before settling down for the night. Danaë blew a kiss goodnight and retired inside.

Before the dawn glowed rose pale the pair met in the lobby, each carrying a small knapsack.

As the light moved from the subtle shadings of mirage, to shifting, to focus, the pair set off in silence for the ten minute walk to the Tholos. Light streaked across the sky, the white moon was low and full, moon shadows on the pavement as they walked distorted their movements, lent an eerie sense of being accompanied by shades of countless aeons past.

The gate was locked but they had noted the way to slip around it and enter the sanctuary. The *Deus loci*, the spirit of place buried there in the rocky cliffs, acknowledged their presence. Danaë spoke softly: "The corpse was left to rot, *paidi mou*, and it was out of *that* the oracular power grew to light. In that fertilizing compost harmony, light and prophecy took root, the dark powers became the light's yeast, so it was, so it is, and so it ever shall be. Alexa is part of this continuum, this *phenomenon*, and something in Aristo knew this which is why he instinctively called her the nearest name his Far Memory could access. He was not, as you know, an educated man in the way she had educated herself in our classics, but he was a man who was nourished by the ocean all his life, supported by it, taught by it. He was a man of intensely heightened instincts, intuitions if you like, think of how the ocean and the winds would warn him of their turning long before any barometric equipment registered. I'm not condoning what he did, I'm not even making excuses for his being unstable for whatever reason ... but, *agapi mou*, it is our *attention to intention* that the gods, those whom we call "*The Watchers*", understand, and they do not judge us. In ancient times only the best, the purest, the highest were selected for *conscious* sacrifice – they *knew* the sanctity of fertilizing the ground with their dead. No, Alexa was not, in all likelihood, conscious of this at that moment, but she was conscious *always* of *love*."

Pericles listened to the words as they blew on the wind, gathering form from the ancient hills, setting themselves into his heart; the powerful winds of Parnassus carrying the ancient Pythic Law. Danaë beckoned Pericles: "lift this slab," she asked, "secure it from falling back until we are finished. It is here."

Pericles did as bid. Danaë took the knapsack from her back, set it down and opened it to produce a small bottle, a small packet, a small handful of grapes, a few olives, two other small bottles. These she laid to one side while she scooped a hollow in the soft soil where had lain the stone slab. Nodding to Pericles he brought from his own knapsack a square of white linen, a small flat olive wood box. Opening the box one last time he and Danaë smoothed the deep green silk that had been arranged as a lining.

Pericles brought from his pocket the heavy gold cross with its weighty chain and the exquisite earring. Onto the green silk he laid the earring, folded the chain around it, allowing the cross fall pendant. He gazed at them a moment, silently intoning his own prayers for the two people he had come to know so well without ever having met them, and closed the lid. He then wrapped the box carefully inside the white linen before laying it in the soil. Danaë reached for her offerings and libations. Opening her container of honeycakes, baked with honey from the island's purest hives, salt from the sea, flour from the local mill, she crumbled them over the linen, speaking too softly for any but the gathering shades to hear. She sprinkled milk, dribbled water and finally poured the pure green liquid of holy olive oil to sanctify the earth from which it came and onto which she laid the symbols of a never-ending love. All the while she was whispering ancient verses long forgotten; she was a woman, and she was Greek, the prayers were held in her blood.

These stones speak, the sacred crossroads remain;
Stones are the priestesses now, choristers the columns;
Take what is eternal of Alexa and Aristo transmute their wounds and grant them peace.
Hear me, oh Holy Ones.

Pericles stood bound to the ground as his mother held her arms up in the *orante* position to greet the dawn. Danaë turned and gently nodded for him to replace the slab and together they scuffed the soil around it. No one would ever know. It was a holy moment.

Walking the dusty path back up to the road each had left their intention on the winds that rose up from the long valley, allowing the sanctuary to reclaim its mysteries of the deep past. A lightness of being suffused them both, it was still early, but half way along the lower road to the hotel a most delicious smell consumed their senses. *Fourno!* Both laughed as they followed the trail to where fresh breads and the day's first pastries had come from the oven and were being arranged along the counters in great square trays. "Breakfast!" said Pericles, re-assuming the authority he had lost since his mother had turned into a priestess of the ancient mysteries, "choose, Mama, we need offerings and libations ourselves!" So much to choose, too many bought, but the day was still ahead of them.

Back in the hotel the pair went to share breakfast on Danaë's balcony. Pericles made a cafetière of coffee, impedimenta for which they had brought with them. Against the sharp chill of the sun's rising Danaë wrapped herself in an old Kashmiri shawl of rose and umber paisley she had found in the Bologna market decades before when markets sold such treasures from the East. The day was their own, they would play tourist: would visit the Charioteer, the lads of Argos, the great Sphinx of Naxos, the Omphalos of course, muse over the Sibyl's Rock, and climb to the gymnasium, the theatre, take photographs, lunch at Patricos for the best Cretan salad beyond the shores of Chania. By mutual consent they would go, as tourists, to the Tholos again later in the afternoon.

In between there was time for a small adventure. Danaë was window shopping, idly, lingeringly, until Pericles met her for lunch. With no real intent aforethought her gaze ran over a collection of jewellery in one of the less ostentatious displays in the main street, and fell on a ring that stilled her breath. It wasn't costly by her standards, though it was 18 carat gold. She knew she had to have it as a symbol of all she had recently distilled from the archives of her own Far Memory. She went inside, a fine looking man her own age, she observed, came forward, offering assistance.

"The serpent," she indicated, "I would like to see it please." And there it was, winking at her from two tiny ruby eyes, uncoiling as its maker had cleverly extended only one of the coils to form the loop to go around the finger. "Oh, delightful," she smiled at the jeweller, "the *perfect* souvenir from the Pythia, *ne*? I'll have it, and I'll wear it, how marvellous that you'd put it in the window or I wouldn't have found it, would I?"

"Kyria," replied the man with the kindly eyes, "you would have found this ring, she is meant for you, look how she fits your finger. Where are you from?"

"Rodos," said Danaë, and before she could say more the jeweller responded with: "ah, Rodos, we goldsmiths can still learn from their ancient skills. I am pleased to think my humble work appeals to you."

"Oh it does, it does," smiled Danaë, her words weighted with meaning heavier than all the gold of Croesus. She handed her bankcard to him, deal over. A smile, a pleasant exchange and she walked back into the sunshine, utterly thrilled with her purchase, *an omen*, a memory, a catalysis. She vaguely recalled some words – perhaps from Sikelianos: *I am the catharsis over the Serpent and the Spring, whose speaking waters never cease to flow ...*"

Pericles noticed the ring at once, chuckled hugely and patted his mother's hand affectionately, "Mama, *agapi mou*, your memory is long ... *Pythia* ... you should have seen yourself this morning, you were magnificent!"

"Yes, I was wasn't I." It was no question, this was self acknowledgement. "Come *agapi mou* no more talk, let's eat!"

The snake ring felt gifted from the Goddess herself, gold from the earth, fashioned by human hands, its significance penetrated Danaë's cellular memory and as she lay wakeful after the afternoon siesta she spoke out loud her gratitude: thank you, *thank you*, ευχαριστώ, to the gods, to her life, for her son, her husband, to her experience of the morning ... to Alexa, whose story had brought her here, whose life therefore had not been lived, or lost, in vain. She pondered these things deeply as she rose, dressed and tapped on Pericles' door as she passed.

He was already waiting for her in the foyer. They walked to the Tholos. The gate was still open and they tripped lightly down the well worn track as the last busload of tourists was walking back up to board their coach. No one else was to be seen. They wandered about, aware the morning's ambiance had transmuted through the day to a shimmering presence, returned to the stillness of frozen time. Two cats were washing themselves on one of the higher slabs of broken stone, all was so normal. Danaë sat close to them as Pericles explored the site. Time passed. Dusk fell, an owl called, a little Athena's owl, *athene noctua*. Danaë did not appear to hear it, but Pericles did. The garden of his childhood had been full of owls until surrounding development had diminished their range and exiled them to the woods closer to Philerimos. He started to walk back to his mother; the caretaker was closing his hut. Dusk. The light around Danaë was dimming as she sat there so still, two cats beside her. Suddenly a flash, wings, too large for a bat, but not too pale for a little owl, Athena's little owl, and there it was again ... it swooped and rose, and rose and swooped, its flight forming a flawless *aeonian ... over Danaë's head.* She sat completely unaware, musing on the middle distance between herself and the centre of the Tholos. Pericles' heart turned over, this was *his* gift, from the witching hour, a symmetry divined from the ancients where the veils were thin, stamped on his soul.

Their claims of conscience now at rest Danaë and Pericles could return to their beautiful island. Secrets were meant to be kept, and Aristo Theohalis would remain as he always had for the islanders of Rhodes. Nothing he had done or not done would change how he would be remembered by them all.

Once the pair had reached home Pericles set to the task of calling Alice and Karen and Jeremy. Each received the details of the story and its magical sequel in assimilable portions, each reacted and responded from their own font of beliefs. Alice, of course, was thrilled by the magic, the mystery, the *assumption* of it all. "How perfect," she chuckled, age having given over to her rare grace, "Alexa would have been delighted to know her life had touched you, that you had seen it for what it was. Pericles my dear, you *and* Danaë must visit me next time, it is such a blessing to be able to speak of more than seas and ships and sealing wax, or even cabbages and kings," she laughed her hearty laugh.

Danaë pondered on the idea of attending the Glastonbury Goddess Conference the next year – she could tell them a thing or two about *Goddesses*.

Pericles had one last promise to keep. He pulled a card from his wallet, reached for the phone: "Hullo, Eve, it's Pericles speaking ..."

Author's Note: For accuracy on Missing Persons I telephoned Interpol and spoke with a charming woman whose name I neglected to note in writing. My apologies. For Forensic Fans I telephoned the Home Office and spoke to an equally charming woman for details, we giggled over the gruesome, and again I apologize for my neglect in noting her name in writing. It was well over a decade ago that I called each, and life has thrown me other curved balls so my unprofessional lapse must be excused.

Missing Persons

Bodies found in suspicious circumstances are held under scrutiny by local police. Dental records and DNA samples are taken and stored. If no person is reported locally as having gone missing the police send a full description to their HQ, which in turn forwards that description nationally. Should there be no report of a person missing nationally police HQ will then contact Interpol who will forward the detailed description internationally.

In the UK the NPIC MPB police will check all recent reports of persons missing. A UK resident missing abroad must be notified to the MPB immediately. Their code advises:

- Send all reports of persons missing for 14 days to the MPB, or sooner if the officer in charge thinks that the case warrants urgent attention.
- If subject is a foreign national notify the Bureau immediately.

- If subject is UK resident missing abroad notify the Bureau immediately.

Send all reports of unidentified bodies or persons to the Bureau within 48 hours of being found.

Notes for Forensic Fans

Strangulation
A ligature such as a belt or rope around the neck, or hands or arm pressure on the neck compresses the internal carotid artery. Fainting or death will occur depending on intention. Apart from the direct restriction of blood to the brain there are two other significant responses produced by pressing on the neck:

Pressing on the carotid arteries also presses on baroreceptors. These bodies then cause vasodilation (dilation of the blood vessels) in the brain leading to insufficient blood to perfuse the brain with oxygen and retain or maintain consciousness.

A message is also sent to the vagus nerve to the main pacemaker of the heart to decrease the rate and volume of the heartbeat, typically by up to a third. In some cases these is evidence that this may escalate into asystole, a form of cardiac arrest. There is a dissenting view on the full extent of how and when a person reaches a stage of permanent injury, but it is agreed that pressure on the vagus nerve causes damage to the pulse rate and blood pressure and is dangerous. This method is responsible for most, but not all, of the reported fatalities due to strangulation. When practiced alone it can be mistaken for suicide.

Fingerprints
Copper or aluminium powder lightly dusted with a soft blusher bruch over surface reveals fingerprints by adhering to the residue of natural body oil.

Odontology Forensics

Teeth tell age, eating habits and abnormalities – bone loss, missing teeth. Computer overlays record bite and bite marks in suspicious circumstances.

How a Corpse Degrades

A corpse – if left exposed outdoors after death – is likely to become predatory food for animals such as foxes, dogs and the like but the most common means of decomposition of a corpse are the myriad of insects and flies who appear within twenty-four hours of the individual's demise.

The locale and temperatures surrounding the corpse indicate the type and species of insects and flies to be found feeding and nesting within the corpse. Blowflies are the prime example and are often to be found laying their eggs in the moist areas of the human body usually *within the first hour following death*. The mouth, nose, groin, armpits, and eyes (if they are open) are all common anatomical locations in which the blowfly's eggs are laid and will normally hatch within twenty-four hours. Blowfly larvae reach half an inch in length and continue to feed on the corpse for up to twelve days; in this time they grow and continue to moult until they eventually transform into the blowfly and then begin repeating the cycle over again.

If a corpse is found outdoors and is only exhibiting the signs of having had eggs deposited upon it then it is taken as a given by the entomologist that the body has been left out in the open for less than twenty-four hours. The appearance of maggots but no pupae means that the body has been outdoors for less than ten days. During this time it is worth noting that - given the ambient temperature around the corpse and the fact that this temperature will rise and fall - rigor mortis will have gone from the body. During this time if the temperature is colder than usual then the blowfly life cycle slows down. The entomologist will collect up live insects and flies as well as those that have expired and also their empty pupae cases, using them to estimate the life cycle and how long they have been in the deceased body as a breeding ground.

Time of Death

As time passes it becomes more difficult to determine when the person died. Once weeks have gone by forensic entomology is essential in deciding, by the evidence of maggots for example, found on the body, the time of death. Pollen is another clue.

Seawater

The challenge really begins when a corpse is removed from the ocean. The body will have been exposed to many changes in the surrounding temperature, pH and salt content. These factors make determination of the time of death a difficult process.

Forensic entomology is rarely useful for a body recovered from the water, mostly because the body would have to float on the water's surface for some time – an uncommon occurrence. Trauma experienced by the body from ocean exposure is hard to differentiate from the trauma that occurs from foul play.

Forensic Science in the Ocean

Pathologists monitor the water temperature, salinity and other factors. The body will be eaten by prawns and other sea creatures. The eyes will be eaten first. A body will often remain on the seabed for some time before it is brought up to the surface by storms or wave surges. When a body decomposes in the ocean, the head as well as the hands and feet will separate from the body. Normally, they don't end up resurfacing.

Categories of Decay

These categories are:

Autolysis: A process of self-digestion where the body's enzymes contained within the cells begin to go into a post death meltdown. The process can be speeded up by extreme heat or retarded by extreme cold.

Putrefaction: Bacteria that escape from the body's intestinal tract after the deceased has died are released into the body and begin the process of melting the body down.

Putrefaction

Putrefaction follows a predetermined timetable in nature. After the first thirty-six hours the neck, the abdomen, the shoulders and the head begin to turn a discoloured green. This is followed by bloating – an accumulation of gas produced by bacteria toiling away within the dead body. This bloating is most visible around the face where the eyes and the tongue protrude as the gas inside pushes them forward.

As the body continues to putrefy skin blisters, hair falls out and the fingernails begin to sink back into the fingers. These skin blisters are also filled with large amounts of liquid.

The body's skin tone then becomes "marbled'; an intricate pattern of blood vessels in the face, abdomen, chest and other extremities becomes visible. This is the result of the body's red blood vessels breaking down which in turn release haemoglobin.

As the process reaches its conclusion the body will now be almost black-green and the fluids - known as purge fluid - will drain from the corpse. This happens normally from the mouth and nose but can also occur from other orifices. The body's tissues then begin to break open and will release gas and other fluids in the same way as a fruit that has been left too long in the sun.

The internal organs will begin to decay in a particular order; beginning with the intestines which hold bacteria as well as various levels of acidic fluid which - when unable to circulate - begin to eat through their surrounding tissues. As the intestinal organs decay so to do the liver, kidneys, lungs and brain. The contents of the stomach may slow down the rate of decay if there is undigested food in and around that area. The last organs to give way to decay are the prostate and/or the uterus.

Hot temperatures will speed up this process while cooler temperatures will slow it down. Septic wounds suffer the effects of putrefaction faster as the bacteria from sepsis spreads quickly and does damage on a larger and faster scale.

Glossary

aeonian symbol of infinity

agapi mou my love

barbaros barbarian, all who did not speak the Greek language were called barbarians from the baa baa sound of their own language according to Greek ears

briki small curved one-handled pot for making Greek or Turkish coffee

dolmathes vine leaves stuffed with rice and mint or lamb rice and mint, steamed under slight pressure to prevent leaves unravelling. Well made dolmathes never require toothpicks to hold them together.

doxa to Theo thanks to God

Dymaheion council, municipal offices

effendi friend (Turkish, from earlier Greek authentes)

efharisto – eucharisto – thank you

El-hamdullilah thanks be to God (Arabic)

filotimo actions to defend a point of honour

FNQ Far North Queensland

fourno bakers oven, shop

Galaktoboureko (γαλακτομπούρεκο) is a dessert of semolina custard (sometimes flavored with lemon or orange) in phyllo pastry.

Gallia France, French

Grigori a race of angelic beings of shining countenance

hos geldinis welcome (Turkish)

kafenion café

kalimera good morning

kalinikta good night
kalispera good afternoon
kyria mrs., madame, as a form of address
kyrios mister, sir
lykóphos wolf light, the dusky sky before dawn
merhaba greetings (Turkish)
Moirae the Fates, weavers of destiny
mou my (possessive determiner)
Né Yes
Ohi! Oxi! No! A one word telegram sent by Metaxas to Italy refusing to participate in war
Omiros Homer
paidi mou my child (pronounced pe<u>th</u>ee moo)
Panaghia/Panayia Holy Mary, lit. Holy Virgin
parakalo please
Petaloudes the famous Valley of the Butterflies some miles south of Rhodes Town
Saganaki a casserole (in this instance) of tomatoes, prawns and feta
S'agapo I love you
sas you ("to you")
skafhandro a truly dreadful, and frequently fatal or crippling, diving helmet used by the early sponge divers.
smaragathi emerald, the colour
then ftaio ego it's not my fault
Theo mou my God!
yahya grandmother
vevaios of course, certainly

CPSIA information can be obtained
at www.ICGtesting.com
Printed in the USA
LVHW011344170521
687652LV00035B/2284

9 781070 2087